D1486518

Scenes of Crime

SCENES OF CRIME

A Crime Writers' Association Anthology

edited by Martin Edwards

with a foreword by Natasha Cooper

Constable · London

First published in Great Britain 2000
by Constable, an imprint of Constable & Robinson Limited
3 The Lanchesters, 162 Fulham Palace Road
London W6 9ER

Copyright © 2000
The right of the contributors to be identified as the authors
of this work has been asserted by them in accordance with
the Copyright, Designs and Patents Act 1988

ISBN 1-84119-221-X

Printed and bound in Great Britain

A CIP catalogue record for this book is available from the
British Library

Contents

Foreword

The first Crime Writers' Association short story anthology was published in 1956. Almost every year since then has seen a successor, compiled by a series of distinguished editors. This is the fifth collection produced under the eagle eye of Martin Edwards.

Throughout the past forty-odd years, members of the association have demonstrated a remarkable ability to move with the times and yet to uphold the standards and traditions they have inherited. It takes great skill to set the scene of a crime and bring its investigation to a credible conclusion within the confines of the short story and yet to people it with characters that live. Martin Edwards's team all show that skill to great advantage. The theme of this collection is the scene of the crime, and it is intriguing to see how different writers have tackled their brief.

Crime fiction has always held up a dark mirror to the society in which it is written, reflecting both factual experience and the febrile fears that uncomfortable knowledge can generate. Sometimes a safety valve, sometimes perhaps a source of even more terrifying nightmares, crime writing leaves almost no one unmoved. The Golden Age tradition was to offer comfort by demonstrating that evil never pays, victims have usually played a part in what happens to them, and evil-doers are always punished. But we all know that life is not like that any more, and probably never was. Justice is not always done; some appalling crimes are never solved; others remain beyond the reach of the law; occasionally the law itself is guilty of imposing suffering on the innocent. And revenge, however satisfying at one level, can never heal a single injury, let alone bring back the dead.

Probing the minds of killers, wrestling some kind of explanation out of the irrational forces that drive them, writers of psychological thrillers have much to tell us all about the deranged monsters of our worst imaginings. What can be explained can be understood, and what can be understood can never be as frightening as the wholly random eruption of violence into our lives.

Violence, real or fictional, is always shocking, but sometimes we need to be jerked out of complacency. Otherwise we trundle along the same old tramlines, understanding nothing of ourselves or anyone else. Crime, more than any other kind of fiction, allows authors to unravel the psychological tangles of their characters, teasing out ideas that can make us all see more clearly.

But, above all, crime fiction is written to entertain. It may shock, it may teach, it may scare, but it also engages the emotions and the intellect of its readers. All the stories in this collection stimulate ideas and therefore well-being. From the skilful traditional locked-room mystery of Edward D. Hoch's 'Circus in the Sky' to the utterly contemporary 'Nice Place' by Mat Coward, they give a good example of the huge range of crime writing at the start of the new millennium. Some of the contributors are senior members of the association, laden with honours and hung about with Daggers of one sort or another; others are near the beginning of their careers. But all of them display that most elusive talent: the ability to grip readers' attention from the first word to the last.

There is much humour to be had here, a great deal of cleverness, insight, drama, and some piercing sadness. It is a fine introduction to the art of the crime writer.

Natasha Cooper

Introduction

Welcome to a collection of crime stories linked by a single theme – in one way or another, they all concern 'scenes of crime'. When I invited members of the Crime Writers' Association to contribute to this anthology, I hoped for an enthusiastic response, but did not anticipate quite how many stories of distinction I would receive. In making tricky choices, I have been guided above all by a desire to show the diversity of the genre. Readers will find all manner of delights: humour, social insight, psychological suspense and classic detective work.

In crime fiction, the setting is often crucial. Locale may impact on the plot, cast light on character and underscore mood and theme. Within the span of a short story, the crime scene itself may serve a crucial purpose. Contributors have chosen a number of memorable settings: a mortuary, a cosmetic surgery clinic, the Golden Gate Bridge. There are stories which explore the past, the world of a chimney sweep in Victorian London and human relationships under strain during the Blitz. Edward D. Hoch sets a baffling puzzle: murder on the seventeenth floor apparently committed by an invisible lion. Peter Lovesey's spin on the theme is very different, but equally compelling: a painting depicts an all-too-recognisable murder scene, but who is the victim and who the killer?

Mat Coward's sleuths of the Neighbourhood Watch return after appearing in an earlier CWA anthology, while Catherine Morrell and Phil Lovesey provide compelling insights into the characters and behaviour of professional police officers. Even such innocent settings as a school reunion and Santa's grotto provide a background for compelling murder stories.

As in previous CWA anthologies, I have aimed to provide a mix of established writers and less familiar names. Two of the contributors, Peter Lovesey and Ruth Rendell, have won CWA Cartier Diamond Daggers while Ian Rankin, like Ruth and Peter, is a past winner of the Gold Dagger for the best crime novel of the year. The CWA's overseas membership is represented not only by Ed Hoch but also by a newer writer, Dr Jürgen Ehlers. This is also the first time a CWA anthology has contained contributions from a father and son: the Loveseys.

I am very grateful to Natasha Cooper, Chairman of the CWA, for contributing the foreword and also to the contributors and others within the CWA who have provided me with invaluable support. I would also like to thank Helena Edwards for help with the proofs and all those at Constable who have worked on this book.

Martin Edwards

Mat Coward

This story marks a welcome return appearance for the Neighbourhood Watch Inquiry Agency run by Doggo and Vincent. The characters first appeared in 'Nice People', Mat Coward's contribution to the 1997 CWA anthology *Whydunit?*. In introducing that story, I expressed the hope that one day Doggo and his vile partner might return and I was therefore very glad to receive this breezy and entertaining manuscript from Mat, which sees his not entirely dynamic duo pursuing another off-beat investigation.

NICE PLACE

Mat Coward

'Easily the most terrifying experience of my entire life,' says the slightly-built, friendly-faced, middle-aged man sitting in the client's chair in my office. 'One of them had a machine gun. Seriously, a *machine gun*, on a strap round his neck. I mean, this isn't New York, is it? This is London. You don't expect bloody *machine* guns in bloody London, do you? Two of them had pistols. You know – hand guns, whatever you call them. And the rest of them had sledgehammers, batons . . . plus of course, that dirty big thing they knocked the door in with. You wouldn't believe the noise that thing makes. Or the mess.'

I would actually. I've used one myself, more than once. But now's not the time to discuss my personal prehistory. 'It must have been awful, Mr Murray. You have my full sympathy, and of course the full sympathy of my – er, my *partner*, also.'

My vile partner Vincent, who is sitting in a chair at the other side of the room, chooses that moment to belch loudly. 'Chooses' being the word, believe me.

Vic Murray ignores Vincent's wind – I always make sure the clients are seated next to open windows, even in the midst of winter; it's the least I can do – and says: 'I'm sorry to go on and on about it, I must drive people mad with it, I'm sure I do. But you see – a thing like that, you just feel as if your life is never going to belong to you again.'

'No need to apologise. But perhaps if you could give us the story in chronological order? That could be a big help. OK? So – it's a Tuesday night, Wednesday morning . . .'

Murray nods. 'Just before one o'clock, Wednesday morning. I was awake, as it happens, because Daisy couldn't sleep, she had a bit of a tummy upset.'

'Daisy?'

13

'Oh, sorry – Daisy's my little girl.' He smiles for the first time since he entered the door marked *Neighbourhood Watch Inquiry Agency, London*. 'We were going to call her Sally, after her granny, but – well, thing is, Mr Pound, once we'd seen her we couldn't call her anything but Daisy. I can't explain what I mean, but somehow she just *looks* just like a Daisy.'

He reaches into his jacket pocket, presumably to pull out a photo of the aforementioned offset, but is frozen in mid-pull by my vile partner screaming: 'She looks just like a *daisy*? Bloody Jesus, man, that's awful! Do the doctors know why?'

Murray looks at me. I look at the window. My vile partner Vincent more or less dies laughing – I should be so lucky – for a minute or so, before hobbling off to the en suite lavatory, clutching his groin and crying, 'Oh God, I'm going to wet myself!'

He leaves the door to the lavatory open, so we can hear his stream as well as his groans of *Oh God that's better*, and of *Looks just like a daisy*!

Murray is still looking at me. When he realises I'm not going to look back at him, he looks instead at his own hand, which is still half in and half out of his jacket pocket. My vile partner finishes pissing after a long time (why do unpleasant men generally have such capacious bladders? Is it deliberate?), and rejoins us. We are not troubled by the sound of a flush. Mr Murray pushes the photo of his daughter – if that's what it is – deeper into his pocket, and then buttons his jacket.

'You were awake?' I say, pretending – as I have spent so much of my life over the last few years pretending – that Vincent simply doesn't exist. 'Awake with your little girl?'

'Right,' he says, looking down at his lap, blinking to re-establish his focus. 'One o'clock in the morning, I was sitting on the bed with Daisy in my arms, and suddenly there was this explosion. Or, that's what I thought it was. Like gas, you know? Or a car bomb. I ran out on to the landing, still holding my daughter, and my wife came out of her bedroom, pulling on her dressing-gown, and I started to run down the stairs, but I stopped on the landing. We both did.'

'What did you see?'

'Coppers,' says Mr Murray. 'Fourteen of them, my wife counted them. When they'd gone, I said there must have been over a dozen, and she said, "There was fourteen of the bastards".' He blushes a little. 'I've never heard her call a policeman a bastard before. Like, we're not that sort of person, you know?'

Not true, I think; everybody's that sort of person, if only potentially. I learned that much in the force, if not much else.

'What were the officers doing?'

'Running everywhere. Some were running into the rooms downstairs, some were running up the stairs. Some were running back out of the door – the doorway, I should say, they'd smashed the door right off its hinges – though God knows why they were running back out the way they'd just come in.'

'So you met them at the top of the stairs?'

Mr Murray nods. 'They were shouting and screaming, and one of them, a female one, took Daisy right out of my arms, and my wife tried to –'

'What were they shouting? Can you remember anything they said?'

'"Armed police! Armed police!" They shouted that over and over, then it was, "Get down on the floor! Do it now! On the floor, do it!"' He sips at the glass of cloudy water which was all he'd accept in the way of the Agency's hospitality. He'd said tea and coffee gave him nightmares. 'Mostly, they were shouting to each other.'

'That's the bit I'm interested in. Do you remember any names they used, or references to what they were looking for, or anything at all like that?'

He shakes his head. 'The thing is –'

My vile partner Vincent belches again. 'Vincent, go and get some sandwiches. It's lunchtime.'

'I'm not an office boy,' says Vincent.

'I know you're not, but I'm promoting you. Temporarily.'

My vile partner slouches out, sulky and noisy. The client smiles at me, uncertainly. I don't smile back at him. I don't say, 'See, Vincent provided the capital for this business, I'm stuck with him.' I make no apologies for Vincent, ever, because if I was ever to make one big enough, I'd need to get scaffolders in.

'The thing is?' I say.

'Well, it was all over pretty quickly. I mean, it didn't seem it at the time, but really – I don't suppose they were there longer than five minutes. Less, probably. Like, one minute me and the wife were lying on the landing carpet with our hands behind our heads, and we could hear all the rooms being turned upside down, and the officers calling back and forth to each other, and then the next minute the one in charge – big bloke, red hair, Scottish accent – he pulled me to my feet, and he stared into my face, and then he turned away and he swore, under his breath, and then he called it all off.'

'What did he say?'

'I think it was "bugger". Might have been "bollocks".'

'No, I meant what did he say after he'd sworn under his breath?'

'Sorry, right.' Mr Murray takes another sip of water, although the level of the glass doesn't seem to go down any. 'He shouted out, "Stop, stop, stop! Everybody stop what you're doing. Clear the scene immediately, everybody out!" And they all ran out again, and we heard vans and that starting up outside, and then it was quiet. Daisy was just laughing, she didn't seem at all scared. My wife was holding her now. But she, my wife, was just shaking and crying. I think I was doing the same. I'd got a burn on my elbow, from the carpet.'

'The Scots copper was still there?'

'Yeah, him and one woman, that was all. And she said, "Sorry about this, our mistake, nothing to worry about, sorry to get you out of bed." And I said it was all right, I was up anyway. The things you say, when you're in a situation, eh? I mean –'

'What was the last thing they said before they left?'

'OK. Let's see . . . the Scotsman said he'd send round a 24-hour repair man, to fix the door, said he'd see to it personally. I said thanks, and the woman said if there was any other damage, ring this number, and she gave me her card.'

I've seen the card. It's a general number for the local nick. No names on it.

'OK, Mr Murray, that's excellent, I've got a much clearer picture now. You sure you won't have a whisky? It is lunchtime.'

'Better not. Don't want to go home reeking. She's worried I'm going to start drinking. You know.'

He shrugs. I shrug. 'A very unsettling experience, Mr Murray. Now, I understand you got our name from a solicitor?'

16

'The lawyer my wife used for the conveyancing.'

Interesting form of words. None of my business, though. Probably. 'So presumably, the legal side –'

He shakes his head. 'I'm not suing, or anything like that. We just want an apology, Mr Pound. We want the police to say sorry, that they got the wrong house. We've only just recently moved into Churchill Road, you understand, we're worried about what the neighbours'll think. No smoke, and all that.'

'I understand. What I'm not so clear about, is what you want *us* to do for you?'

The client takes out his cheque book. Always a sight that lifts my heart, no matter how often I see it – which hasn't been all that often, lately.

'This is the thing, Mr Pound. I'm told your agency checks out neighbours for people who're planning to buy a house.'

'That's right. Usually before they've bought the house, obviously.'

'Well, too late for that. But what I can't get out of my mind is that the police raid, it was meant for *someone*. And presumably, unless the whole thing was a total cock-up from beginning to end, then it's someone living near us.'

'And you want us to find out who?'

Mr Murray nods, and grits his teeth. 'I do. I want to find out what we're up against. If we're living next door to a drug dealer or a gun smuggler or a pornographer – well, yes, I want to know who. For Daisy's sake, you see.'

'I see.'

The cheque is filled in, and exchanged for a receipt. As I show him to the door, the client says, 'And you can tell that partner of yours, she doesn't look like *a* daisy. That's not what I meant, and it's not particularly funny.'

'I'll tell him,' I promise. I'm lying: I wouldn't tell my vile partner if his hair was on fire. I never speak to him at all except when it's absolutely unavoidable, or when I think it might cause him pain.

Two nights later, my vile partner Vincent and I are doing what we do best: sitting in a car in the dark, staring at houses. I can't

17

complain – it's been a living for me for many years, both as a policeman and since.

A great deal of neighbour-checking can be done by bureaucratic means, technically legal or otherwise, involving telephones, computers, filing cabinets, electoral registers, former colleagues and twenty-pound notes. By such methods, the Neighbourhood Watch Inquiry Agency will soon discover if any of your potential neighbours are known to the police, or are undischarged bankrupts, or have a history of unneighbourly violence.

But there is a place, too, in our specialised trade for the more primitive approach: for walking a street, for listening to its noise and its quiet, for witnessing its days becoming its nights, for conducting cavity searches of its back alleys and dustbin shacks, for watching its comings and goings.

I let Vincent do the paperwork. He used to be a lawyer, he should be good at dusty searches. He's *not*, needless to say, but if I threaten him often enough he usually gets the job done in the end.

This – the sitting and the watching and the poking about – this is the bit I fit.

'Funny sort of street this,' says my vile partner, sometime after midnight. I say nothing, I don't even grunt, so after a while Vincent says, 'Well, what I mean is, all down the north side you've got council houses, and then opposite them you've got flats and bedsits at one end, and half-way decent semis up this end. Bit mixed, isn't it? Who'd buy a house opposite a bloody council estate?'

Like many who are themselves universally shunned, Vincent is a snob.

'The client,' I say because I wouldn't want my vile partner getting the idea that he is sufficiently important to me for me to go to the trouble of not talking to him, 'is convinced that the police raid that mistakenly rammed his door in was supposed to be keeping an appointment at one of the bedsits. Probably just suburban prejudice, but he says there's a lot of shady characters down that end.'

My vile partner snorts his malicious laugh. 'Coppers who can't tell the difference between a third-floor walk-up and a four-bed semi? Yeah, well, wouldn't be the strangest thing I've ever

18

heard.' Vincent has an exceptionally low opinion of police officers, even for an ex-lawyer.

Still chuckling, he begins to unwrap a sandwich. 'That had better not be pilchard and yoghurt again,' I warn him, 'or it's going straight out the window.'

He gives me a look intended to convey innocent bafflement, and says, 'It's just cheese and tomato, Doggo.'

I roll down the side window anyway, as a precaution and as a territorial display – it is *my* car – and I hear a cry of pain.

'Shh! Vincent, shut up chomping, I heard something.' My vile partner obediently freezes in mid-chew, his mouth open. 'And stop breathing through your bloody nose, will you! That's even louder than your –'

There it is again. Unmistakably a sound of suffering and fear, it couldn't be anything else.

'Someone's having it off,' says Vincent, spraying flecks of sandwich over my dashboard. 'That's all that is, Doggo. You're so old you've forgotten what it sounds like.'

I open the car door, and get out. 'Come on, we're going to have a look.'

'Oh, kinky,' says Vincent, predictable and inappropriate as ever. 'Count me in!'

It's a windy night, and sounds aren't easy to track. Now we're standing outside the car, I can't hear anything except a faint rumble of traffic from a nearby main road, and a burglar alarm ringing, in that pointless and irritating way they do, from one of the houses further down the street.

'It's cold,' says my vile partner. 'Can I finish my sandwich now?'

'Shut up, Vincent! There – did you hear that?' I don't wait for an answer – Vincent's answers are rarely worth waiting for – but set off at a trot towards the sound of suffering, which the shifting breeze has again brought to my ears.

I've got it narrowed down to a group of six semis thirty yards up from where we're parked, but then I lose it again. 'That stupid burglar alarm – I can't hear anything over that. Why doesn't someone switch it off?'

'Perhaps –' says Vincent, coming up behind me, panting even though he's only been proceeding at normal walking pace.

I'm in no mood to hear Vincent say something sensible, so

19

I interrupt him: 'Perhaps because they can't. Look, it's that house at the end – you can see the alarm light flashing.'

As I reach the front of the house, I can hear the human noise clearly, even through the alarm's blare. I bang on the door, press on the bell, then drop to my knees and yell through the letterbox, 'Hello! Anybody there?'

'Tell them you're a singing telegram,' says Vincent, strolling up the path.

'You get round the back,' I tell him, and he wanders off, muttering obscenities.

The screaming has given way to whimpering, not so easy to locate with the ears. I give the bell another push, the door another thump, and am busy peering in through the downstairs windows, looking for a chink in the curtains, when my vile partner returns.

'Found him,' he says, giving me a thumbs-up. 'I think we might need an ambulance here.' At that moment, the whimpering ends in a choking gasp that must be audible a block away. 'There again,' Vincent adds, 'we might not.'

We don't. The man at the back of the house is dead. I can tell that by looking at his face. The cause of death, at a guess, is having a large, very heavy, double-glazed patio door lying across his body. He's about twenty, white, with shoulder-length hair.

'Well,' says my vile partner Vincent, 'the government did say they were going to get tough on burglars.'

I look around. There are some lights on in nearby houses. 'For God's sake, I know no one bothers to report burglar alarms, but the noise that kid was making – you'd think *someone* would've called the cops.'

A torch beam hits my face. 'Are you the householder, sir?'

Someone's called the cops.

'The theory the police are going on is that the kid was breaking into your neighbour's house, presumably to rob it, that he managed to get that patio door off its frame somehow, perhaps with some special glazier's tool, but that he'd underestimated its weight. It fell on him, and crushed him. He would have died pretty slowly, unable to shift the door unaided. Unfortunately, the house was empty that night – but then, he knew that before he broke in, presumably.'

'Jesus,' says Mr Murray. 'What a way to go. I'm starting to think that bloody street's cursed.'

We're sitting in a café round the corner from his house. He doesn't want the wife to know about us, he explained, doesn't want to worry her – which may be true, and there again may be an excuse for keeping Vincent's bottom off his sofa. Understandable, either way. There was nowhere to park, so I've got my vile partner driving around the block for the duration. He'll hate that.

'I don't think your street's cursed. There's no connection as far as I can see between the police raid and this burglary-gone-fatal.'

'Just coincidence?'

'Must be. Every street gets burgled, Mr Murray. There's been several round your way this month.'

'I think I know the guy who owns that house. At least, he said good morning to me once. From behind, in the dark; I nearly jumped out of my skin. Have you made any progress with – you know, what I asked you to find out?'

'Negative progress, which is progress of a kind. There are no obvious suspects as yet.'

He chews a hangnail, and looks out the window. He doesn't look at me as he says, 'Couldn't you, like, get into the police computer?'

Ah. I wondered when that would come up.

I wait until he's looking at me before I reply. 'Not without causing a police officer to commit a corrupt act, Mr Murray. Which would be a very serious criminal offence.'

The client back-pedals so fast it's a wonder he doesn't fall off his chair. 'No, no, sure – I understand. I didn't mean, you know . . .'

'Of course.' And besides (I don't add), I no longer have those kind of cop contacts. My old mates are mostly retired, and those that are left pretty much severed all diplomatic relations the day I joined up with Vincent. 'Listen, Mr Murray. We can leave it as it is –'

'No!'

'Or, if you're happy to carry on paying, we'll carry on in our

21

quiet, law-abiding way, and the chances are pretty good that sooner or later we'll get a result. It all depends on how much you want to spend on this.'

'Right,' says the client, and he gets his cheque book out again. I like this man: he takes hints the way a circus seal takes fish.

'He seems to have plenty of money to throw around,' says my vile partner, driving back to the office. 'Funny. Doesn't look like a rich man. Doesn't live in a rich man's house.'

'People find the money for things that are really important to them, don't they? Heroin addicts find the money for heroin, don't they?'

'Yeah,' says Vincent, smugly. 'And where do they get it from, hey?'

'What are you suggesting?'

'I'm not *suggesting* anything,' says my vile partner, who is a part-time pedant when he's not too busy being a snob. 'I am simply saying, he seems to have plenty of money. What does he do for a living?'

'Early retirement. From an insurance company. Probably got a big pay-off. Now stop gassing, and drive. You know you can't do both at once – any more than you can breathe and think at the same time.' That's true, in fact: my vile partner holds his breath when he's thinking. I once gave him a cryptic crossword to do, in the hope that he'd asphyxiate, but he just blew his nose on it.

All the same, Murray does indeed seem remarkably unconcerned about how much he pays us. Refreshingly so; but suspiciously so?

'What *are* you saying, Vincent? That he's some sort of gangster, checking out the local opposition? To which he was alerted by the police raid?'

'I'm not saying anything,' Vincent replies. 'I've been told to shut up.'

It's possible. There's something about Murray that makes me slightly uneasy, I can't deny that. Perhaps it's just that he's a client who pays up without arguing, but when he first came to us, all that long story about the police raid, it was all a bit . . .

well, *effusive*, perhaps. He doesn't strike me as the naturally effusive type.

And if our esteemed client is playing games, then everything else in the case warrants a second squint, too. Including, just possibly, the fatal burglary.

'Pull over by the Tube station, Vincent.'

'Why, where are you going?'

'You're going to the newspaper library. We haven't done a local paper search for the Churchill Road area yet. Meanwhile, I'm going to go and talk to the burglary victim. Put my mind at rest.'

Vincent starts whining. 'Oh, how come you always get to go swanning around chatting people up, while I have to spend days on end aggravating my dust allergy in newspaper libraries?'

'What, *you* want to do the chatting up instead?'

My vile partner looks at me like I'm an idiot. 'Christ, no! I want *you* to do *both*, Doggo, while I look for pornography on the internet.'

He's not joking. He means it. He is genuinely puzzled when I decline to respond to his suggestion.

If he's not bent, I'm thinking on the drive to Churchill Road, then why exactly is Mr Murray so desperate to identify his crooked neighbour? To clear his name in his new neighbourhood? But surely the police apology will see to that. Besides, these days, people are used to the cops making mistakes. Nobody believes anything the police say, anyway.

To protect Daisy from harmful influences, then? That doesn't really wash either. If he's that worried that he's moved to a blighted neighbourhood, then he ought to move out.

Conclusion: he has an overwhelming personal necessity to know who and what the real target of the raid was. He's looking for someone, sure, but he's looking for someone specific. Or else, he wants to be certain that someone specific hasn't found him. Maybe Murray's in Witness Protection. Or maybe the person he's looking for is in Witness Protection. Or maybe Murray's just an old-fashioned cuckolded husband. Or maybe a thousand things, none of which the Agency wants to get involved with.

One thing any kind of private investigator has to be very wary of, is tracking someone down for a client, without knowing why the client wants that person tracked down, or what the client plans to do with that person once they've been tracked down.

It's started raining by the time I reach Churchill Road, heavy and blustery, so I stay in the car to make my phone call.

It rings ten times, then: 'Yeah, what?' says my vile partner.

'Where are you, Vincent? You sound flustered.'

'It's raining.'

'Oh, really? How strange, it's gorgeous here. Listen, before you go to the newspaper library –'

'I'm standing outside the bloody newspaper library right now!'

'– I want you to do something else. If the client *is* up to something, then we need to have some idea what's going on. So what you do next is –'

'It's raining!'

'– go back to the office, and do a computer search on all the electoral register names for Churchill Road. Starting with the client. See if any of those names don't exist, right?'

I hang up, because it seems to me an inefficient use of Agency resources to run up the company phone bill listening to Vincent moan and curse. He can moan and curse on his own time, and I've no doubt he does.

The doorbell at number 81 Churchill Road summons a pale, balding man in his forties, with sweat on his upper lip and a spot of tomato sauce on his striped shirt.

'Mr Duncan Hinton?'

'What is it, please?'

'My name's Pound,' I tell him, slipping past him into the hall, using the technique for gaining entry past a reluctant house-holder that was one of the first things I learned in my police career. 'I'm from Neighbourhood Watch, just wanted to ask a few questions about your tragic burglary. I don't think we've met before, have we?' Not that he needs security advice; there are burglar bars on all the windows, and the door's a solid job.

'I'm afraid I've never quite got round to joining the Neighbourhood Watch. I travel a lot for my job, you see, I don't really know any of the neighbours that well.'

'Thinking of buying one?' I ask, smiling, picking up a conservatory brochure from a pile on the telephone table. 'Very nice, adds value to the property.'

'I'm not buying one,' says Hinton, taking the brochure from my hand, rather firmly, and replacing it on the table. 'I'm – well, I sell them. Come through to the kitchen, if you like. But I'm afraid I'm in rather a rush today.'

'Cup of coffee'd be lovely, thanks. Won't take long,' I assure him. 'It's just that when something terrible like this happens . . .'

'Wasn't my fault,' he says, spooning coffee into two mugs. 'I didn't want that boy to die!'

Odd thing to say about an accident. 'Of course not, Mr Hinton. I mean, a death caused by a faulty patio door – that's nobody's fault, is it? Well, except for the little toerag who broke in, I suppose.'

He hands me my coffee, without looking at me. 'I was meaning to fix it.'

'Thanks.' I take a sip. 'Lovely. Well, I presume you've not been here long. Otherwise you would have fixed the door, wouldn't you? What with you being in the double glazing business, and all.'

Hinton attempts a shrug, and a wry smile. 'Just never quite got round to it. You know what they say – a builder's house is always the biggest tip in the street. Window cleaners always have dirty windows.'

'Right. And hairdressers are all bald.' I put the coffee down, and take out my notebook – purely for theatrical purposes. Another trick I learned in the force. 'How long have you known Vic Murray?'

'What?'

'Come on, Mr Hinton – the bloke that recently moved into number 77. With the little girl, Daisy.'

He takes a sip of coffee, chokes on it, puts the mug down. 'How do you know I know him?'

I don't. Or I didn't. But it's just struck me that this is a guy who, by his own admission, doesn't have anything to do with his neighbours and yet he made a point of saying hello to Murray – from *behind*, so that Murray had to turn round to acknowledge him. Why? To get a look at Murray's face, it can't have been any other reason.

25

'Well, if you don't know him, you don't know him. Doesn't matter, I was just wondering.'

'I was at school with his son, that's all. Thirty-odd years ago.'

Hinton bites his bottom lip, picks up his coffee, takes a slurp, burns his bitten bottom lip, and says, 'Oh Christ, what a mess! This is all his fault, you know, all this with the burglar.'

'It's Vic Murray's fault that a burglar was crushed to death under your patio door?'

Hinton looks as puzzled as I feel. 'Vic Murray? No, he moved away years ago. I'm talking about his dad, Eddie Murray. That psycho at number 77.'

Dad? What dad? And who's Eddie?

Something I do – something I started doing when I was in the force, I don't know if you'd call it a habit or a neurosis – is when I'm trying to figure something out, and the whole surface of my brain feels like someone's been after it with a cheese grater, I rewrite old popular songs in the unoccupied zones of my mind. At the moment, I'm silently singing *I'm puzzled now, but I won't be puzzled long*. Because bits of this are beginning to make sense.

I phone my vile partner to give him the bad news: he's going to be taking up permanent residence in front of that computer screen, until he finds what I'm looking for.

Then I sit Duncan Hinton down, dry his tears with a bit of kitchen roll, and encourage him to unburden his fears. While I'm doing that, Vincent phones me back to tell me Vic Murray is dead.

'Well, Mr Murray, there have been some developments since we last spoke.'

'Great,' says the client, leaning forward on my desk to catch my every word. 'You've found out who the police raid was meant for.'

'Not quite, no. To be honest, we've pretty much exhausted possibilities on that one. Think about it – even assuming their information was accurate to begin with, the cops could have got the wrong street, not just the wrong number. Or the wrong borough, even.'

Vincent enters the office carrying three teas. To punish me for making him fetch them, he says, 'In fact, you said the bloke in charge had a Scottish accent? They were probably Edinburgh police. Took a wrong turning off the motorway.'

Mr Murray's met my vile partner twice, which is once more than the minimum needed to know that he's best ignored. To me, he says, 'I've already said, the money aspect is not crucial here. If it's a question of widening the search . . .'

I shake my head. 'Not necessary. The fact is, we've already discovered what you hired us to find out.'

The client looks puzzled. He stares at me. He even stares at Vincent. Then he looks back at me, grins, relaxes back in his chair and lights a small cigar. He still looks friendly, he still looks slight, and he still looks middle-aged, the way he did when he first came to this office. It's just that now, he doesn't look like some friendly, slight, middle-aged bloke. And that's quite a difference.

'All right,' he says. 'You tell me what you know – that's what I've paid you for, after all.'

'First of all, Mr Murray, my condolences on the loss of your son.'

He stops in mid-inhale, and looks at me very hard. For a while, it occurs to me that he might punch me, but finally he nods, and starts smoking again. 'Vic was a good kid. Thank you.'

'May I ask you something?'

He smiles. 'Something you don't know? I'm amazed.'

'How long have you been . . . missing?'

This time he laughs. 'How long have I been on the run? Thirty years. I started young.' The client licks a finger and smooths his eyebrows. He laughs again; he seems to be enjoying himself. 'I was twenty-five when my wife died. Left me alone with a five-year-old kid. Neither of us had much family – not that we had anything to do with, at any rate. Anyway, I needed a job I could do from home, see? So I could look after the kiddie. I grew up around here, twenty minutes' walk from where I live now, I knew everyone, everyone knew me. People trusted me.'

'So you became a receiver of stolen goods.'

'Caretaker, basically, is what I was. People'd bring me pack-ages, boxes, whatever. I'd store them in my shed, or my loft, or

27

in the spare bedroom, in exchange for rent. Easy money. Better than taking in lodgers – boxes don't hog all the hot water.'

'You got caught, though.'

'Usual story, someone turned me in, hoping to get a lighter sentence themselves. I don't bear a grudge, I'd have done the same. It wasn't too bad – I only got six months, I made arrangements for a local villain's widow I knew to look after Vic for the duration. I wasn't too worried.'

'But three weeks into your sentence, you went over the wall.'

'Couldn't take it.' Mr Murray spreads his hands wide, and stretches his mouth and eyes in a look of amazement, as if, after all these years, that one weakness of his still shocks him. 'Prison – some people can do it, and some people can't. I simply couldn't. Tried to kill myself at the end of the first week. Tried again at the end of the second week. Escaped at the end of the third week.'

'And you've been on the run ever since.'

'Thirty years,' says Mr Murray. 'A British and Commonwealth record, I believe.'

'It's not,' sniffs my vile partner. 'There was this Irish bloke in the paper last year, still missing after forty-two years. Thirty years probably isn't even the British *amateur* record.'

'How come you've never been caught?'

Eddie Murray looks around the office, grinning. 'It's like the estate agents say: location, location, location. Listen, when it comes to non-violent, petty criminals like me, the police don't exactly get sweaty hunting for us. Why? Because they know for sure that sooner or later we're going to turn up somewhere we're known. The ex-wife's, the local pub, Mum and Dad's. And when we do, there'll always be someone with two pee to spare for a phone call to the local nick.'

'But not in your case?'

'No way. I was *never* going back inside, and that was that. As soon as I was clear of the walls, I headed for somewhere I'd never been before, had no earthly connection with, and I set about creating a life for myself that could never possibly intersect with my old life.'

'But you kept in touch with your son?'

'Not with Vic himself. But the woman who was looking after

28

him, she was a good person – still is, as it happens – and twice a year I phoned her, Boxing Day and Vic's birthday, and she spent ten minutes telling me his news. And that was it.'

'Until he died.'

'Yeah. Knocked off a bicycle, same as his mother. What are the odds on that?'

'Maybe it's hereditary,' says Vincent, and just for a second, Mr Murray's shoulders tighten and his eyes flicker Vincent-wards.

I jump in. 'By this time, your boy was a married man, with a young daughter. So you broke your rules, came home?'

Mr Murray nods. 'My fear of prison kept me from doing anything for Vic when he most needed a father. I couldn't let the same thing happen with my granddaughter.'

'How did your daughter-in-law react to you suddenly materialising in her life?'

He chews his lip for a while before replying. 'Stoically. She's a mother; she wants what's best for her child. A grandfather's better than no father at all.'

'I don't understand why you came back to Churchill Road. You had to leave where Vic and his family had been living, sure, but why not just start again somewhere new?'

He shrugs. 'It was a crazy risk, I suppose. Well, *definitely*, as it turns out. It's just – I always liked it around here, always missed it. Thought I'd been gone so long it'd be safe. What can I say? It's a nice place.'

'It's a boring, dead, anonymous, suburban dump, same as a million others,' sneers Vincent, who thinks 'nostalgia' is the name of a perfume they advertise on telly at Christmastime.

The client stands up, walks over to my vile partner, grabs a handful of his hair, tugs it out and shows it to him. Vincent yelps. 'What can I say?' Mr Murray says again. 'Roots: you've either got them or you haven't.'

Having heard the majority of Eddie Murray's life story from his own lips, it's my turn to tell him the rest. There's a tension in the air between us now, because we both know that we're getting to the crunch.

'The police raid panicked you. You thought that maybe it wasn't a coincidence, that it meant that someone had recognised you. Or at any rate, that it would draw attention to you. That's why you hired us – you needed to know if there was a serious, connected villain living locally, who might be a threat to your secret.'

'And I was right?'

'No, I don't think so. The raid was just what it seemed, a clumsy police error. It happens from time to time. The burglary at number 81 was a coincidence, too – but the death of the burglar wasn't. You were right about one thing – someone had recognised you: a guy called Duncan Hinton.'

'Never heard of him.'

'He was at school with your son. Unlike your son – unlike most of the old residents – he's stayed in the same area all his life. He happened to see you coming out of your house one day, shortly after you'd moved in, and something about your face, your body language, niggled at a vague memory in the back of his mind.'

Mr Murray shakes his head. 'He couldn't possibly have known my face – not after all those years.'

'No. But he knew your *son's* face. Seems there was a strong family resemblance, in adulthood.'

'Oh,' says Mr Murray. 'I see.'

There's a moment's quiet, to allow the ghosts to pass by.

'When Hinton recognised you, he was sure you'd recognised him. He was terrified.'

'Terrified? Of *me*?'

'Mr Murray, you were a bit of a legend amongst Vic's school-mates. Stories grew, the way stories will. As far as Hinton's concerned, you were a bogeyman from his childhood – a mad axeman, a master criminal, a remorseless monster from gang-land.'

The client splutters a puzzled laugh. 'I kept boxes in my spare room,' he says. 'That was all.'

'Duncan Hinton is a lonely man. No wife, no kids, doesn't have much to do with his neighbours. There's nothing more dangerous than a lonely coward with a lively imagination, Mr Murray. He became obsessed with the fear that you would think the police raid was down to him. In which case, you would come after him.'

30

'I've never *gone after* anyone in my life!'

'OK, but it wasn't the real you he was scared of. It was the myth of you, the ruthless gangster, that he'd grown up hearing about in and around Churchill Road. So, he set a trap for you. When you came to get him, he'd be ready for you. Every door and window in his place was well secured, but he deliberately made the patio door vulnerable – turned it into an irresistible invitation to break and enter. You see, double glazing is his business. He knew just how to –'

The client cottons on. 'That's – that's attempted murder! Or is it manslaughter?'

'I'm not a lawyer, Mr Murray, but certainly he'd hung the door in such a way that as soon as it was tampered with – either subtly with a tool, or bluntly with an object – it would swing out and pinion the intruder. Then he arranged to be away on business for the next few nights; nothing unusual in his trade. I believe he'd forgotten, or else didn't know, that there'd been a recent rash of break-ins in the area. He didn't have much to do with his neighbours. Double-glazing salesmen rarely win popularity polls.'

Mr Murray's gone pale. 'And if I hadn't gone for it?'

'He'd have tried again. Or tried something else. He was desperate.'

'I've never hurt anyone in my life, Mr Pound. Never.'

'You hurt me,' my vile partner mutters, rubbing his scalp.

'And he admits all this? This Hinton geezer.'

'Ah, well. He admitted it to me. But by the time the police ask him about it, I suspect the confession fever will have passed. If his lawyer's not too dozy, he'll see that it's going to be difficult to prove intent, provided he doesn't bring your name into it.'

The client takes out another small cigar and lights it. 'The police,' he says.

The crunch. It's arrived. And I'm still not sure what I'm going to say, let alone what I'm going to do.

'They're not stupid,' I say. 'The police. People using lethal means to defend themselves from burglars, it's far from an unknown phenomenon.'

Mr Murray inhales. 'But they won't know about me.' He exhales. 'Or will they?'

My decision enters my mind and exits through my mouth in one, fluid motion. 'They'll have to, I'm afraid. I run an honest business, Mr Murray. I'm an ex-copper. Reporting the whereabouts of an escaped prisoner – it's not a matter of choice for me.'

'I understand,' says Mr Murray.

'You're not going to kill us, are you?' says Vincent.

Mr Murray gives Vincent a look of intense loathing – which endears the client to me considerably, needless to say. 'I have never killed anyone, you prat. The last person I ever so much as slapped was my son when he was three years old, and he'd scratched one of my Elvis records.'

'Let's see,' I say, trying to sound casual. 'It's Friday night. The CID boys don't work weekends. I'll ring them first thing on Monday morning. Tell them what Hinton told me – how I thought it sounded pretty far-fetched, but eventually decided I ought to pass it on nonetheless.'

The man who had loved his son, and failed him, says, 'Thank you, Mr Pound,' and means it. He insists on settling up what he owes us before taking his leave. We shake hands, and I tell him it's a pleasure doing business with an honest man for a change.

After he's gone, Vincent – his bravado recovered – says, 'Maybe we should turn him in straight away, Doggo. I mean, there might be a reward.'

'If there is, it'll be in pre-decimal currency.'

We sit and drink whisky from coffee mugs for a while. I don't like drinking with my vile partner, but it's marginally less depressing than drinking alone.

'He's got three options, hasn't he?' says Vincent. 'Go to prison, do a runner, or top himself.'

I nod. 'And two days to decide.'

Vincent belches, but not very loudly. Perhaps even *he's* a bit subdued. 'So, what do you think he'll do? Run, or kill himself?'

I screw the top on the whisky bottle. 'Come on,' I say. 'Let's lock up and sod off.'

'It's his own stupid fault,' says Vincent. 'He shouldn't have gone home.'

'Places *call* to people, Vincent.'

He snorts that snotty, contemptuous laugh of his. 'Not to me, they don't.'

'Yeah, well. You're not people, are you?' From his self-satisfied expression, I gather that my vile partner takes that as a compliment.

Carol Anne Davis

Carol Anne Davis is a writer who successfully walks a tightrope, describing chilling and sometimes grisly events with a sharp wit. One of the pleasures of the crime story is the opportunity it affords to writers to address changing social fashions, and in 'Stitched Up', Carol pokes fun at the contemporary obsession with outward appearances as well as implying more serious comment on those who crave, and those who practise, cosmetic surgery. At the end, there is even a sly dig at Internet geeks.

STITCHED UP

Carol Anne Davis

She doesn't want to kill him, not at first. She just doesn't want to stay married. The eight-roomed villa would be so much more peaceful if it was exclusively hers. But if she asks for a divorce he'll go to the tabloids and then . . .

She runs her clinic all day and returns home to find his publicity photos all over the lounge. Goes to hang up her suit and finds a new toning table in his half of the dressing-room. He's in the drawing-room, watching a video he appeared in circa 1983.

'Fully booked?' he asks as she loosens her support stockings and pours herself a gin.

'Two abdominal reshapes today and a rhinoplasty job tomorrow.'

'Noses R Us,' a male-menopausal Justin says. Is he alluding to her first ever rhinoplasty? Roz drinks fast and soon refreshes her glass. Then she winces as she reads the latest bill from the wine club. If only he'd settle for a more affordable life.

'So, what did you do today?'

He stares more intently at the screen. 'Costed a new portfolio, but I think I'll leave it for a week or two.' That'll be a week or two spent on the toning table, then.

She realises the machinery she's looking at has changed. 'You've bought a new video player.'

'That was last month. A DVD.'

She's too busy – and too aware that he can blackmail her – to challenge him about their joint account but she's sure he's spending more than his royalties from UK Gold.

The tummy ops went well, as they usually do. She's given money to Oxfam, helped a child across the road, avoided walking on the cracks in the pavement. But rhinoplasty – nose

35

reshaping – is much more intricate as she'll have to break and trim and reset the bone.

The patient arrives early, as does the paid-by-the-hour agency nurse. Roz breaks and cuts and tries to forget her first ever nose-trimming procedure. The nurse calmly hands her the implements and watches the patient's vital signs. Once Justin used to hand her the implements. The patients loved him. Everyone had just assumed he was a doctor when he wore his neat white coat.

She'd put on her own coat and left the clinic that fateful day twenty years ago. It had only been for an hour during her first year in practice. An hour whilst the patient recuperated from the op. 'Page me if there are any problems,' she'd said to Justin. But the pager had failed and the patient had been a bleeder who choked to death . . .

She forced her thoughts to return to the present. The past and the future involved too much uncertainty and fear.

'I've got a commission from the Countryside Clothing catalogue,' Justin told her the following night, happily turning away from the DVD player. He spoke about it for an hour then seemed to belatedly remember the need to keep breathing. This was as good a time as any to tell him of her plans.

'I've decided to give up the clinic.'

'*Give it up?*'

'Yes. I don't . . . I'm not getting anything out of it any more. I thought I'd buy into a GP practice instead.' She named a couple of the larger ones which often had need of a practitioner. 'They have a refresher course for people like me who haven't worked as GPs for many years.'

'But you wouldn't be able to . . .' He ran a manicured hand over his abraded and reshaped fifty-year-old head.

'No more homers, I'll admit – but I can give you a recommendation.' She pretended to smile. 'I know a few people in the trade.'

'Word might leak out. I don't want the bloody tabloids sending me up,' Justin said.

You're yesterday's news, Roz thought, but she didn't say it. She was still at the stage of biting back her more hurtful replies. She felt that if she started to say what she really thought she might be shouting for ever, would unleash insults and accusations going back more than twenty years. And that wasn't fair – she had married him partly because he attracted her so hugely. Now she couldn't blame him for trying to maintain those exact same looks.

'We'll find you someone discreet.'

'I can't afford it.'

'Justin – you must have some money put away.'

She watched a guarded look enter his eyes. 'Just for our old age – assuming your changing career plans don't drive me to an early grave.' When he grimaced like that a series of little lines stood out at the corners of his lips. His frown fanned similar wrinkles. I'm damned if I'm giving him a skin peel, Roz thought to herself. If she was to buy into a general practice and keep paying the mortgage and antique furniture repayments on this house then she'd have to save like a miser. And have to spend her last surgical weeks bringing in much more cash.

She booked in extra patients for the four months which stretched ahead. She added new procedures like permanent micropigmentation. The results gave lasting eyelid and lip colour to women who didn't have time to put on make-up every day. 'You could do *my* brows with that. I'm always repencilling them,' Justin said, walking restlessly around her clinic till he found her new eyebrow colour charts.

'Mm?' She looked up from her book on refractive surgery, wishing that he wasn't always turning up here at her work and stealing her professional cosmetics. He often borrowed her keys and waxed his bikini line, leaving the sinks and surfaces coated with his hair overnight.

The days fused into the nights as she augmented lips and enlarged girlish breasts and reduced womanly buttocks. Removed eye bags from still vain fifty-somethings and enhanced teenage ears and cheeks. The basin swam with blood and bone and flesh. Her surgical gloves dripped crimson. Roz strove to keep her hand from shaking as silicone implants undulated on the table without benefit of touch or breeze.

Four months till countdown. The surgical seconds all dragged. Was it her sight, her steady hand or just her nerve that was declining? Was this simply the culmination of years of volatile operations? Or was some premonition at work, trying to save her from a catastrophic operating end?

'My wife the doctor doesn't sound as good as my wife the plastic surgeon,' Justin said. He'd taken to putting on his videos whenever she picked up a book. It was his equivalent of sulking.

'Act like it does. It's what you do, isn't it? Or are we just modelling for clothing catalogues nowadays?'

She watched him redden under the foundation he'd so carefully applied. 'You're a real bitch, Roz. I'm getting tired of it.'

She knew what he really wanted to say was, I'm getting tired of you. But he couldn't leave her unless he was willing to live on his savings. And if she left him he'd go to the newspapers and tell about that long-ago negligent death. At the time she'd begged him not to tell the police or the girl's parents that she'd been absent – and he'd agreed to cover for her. But they'd been in love then, whereas now . . .

At least a GP treats sickness that she hasn't caused, she said to herself several times a day. There was no one else to hear her. Justin was either out failing auditions or lying in the solarium he'd had installed and added to the existing mortgage on the house.

As her lease of the cosmetic surgery clinic neared its end, he grew ever more frantic.

'Maybe you should give me pectoral implants,' he said, flexing his arms before his dressing-room mirror.

'Maybe you should pay a few more of the bills.'

'If I look good I get more work. It benefits us both.' He looked ridiculously pleased at his cursory answer.

'It benefits these girls you screw,' Roz said.

She watched him grit his porcelain crowns together and remembered how much his private dentistry had cost them. 'Well, maybe if you made more of an effort I'd screw you too.'

So there it was, out in the open. The bookworm versus the male bimbo. Depth versus shallowness. Intellect versus looks.

'You're getting old, d'you know that?' she said with deliberate cruelty, 'You're starting to go bald on top.'

'Don't confuse me with someone who gives a fuck,' he said. She knew that he'd used that line in a film, that he'd repeated it since in the exact-same screen voice. She felt a small rush of pleasure as he put his right hand back and touched his slightly-thinning pate.

'I'm not doing your pecs,' she said resolutely, 'Extra surgery is madness. You can go to the gym like everyone else.' He could take charge of his own body there, instead of relying on her increasingly shaky hand and jaundiced eye and weary spirit. He could be manufactured rather than womanufactured for a change.

'My eyelids, then? It's years since you did them.' He was like a kid in a sweetshop trying to figure out just how much he could get away with.

'Told you – I'm only working for cash.'

She watched his fingers curl into fists and knew that he wanted to hit her. 'In that case I'll have to spend my life savings on another surgeon instead.'

It took Roz three days to decide what to do. Three days of mulling over the various ugly options. Finally she decided that she would operate.

'It's those little facial lines that really need to go,' she said.

'The ones around my eyes?'

'Yes, at the corners. And I could do your forehead.'

'A chemical peel?'

'No, more deep-seated than that – I can relax the muscles in your brow for a few months with a botox injection. After a few injections it gives a permanent result.'

'Something new?' He looked pleased, even hopeful.

'Well, new to me. I saw it done last month at that video presentation. But American ophthalmologists have been using it for twenty years.'

'Does it hurt?'

She shook her head at him as they sat across from each other in her beloved lounge with its restored original fireplace. 'No, the needles are tiny – after all, in some cases they're going into the muscle beside the eye.'

'And will there be bruising afterwards?' He flicked through his engagements diary. 'I'm doing that blood donor advert – a nationwide screening – at the end of the month.'

'No, the actual injection will just take a few minutes and then you must sit upright for a few hours rather than lying down. And it's a few days after that before the solution works.'

'And if you give me a few over the next year or so I may never need another facelift?'

She used all of her strength to keep her smile from being too knowing. 'That's right. Repeated treatments can make the smoothness permanent.'

He was laughing the next day as she injected the protein into the corrugator muscle between his brows. He winced only slightly when she injected the muscles beside his eyes. When she pushed the needle into his throat he stopped smiling.

'I didn't know that you planned to . . .' She watched him grow pale beneath the carefully layered damage of his tan.

'Just smoothing out a few lines on your neck.'

'And now I just sit here?'

'For four hours,' she confirmed, handing him his slender blood donor script to memorise. 'You can use the en suite toilet if you need to but don't go moving around unnecessarily and don't take any aspirin.'

'Don't need it anyway. Didn't hurt a bit,' he said with macho pride.

It would start soon. She went out and locked the door to her once-loved clinic. Went to the medical library and took out three books on general practice. 'Just doing a quick refresher course,' she said to the librarian, her unwitting alibi. 'My husband can't wait for us to spend more time together when I return to being a GP.'

Then she went and sat in Trafalgar Square and read a book and watched tourists in the joy-inducing sunshine. She'd be able to do this every weekend once she was a doctor again. Roz smiled to herself as she bought a carton of birdseed and threw it to the hungry beaks which soon surrounded her. There was much to be said for a quiet, single life.

It was encouragingly quiet when she returned to work. Slowly she unlocked and eased open the surgery door. Justin had fallen from the treatment couch and was lying on his back, his trousers soaked with urine. He was gasping like a fish on hot dry land. She watched his increasing respiratory paralysis, noted his vision was blurred or non-existent. Leastways, he didn't seem to be aware of her staring down. Another two or three hours should stitch things up completely. Roz left, leaving the door unlocked this time.

When she next went back he was clearly dead. Her heart started to speed guiltily in her chest and she backed away from his sprawled intractable body. She had to phone right this second whilst she felt genuinely ill at ease . . .

999. She'd never phoned it before though her patients had occasionally looked so grey that she'd known that she ought to. 'Ambulance!' she gasped when the strangely mechanical voice asked which service she required.

'And what is the nature of the complaint?'

'I . . . think my husband has . . . harmed himself.'

'Can you tell me his condition?'

'I . . .' A vocal tremor here for benefit of the recording equipment. 'I think he's dead.'

After that it was all blue lights and black tea and orange comfort blankets. 'He wanted to try the latest injections,' she said in the hospital side room.

'A drug, ma'am?' the WPC inquired.

'No, botox – it relaxes specific muscles in the face to erase wrinkles.'

'And you injected him?'

'Oh no.' Roz had practised looking indignant in front of the mirror. 'I would have given him a little injection to help erase crow's feet – but he wanted every part of his face and neck done in larger doses. I explained that that was impossible, that the jags caused mini-paralysis.'

'So, could he have entered the clinic and treated himself?' the male colleague asked.

'Yes.' She wished she had the acting talent to summon up a few tears. 'He was my receptionist when I first went into private practice. He knew his way around the surgery.'

'He was qualified?'

'No, no. He was an actor. But when we were first married and he was resting, he'd send out testimonials to potential new clients and answer the phone.'

'And you think he used your medicines on himself?'

'He must have done.' Roz nodded. 'I came back from the city to find him . . . well, like you saw him. My entire stock of botox is no longer where I stored it and Justin's body was half covering the empty bottle and a syringe.'

41

'Imagine dying to look good,' said the PC, shaking his wrinkle-free head.

His time as a troubled mirror man would come. 'The sad thing is I was about to give up the clinic, move into general practice. Another few days and Justin wouldn't have had access to this stuff.'

'Suppose that's why he did it,' the WPC said, looking pleased with herself. 'We've people at the clinic now searching for clues.'

Later she phoned. 'We found an R pencilled in his diary for today. Can you tell me what that means?'

'R stands for rehearsal.' But he hadn't had a formal engagement today. Hell, he'd have hired a skywriter to tell the world about it. 'He must have meant reading over his blood donor script.'

Both police people seemed to be reading from a script when they came to the house later that night. 'Roz Wayborne, I'm arresting you for. . . .' She only half heard the rest.

'But I didn't.' She denied it till she reached the station, till they showed that they had it all on film. Roz watched herself walk into her pristine sunlit clinic. Justin was already sitting there, fidgeting about on the surgical couch and admiring his tanned arms and legs. She watched as she greeted him then injected him, as she left and he collapsed and she came back to watch him nearing death. She saw herself leave his gasping body at the hour the clock showed and return a second time.

'Why would he film it?' she asked, still disbelieving, 'I mean, he always wanted to look good. He thought he was having cosmetic surgery.'

'We think he wanted to rehearse his blood donor advert,' the policewoman said. 'We understand it would've been his first TV appearance in over a year.'

That was in character, made sense. It would have been so easy for him to set up a camcorder in one of the shelving units or on top of a cabinet. She didn't know that he'd bought one, had never thought to check.

They took her away, then, but she read later that the film of Justin's death had been stolen and finally played on the internet. The papers said that dozens of people had consequently set up Justin Wayborne tribute sites. Roz herself didn't see the sites because she no longer had access to the internet – and she couldn't watch the televised documentary about Justin's life because the prison warden turned off the TV at 8 p.m.

She hoped, for a while, that when she was eventually paroled she'd get all of Justin's worldly goods and his life savings, but a murderess cannot benefit from her actions so the estate went to the Indigent Actors Fund instead.

Eileen Dewhurst

Christmas crime stories have a long tradition: according to *The Oxford Companion to Crime & Mystery Writing*, there are at least 130 novels and eight anthologies of short stories with Yuletide associations. Here, however, Eileen Dewhurst has managed to come up with a fresh variant on the familiar theme. The police investigator is a young detective constable and there is passing reference to one of Eileen's regular heroes, Detective Chief Superintendent Maurice Kendrick, and his last recorded case, *Roundabout*. But it emerges late in the story that Eileen's interest lies not in the police work, but rather in the motivation of the culprit. And so the traditional themes of Christmas and the scene of the crime are put to effective use in a tale that in the end proves to be unexpectedly poignant.

A DATE WITH SANTA

Eileen Dewhurst

October was going out in a blaze of glory – calm blue skies, thick warm yellow sunshine – so it made municipal sense, Detective Constable Jim Martin reflected philosophically, for council workmen to be putting up Christmas decorations in Seaminster's main shopping street.

Trying not to imagine how tatty they would look by Christmas Eve, the DC plunged into Curley's, the town's normally elegant department store, to find it even more glaringly anachronistic: a carol was already trilling, ice-cream-van style, in the fancy goods department, and a one-dimensional Father Christmas was indicating a huge decorated Christmas tree. And you couldn't get away from it, the DC discovered as he began his patrol of the ground floor: everywhere you looked there was at least a bunch of ersatz holly or a golden fir cone in your field of vision. The transformation from Saturday was so total, they had to have had armies of overtime seekers at work on Sunday.

The grotto was the only Christmas item that had been under construction the last time he'd done his tour of duty, but now it was up and running; already, at ten o'clock on a Monday morning, a line of mothers and infants was forming. Jim exchanged a wry smile with the girl behind the glove counter. He or Janice or both of them would have to bring the two kids along, but he'd make them wait till December; he'd be as resistant as he could get away with to this commercial exploitation of an event which had allegedly taken place at the coldest time of the year. As if conceding the rightness of his reaction, the tinkly music began to play 'In the Bleak Midwinter'.

Over the past few weeks Curley's ground floor had been subject to a bout of shoplifting so consistent and intense that, with the imminent display of seasonal goods and the prospect of cover being provided for the thief or thieves by the hoped-for crowds of Christmas shoppers, the management had asked the local constabulary if they could provide a plain-clothes presence for as long and as often as one could be made available.

So for a week now, twice a day at ten and three, DC Martin had presented himself at the Information Desk and begun a random patrol. Despite the presentation by the management of a desperate situation, the only person he had so far apprehended was an old lady who had pocketed a hairnet, and as she was so small and gentle he had accepted her plea of absent-mindedness and let her go without referring her to the store's own detectives. Management's expressed interpretation of the hiatus was that the felons were gathering their forces for the richer seasonal pickings, but DC Martin had started to experience an uncomfortable feeling that Curley's staff were beginning to be disappointed by his lack of performance.

So that this morning, mingling with his personal disapproval of Christmas in October was a sense of professional relief that battle was about to be engaged.

The grotto theme this year was a fairy glade. Stone-coloured cardboard toadstools dotted the cordoned-off tableau lining the back of the grotto area – normally a section of the electrical goods department – and an upholstered one awaited any child too shy to climb on Santa's lap. On the cardboard toadstools, out of reach of stretching hands, sat elves, fairies, pixies and gnomes fashioned in fibreglass and helped to a semblance of reality by the dim yet clever lighting. Small animals were frozen in mid-flit between the fungoid growths, but there were two – a squirrel and a rabbit – which actually moved about the simulated forest floor, while the heads and arms of a couple of fairies and one of the gnomes were mobile too. The trees that framed the scene were white with rime, and there was a constant slow fall of fat white flakes which DC Martin was told by the girl behind one of the perfume counters was an illusion created by the play of light on a static backcloth of white blobs. Mildly curious, he put his head for a moment round the heavy velvet curtain framing the entrance, nodded apologetically to Father Christmas on his rime-encrusted throne, and reluctantly admitted that, in one small corner of Seaminster at least, the weather did appear to be in tune with the season that was being so assiduously mocked up.

By eleven o'clock, Father Christmas was ready to call it a day. He detested children, and an hour was time enough in which to be kicked about the shins by the embarrassed wriggling feet of little boys, wetly kissed by deluded little girls, and twice have his beard pulled, the second time so hard he'd been afraid of losing it. And there were another six hours to go, with just one half of one – unpaid – for his lunch at two o'clock when the grotto briefly closed. At least all the facial hair and the rosy-cheeked, bulbous-nosed mask meant he didn't have to smile, and he'd won one reluctant concession from his temporary employers: after every ten visitations, the member of staff currently on the entrance was to allow him a five-minute break.

He was longing for a fag, but the miserable little respites were too short for him to leave his post. At least Curley's paid well apart from the lunch break – or he wouldn't be sitting there like a prat saying 'Ho, ho, ho' every few goddam minutes – and while he awaited each renewed onslaught he kept himself going by thinking about what he would do with the extra cash. Go digital with his TV, increase his regular stake at the bookies, pretend to be generous with that loaded old bird down the Royal Oak . . .

The last family had been particularly large and unruly, and as they disappeared between the curtains he closed his eyes after waving an acknowledging hand at the young chap on duty who was nodding to him as he drew the entrance curtain which would ensure his peace for the statutory five minutes.

So the surprise was big enough to make him jump when he felt another small body nestling into his lap. Another small boy, he saw as reluctantly he opened his eyes, the skin of his face noticeably smooth and clear even in the dim light that surrounded them, his rosy mouth widening in a smile.

'Hi, Thanta!' the mouth lisped.

'Hello, my little man.' He'd better get a move on, cut the usual cackle, before an irate mother came storming back in to accuse him of molesting her little innocent. It had happened before. Not

47

always without cause, but these days he seemed to be past it . . .

'So, what would you like from Santa Claus?'

Girls' presents were on the floor to his right, boys' presents to his left, and he began to lean leftwards.

'*I've* got a pwethent for *you*, Thanta,' the child said.

'Well, isn't that nice,' Father Christmas responded on a reflex, placing a kindly hand on the little chap's shoulder.

It was the last thing he ever did.

It was another child screaming that alerted everyone, the boldest child of the next family in the queue, whose mother told DC Martin how he had run up to Father Christmas and clambered on to his lap in one rush from the entrance as the curtain was drawn back. The child had held up a pair of red hands as he cried out, and the subsequent flurry of snatching him away was what caused Father Christmas to loll sideways on his throne and confirm the terrible truth. By the time Jim arrived at a run from men's toiletries, alerted by the panic in the summoning voice, overhead lights were blazing and the little world of the fairies seemed to him to have shrivelled to nothing, its illusory magic fled.

Someone had opened the red uniform, and the handle of a kitchen knife was visible in the gap.

'When was the last time anyone saw him alive?' Jim demanded of the small group clustering around him, thanking fate that a cordon to keep out the curious – inadvertent vandals at the scene of any crime – already existed in the form of the grotto boundaries. He had alerted the station, and uniforms, senior CID, SOCO and the doctor would be on their way, so he could turn his full attention to any possible witnesses or clue-holders. Somewhere at the back of his shock he realised that he had never yet been in so important a position . . .

'I saw him just five minutes before . . . before I heard the scream.' The young chap who had been on the entrance was pale and sweating, the planes of his face gleaming in the unmerciful light. 'I nodded to him through the door to tell him I knew it was his break time, and he waved a hand at me. Then . . . then I just drew the curtain and stood talking to the family at the head of the queue' – he nodded to the little group beside him, motionless

48

but for the sobbing child in the arms of its mother – 'until my watch told me it was time to get going again. I might have exchanged another look with Mr Burnett when I drew back the curtain, but I didn't, I suppose I was just about aware of him sitting still in his chair – oh, God – but I just said to this lady ... OK, in you go, and the little boy started running ... I swear –'

'That's right, officer.' To Jim's relief the mother's voice was strong and steady, sounded as if it was used to being heeded. 'I watched this young man raise the curtain without really looking inside the grotto, and then my poor lamb ...' The woman bent her head to kiss the curls of the child folded foetus-like in her arms.

'I'm so very sorry, madam,' he said automatically. His job, if courteously done, constantly entailed being apologetic over events for which he was not responsible. He turned to the two men. 'Are there other ways in and out of the grotto?'

'All the way round except for the tableau area!' Jim saw the relief of this fact in the younger man's desperate face. 'There are breaks in the curtains, but apart from that you'd only have to bend down and crawl under anywhere at the sides. Our store detectives – and you too, of course, officer – walk around regularly, but no one thought there was any particular danger. I mean ... the gifts aren't valuable – I mean ...' His pallor suddenly flooding pink, the young man glanced uneasily at the small stout man standing impatiently beside him.

'Compared with many of the goods stocked by Curley's,' the store manager took up smoothly. 'It did not seem to us, officer, that with the erection of the grotto we had acquired a new safety hazard. It surely has to be someone with a personal grudge –'

'Or a hatred of Christmas in autumn,' the child's mother interrupted, and DC Martin, who had already decided she was attractive, shot her an involuntary approving look.

The store manager politely inclined his head in her direction, but turned back immediately to the detective constable to reiterate his own suggestion. 'I've heard that Mr Burnett was – a somewhat difficult man,' he added.

'His background will have to be investigated, of course,' Jim responded. The mere thought of it made him feel tired. 'But for now, CID's priority will be to interview staff and customers and

I'll be glad if a suitable room can be prepared. I know it's hard to imagine the murderer lingering in the store after the killing, but I'm afraid I've had to give orders, sir, that for the time being no one be allowed to leave.'

Jim steeled himself for the expected explosion of outraged protest, but to his surprise and relief the manager shrugged and said crisply that he was aware of the need for such an action while relying, at the same time, on the skill and understanding of the police to let the imprisonment continue for as short a time as possible.

'Of course, sir. Now, if you'd be good enough to set up a tannoy message to all those still in the store who have visited the grotto . . .'

Shadowing the manager and approving the quarters allocated for the interviews, Jim Martin thought warily of the Big Chief. A body in a Christmas grotto wasn't quite so frustrating as the two bodies on a traffic island Detective Chief Superintendent Kendrick had elected earlier in the year to investigate hands-on, but it was tending that way and the DCS, though well liked, was known for his short fuse. Not quite so short though, Jim tried to console himself, since the DCS and his wife had got back together. But having seen today's set-up, Jim Martin was convinced that the killer of Father Christmas had planned his actions over time and with care, and his instincts were telling him that this was a murder which would never be solved. There were storms ahead.

The small boy was just old enough to be out on his own without causing concern to the mothers and the bobby he passed in the street, but when he reached the station and showed his ticket for the London train to the man at the barrier he got a searching look and a question.

'Well now, sonny! Where's your mum?'

'It's all right, thanks. Honestly. I've done it before. And my mum's meeting me the other end.' The child was no longer lisping.

'OK then, off you go. But don't talk to any strangers!'

'Promise!'

The boy could feel the man's eyes on him as he skipped

50

childishly along the platform and hopped nimbly up the steep steps into a coach. The little lobby was empty and he stood leaning against the wall, breathing heavily and flexing his protesting knees, before flinging himself into the corner of the nearest empty pair of seats, where his eyes immediately closed in exhaustion.

There was another overtly wary reaction during the course of the hour and a half's journey – from the ticket inspector, who was a little more difficult to convince that he was old enough to be in charge of himself – and a few smilingly indulgent glances from his fellow passengers.

He had learned that the train remained stationary for several minutes at Clapham Junction, and just before its arrival there he made his way to the nearest toilet. Standing on tiptoe to stare into the pockmarked mirror, he had to congratulate himself on the appearance of the face staring back at him, its fresh bloom, the thin scattering of freckles over the nose, the soft lock of dark hair falling carelessly on the forehead. No wonder he had awakened so many protective instincts since leaving the department store! To his ironic amusement, he found himself reluctant to lift his hands to his face, but when he had placed them to each side of his chin he raised them roughly and whipped their contents above his head.

'Jesus!' he muttered then. 'I hadn't realised . . . You're an old man as well as a freak.'

But a freak and an old man – a man on the verge of middle age, he amended, as he reluctantly reaccustomed himself to the heavy jowls, bulging forehead and coarse skin of his normal appearance – who had at last earned his place in the community. Cursed with a little boy's body while his head and its contents grew up, he'd been an outcast for years. First there had been the slow withdrawal of his parents' caresses as gradually they realised what they had given birth to, then the mockery of his fellow inmates in the home for unfortunates to which they abandoned him. The staff didn't caress him either but they didn't mock him, except for the man in whose immediate care he and another midget had been placed. Even now he couldn't think of his little friend Peter without pain. The man in charge had so sadistically abused them both that one day Peter had gone down to the nearby railway line and laid his neck on the track. Escaping his prison to go in search of his missing friend he had come across the decapitated body and then, a few feet away, the grimacing head.

After the initial shock he had envied Peter the courage that had brought his suffering to an end, and for the next few years he had desperately tried to follow his example. But his own courage had never reached the level of his friend's, and he had continued to suffer the miseries the monster so secretly inflicted – no chance of complaining, the threats of retribution were even more terrible than the horrors he was already undergoing. Mr Burnett detested freaks; they were the detritus, he said, left over from God's nobler creations, and he made sure the midgets, and the other poor souls with misshapen bodies, were left in no doubt of his contempt. The reluctantly surviving midget had escaped at last only because his head gave up under the onslaughts and he was sent to a hospital for people with freakish minds.

And there, a kind and enlightened member of staff, as he recovered, had found him a trade: his superb eyesight – operating so improbably out of narrow sunken sockets – fitted him well for the office of watchmaker, and he had a feeling for beauty. Over the years that followed he had extended his skills to include the making of jewellery, and had eventually set up his own small business.

And now, at last, he was being accepted as a human being: his customers were recommending him to their friends, he had been invited to become a founder-member of a Neighbourhood Watch, and he was discovering a small gift he had not known he possessed, the gift of listening. His customers and his new friends were confiding in him, using him as a sounding board for their frustrations and dilemmas, so that he had begun to experience, if vicariously, a number of normal lives.

But there had been another ambition. All the time, as he searched for, and found, his self-respect, he had slowly but steadily pursued the other search that had culminated in the execution he had carried out that day. Ever since he had escaped the sadistic clutches of Cecil Burnett he had known he had a duty to rid the world of an evil brute. The man, he was convinced, had no soul, it was he who was the detritus of God's creation. So that, although he had never so much as killed a fly, as he struck the blow he had so carefully set up he had had no qualms.

But now?

Underneath the certainty of what he had to do there had run a current of fear that when he had done it, righteous as he believed it to be, he would be doubly crippled by his knowledge that he was a murderer . . .

After combing his sparse hair and straightening his tie he went back into the lobby and stood staring through the window above the door. The train was gathering pace, it would soon reach Victoria. And he would soon know what he had done to himself through a deed that in the end had been an act of altruism as much as the settling of a personal score. If remorse came, there was no place in any community that would shield him from it.

But the rail track was very near, and Peter had always beckoned . . .

The train whistled as it entered the tunnel, and against the sudden blackness beyond the window there sprang up in the grubby glass a dim reflection of his face. It seemed for a moment to be unfamiliar, and then, to his infinite relief, he realised why: this was the first time in his life that he had seen it smiling.

Martin Edwards

This is the first time I have set out to build a crime story upon the foundation of a real-life (although non-criminal) incident. Although many fine mysteries have their origins in actual occurrences, my preference is to make everything up. But the germ of 'The Basement' came from my mother's reminiscences of life in war-time Yorkshire and the setting of one tragedy she recalled struck me as especially evocative. Beyond that starting point, everything else is of my own devising.

THE BASEMENT

Martin Edwards

I hated that basement. Hated it from the moment I first climbed
down the old stone steps. It wasn't only the smell of damp,
which made me want to heave. It wasn't even the sound of
scurrying feet as an unseen rat fled at our approach. I loathe
enclosed spaces; since childhood, I have suffered from a mild
form of claustrophobia. The prospect of spending a night underneath Prince Albert Chambers in my uncle's company started a
pounding in my temples and I found myself gasping for
breath.

I kept trying to reassure myself. It was at least safer here than
when we were checking that all was well in the offices upstairs.
But there was no point in pretending. I would sooner have taken
my chances outside, even if this turned into one of those nights
when the Luftwaffe, on the way home from blitzing Liverpool,
dropped their remaining bombs on the city centre.

'You all right?' my uncle muttered as I followed him back
down, a bucket of water in each hand, taking the uneven steps
gingerly and one at a time.

'Fine, fine,' I assured him. It was a lie, but he simply responded with his characteristic sceptical grunt.

I could say nothing about my fear of the night ahead, could do
nothing but endure his quiet scorn. Besides, I'd always suspected that Uncle George had never had much time for me. As
a child, after my epilepsy was diagnosed, I'd overheard him
describing me to Auntie May as sickly, and although it was true
enough, the scorn in his voice made me cringe. For a few short
hours, I wished I was dead.

I was acutely conscious that he regarded me as a poor specimen in comparison to my cousins: Tom, the handsome one, and
sporty Ronald, who played soccer in the Manchester League in

55

winter and transformed into a dashing batsman each spring. Ronald was George and May's son, a boisterous, good-humoured young man who had combined his weekend game-playing with a job as an insurance broker before the call-up. Ronald and Tom enjoyed the rudest of health, but I was never jealous. At least, not much.

'Come on, then,' Uncle George muttered as we put the buckets down.

He led me back upstairs to make sure that on each floor there were more buckets, each filled to the brim with water, in case the worst happened. Darkness had fallen outside and even above ground there was a March chill in the air. To keep my mind off other things, I chattered nervously about one of the ARP wardens I had got to know while helping to man the telephones. Twenty years ago, I'd learned, he had played county cricket for Lancashire. I wondered if my uncle, a keen lover of the game, remembered him.

'Once saw him drop three catches on the first morning of a Roses match at Old Trafford,' my uncle said grimly. 'We lost by an innings.'

So that was the end of that conversation. I cast around frantically for another suitable topic to talk about. Tonight I felt apprehensive in his company, more so even than when I was a boy. As we did our rounds, I gabbled about the trivial incidents of my daily routine. He didn't show the slightest interest in what I was saying, did not even bother to grunt, but I could not blame him. I knew I ought to pull myself together, but I found it almost impossible to keep a grip on my emotions. Especially each time we returned to that cold and musty basement.

'Jerry scored a couple of direct hits on shops in Market Street last night,' I said, panting as I put the last bucket in place. 'It makes you think ...'

'Not much point in thinking about bombs, lad,' my uncle said sourly. He was straightening a length of hosepipe. 'If it's got your number – that's it.'

He was right, of course. Eighteen months since we had sat around the wireless and heard Mr Chamberlain's declaration that a state of war existed between ourselves and Germany, I had almost forgotten what it was like to live in a time of peace. War is strange. It affects people in different ways; it can break down

56

barriers, and inhibitions too. When that mournful siren wails, no one can be sure that they will live to see the dawn.

We made another journey downstairs with bedding for the night. My uncle had suggested that after midnight we should take it in turns to grab a bit of shut-eye while the other kept a look-out. His own office was on the second of Prince Albert Chambers' five floors, separated by a dusty corridor from a bespoke tailor's. The tenants of the little businesses which filled the building took it in turns to firewatch each night. They had to do what they could to protect their livelihoods. Even if no bomb struck, there was always the danger that sparks might set off a blaze with consequences no less devastating.

I shivered at the thought of sleeping in that basement. Perhaps it wasn't so safe after all. What if the building above was destroyed and the entrance to the basement became blocked by tons of fallen masonry? The two of us would be entombed together. How long would the oxygen last – in time for help to arrive? I found myself breathing hard as my imagination did its worst.

'Cold?' Uncle George demanded. 'You're shaking, lad.'

He could never quite conceal his impatience with me. I felt myself blushing as he checked his keys. In the candlelit gloom, I could see a huge old coke boiler in front of the far wall. Presumably it was supposed to provide the heat for the whole building. By the look of it, the boiler had been put in at the time that Prince Albert Chambers was built. No wonder everywhere was so draughty. I went over and warmed my hands on the rusting metal.

'No time to be mollycoddling yourself,' my uncle said sharply. 'We need to get back up there.'

I felt as though he had slapped my cheek, and for a moment I almost said something that we would both have regretted to the end of our days. Fortunately, I managed to hold my tongue and, without another word, I followed him upstairs to fire-watch.

How I wished I had not agreed to take the place of Manny Shimkus and thus spared myself the misery of a whole night in the basement with my uncle. A misery compounded by the inescapable fact that I owed him a great deal. Uncle George had always had a soft spot for my father, the youngest of the three brothers, and when Dad died suddenly of a stroke four years before war broke out, he made out an allowance to Mum so that she and I would not starve.

George was the success of the family. An accountant by profession, he had established his own small practice in the city centre. My father worked in a foundry and had never managed to scrape enough cash together to save, while Arthur – Tom's father – worked in a department store in Bolton. The Chadburns had never been moneyed. My grandparents had met while both in service at one of the big houses in North Lancashire. But George had a good brain and, even more important, a resolute character. He was practical. Once he set his mind to something, he did it. Fortunately for my mother and me he had determined that we should not suffer because my father had failed to provide for us. Yet, although it may seem ungrateful, his generosity did not strike me as entirely unselfish. George Chadburn did not say much, but I had no doubt that he cared about appearances. In his own way, he was a man of substance in Manchester. Like many of his age and class, he disliked nothing more than to be embarrassed and he would have felt uncomfortable about what people might say, had his sister-in-law and her invalid son been left destitute. At the time of Munich, he even offered me a job as a clerk in his office, on a weekly wage ten shillings more than I was paid by the solicitor for whom I worked. When I declined with profuse thanks, however, I sensed his relief. He was a man who would always do his duty, but sometimes he made it a little too obvious that was precisely what he was doing.

Increasingly, I felt a sense of guilt so far as Uncle George was concerned, and not simply because I guessed that, secretly, he wished that I had died and his son Ronald had lived. Since I was in debt to him, it seemed right to seize any opportunity to redeem that debt, even if only in small measure. My chance had come at a family gathering at Uncle George's home the previous Sunday afternoon. George was complaining that the tailor, his fellow tenant on the second floor of Prince Albert Chambers, was not pulling his weight when it came to firewatching.

'But he's ill, isn't he?' Lucy asked, smoothing the hem of her silk dress and pretending not to notice my cousin Tom's admiring gaze.

Lucy was George's second wife. They had been married for

two years. The wedding took place barely six months after he had laid Auntie May to rest. She had been suffering from cancer of the liver, a dreadful illness but mercifully swift. Lucy had been George's secretary, sharing an office with him on the second floor of Prince Albert Chambers. No one doubted that George had been bereft, although a few tongues wagged at the shortness of the interval of mourning before the happy couple announced their engagement. But George was one of those men who needed someone to look after him. To iron his collars and put out clean clothes for him every morning. And someone, perhaps, to give him the respect that he considered his due. Lucy was thirty years his junior, a pretty and slender young woman from Ancoats who knew exactly what she wanted. Her family was as poor as church mice and even though people sniggered at the mismatch in age, looks and state of bank balance, I could not in my heart blame her for seizing the chance to escape from the tawdriness of the terraced back streets and a job in a bolt factory.

'Everyone ought to do his bit,' grumbled George. It was a favourite refrain. 'And that includes Manny Shimkus.'

Shimkus was the tailor, a fat breathless little man who had sold me the suit I wore for my uncle's wedding. I never remember meeting him on a single occasion when he did not complain about his health. I suspected he would probably outlive us all. My uncle didn't much care for him. Whether that was because he was a Jew – and my uncle had, in years gone by, been known to say that Mosley knew a thing or two – or simply because my uncle didn't like many people of any kind, I was never entirely sure. Probably it was a bit of both.

'Short of someone to help you out on the rota?' Tom asked. 'Don't worry, Uncle George. Reg and I will help you out. Won't we, Reggie boy?'

I was taken aback by Tom's suggestion. He was an entertaining companion, but I had never associated him with spontaneous acts of selflessness. Without thinking it through, I nodded enthusiastic agreement. 'Glad to. Any time.'

Of course, I had never visited the basement then. Never had cause to.

My uncle replied with his customary grunt, but I could tell that he was pleased. 'All right,' he said at length. 'If you want.'

After Tom and I had said goodbye, and while we waited for our parents to collect their coats before we all set off on the short walk to our respective homes, I asked, 'What gave you the idea of volunteering our services?'

'Everyone ought to do his bit,' Tom said, imitating our uncle's gruff tone to such perfection that I could not help laughing. Tom often had that effect on me. The wickeder his wit, the funnier I found it.

'Speaking of which . . .' he said, after a few moments.

'What?'

'Oh, nothing,' he said, with a smirk and a shake of the head. 'So tell me, Cousin Reginald. How's your love life?'

I shrugged. Tom had always enjoyed much more success with the opposite sex than I did. He enjoyed talking about his conquests and prospective conquests, too. 'It was bad enough before war broke out. Now . . .'

'Come on,' he said, clapping me on the back. 'No need to be downcast. You're not a bad-looking fellow, you know. And let's be honest, there aren't many presentable chaps like you and me around these days, are there?'

It was true enough. Neither Tom nor I would be going to war. Tom was a fit young man, who often said that he would have loved to join up, if he hadn't been in a reserved occupation. He was a draughtsman at Goldsborough's Steelworks; it was a skilled job, vital for the war effort. As for me, the epilepsy ruled me out of active service, and even though I had thrown in my lot with the ARP, I found it difficult to suppress a sense of inadequacy. In appearance, I was like any ordinary young man of twenty-two. I imagined strangers thinking that I should have been away with my peers, helping to overcome tyranny. But what was worse was the sense of relief, of which I had never spoken to another soul, because it made me burn with shame. I was glad that I had been spared the ordeal of fighting. Impossible to deny that I was a coward: come what may, I wanted to survive, not lay down my life for the greater good.

Ronald had not been so lucky. Like so many other young men of our age, he had dreamed of becoming a pilot and joined the Royal Air Force at the first opportunity. His Spitfire had been shot down over the North Sea six months ago. To make matters worse, during his last leave, he and his father had quarrelled and finished up not speaking to each other. I never learned the details, but the two of them hadn't been getting on too well since Lucy's arrival on the scene. Ronald had never liked the woman who had filled his mother's place and lacked the subtlety to conceal his true feelings. Uncle George had been devastated by his son's death. Perhaps he felt an obscure, illogical sense of guilt about it. Always a hard-working man, he had tried to shut out the pain by throwing himself into his office duties with greater zeal than ever. He was a member of the Home Guard and never missed a turn on the rota when it came to the firewatch at Prince Albert Chambers.

On one occasion, a fortnight or so earlier, Tom had talked about our uncle's restless activity. 'Makes you wonder, doesn't it?'

'What?'

'Well, Uncle George. I mean, there he is, filling each unforgiving minute either with his business or with war work. I can't help asking myself what his lovely bride reckons to it all.'

'I don't understand.'

He uttered a stagey groan. 'You've never been too quick on the uptake where the ladies are concerned, have you, Reggie? I've seen the way she yawns sometimes, when she thinks no one's looking. Although I can't help looking, I tell you straight. The woman's bored out of her tiny little mind. And who wouldn't be?'

I tried to match his knowing tone. 'Shouldn't have married an accountant, then, should she?'

He raised an eyebrow, just to make me aware that his question had been rhetorical. My role was to be his audience. That was the nature of our relationship. 'Ever taken a good look at her legs, Reggie? I mean, a really good gander?'

I frowned as he whistled in appreciative reminiscence. 'I don't think it's right . . .'

'Only commenting, Reggie boy. Don't get on your high horse. I was only passing the time of day.'

But the remark stayed with me and it echoed in my head as Uncle George and I settled down in the basement after our eleven o'clock reconnaissance of the upper floors. The night had been oddly quiet. No pyrotechnics, no shells or searchlights. The noise of a raid could be deafening, but the calm was, if anything, more sinister. Especially down in the dank gloomy basement, waiting to see if the familiar world would still exist tomorrow.

'I wonder what Lucy is up to,' Uncle George said suddenly.

It was an inconsequential enough remark, but it sent a shockwave through me, just as much as if the building had been struck by a shell. I could never remember Uncle George uttering a sentence that could remotely be characterised as either personal or ruminative; it was not his way. He never spoke about Lucy. Or Auntie May, come to that. Strong and silent men of his generation were not accustomed to wearing their hearts on their sleeves. Especially not when they were in the company of a handicapped weakling who had dodged the call-up and lived, while his own boy had died.

I hesitated before replying. I sensed he had been talking to himself rather than to me, but I felt it important to offer reassurance in my clumsy way. 'I'm sure she will be all right. She – she never seems to worry about the air raids.'

'No,' he said. 'No, she isn't a worrier, isn't Lucy.'

For a moment, I thought he was about to say something else. I held my breath, but he simply shook his head and suggested that I take a nap. At first I thought I would never manage even to doze in that ghastly basement, but I must have been more tired than I realised, since before long I was asleep. I remember my dream vividly. It resembled a nightmare. Tom and I were together and he was boasting of his latest conquest. She was a married lady, he confided. He would not tell me her name, instead giving me nods and winks. Enough for me to guess her identity.

When I woke later, my uncle was sitting on a blanket a few feet away from me. His back was resting against the wall and he was staring into space. Never before had I seen such an expression on his face. The old self-assurance was nowhere to be seen. Instead he wore a haunted look. I thought I could guess what was passing through his mind.

Tom had always, I knew, found Lucy attractive. What red-blooded man would not? She was a beauty; not a natural blonde, but with hair Hiltoned at the front and sides in the fashionable manner. Her figure was full, her legs elegantly curved. She had long ago mastered the art of flattering her husband; whenever she thought his eyes were upon her, her manner was meek and attentive. It was a habit she must have acquired after first starting to work for him. At the time their engagement was announced, Tom had joked with me that now they were making it legal. I was shocked when he suggested that their affair had begun while Auntie May was still alive.

To this day, in public, Lucy played the part of the devoted little woman. But Tom was right: every now and then, and to my mind with increasing frequency, she allowed the mask to slip and her dissatisfaction to show. I did not find it difficult to believe that when they were alone together, he fawned on her, desperate for a sign that she still loved him, in the way he believed she once had.

I coughed. 'I'll have a look around upstairs. Why don't you try and get forty winks?'

He shook his head. 'I won't sleep tonight.'

'It's been quiet so far.'

He shrugged. 'You go on, make sure all's safe.'

I climbed up to the top of the building and worked my way down, prowling the length of every corridor, taking my time as I peered at the business names on the frosted glass of each office. I did not want to spend any more time in that basement than I needed to. I rattled every door handle in the place, half-hoping to find something amiss, something that could take my mind off the fears that were forming in the back of my mind. But Prince Albert Chambers was as quiet as a graveyard.

My tour of inspection took upwards of half an hour. When I returned to the basement, Uncle George was dozing. The sound of my footsteps on the stone steps must have disturbed him, for his head shifted and he muttered something. Then repeated it.

'Lucy. Say it's not true. Oh, Lucy.'

'It's all right, Uncle George,' I said. My voice echoed around the basement, sounding unnaturally loud. 'There's nothing doing. Jerry's given us a wide berth tonight, it seems.'

He opened his eyes and groaned. 'Oh, it's you.'

I felt the need to fill the embarrassed silence. 'Did I hear you calling me?'

It was too dark to see his features, but I could picture them reddening. 'No, no. Maybe I was talking in my sleep. You didn't hear?'

'Not a word.'

'Well,' he said, his relief scarcely disguised. 'It's nothing to mither yourself about.'

Somehow or other the two of us hung on together in that chilly basement until the dawn came and he uttered a few gruff words of thanks for my help. I said it was nothing and we went our separate ways. As I wrapped my scarf tighter around my neck, I vowed to myself that it would be the one and only time that I shared the firewatch with Uncle George at Prince Albert Chambers.

A couple of days later, I saw Tom again. He lived a few streets away and was in the habit of dropping in to invite me out for a beer every now and then. We headed off to the Eagle and Child and midway through his second pint he asked me about the firewatch.

'The basement's a creepy place,' I said.

'Spooked you, did it, spending a night there?' He wiped the foam from his mouth. 'Matter of fact, I happened to be passing by Uncle George's house that evening. Thought I'd look in, make sure that Lucy was all right.'

I hesitated before saying, 'And – was she?'

'Oh fine.' He laughed. 'Fact of the matter is, I stayed a lot longer than I meant to.'

'What?' I was genuinely shocked.

'Oh, take that worried look off your face. It's just that we were having a chat and all of a sudden the siren went off. I said to Lucy that I hadn't realised that was the time.'

I bet, I thought to myself.

'Anyhow, she and I had to pile into the Anderson shelter in their back garden.' Tom laughed. 'Very cosy, it was. But I prom-ise you, I kept my hands to myself. Softly, softly, catchee monkey, you know.'

'She's married to our uncle,' I said tightly.

'Right enough. All the same, she's like a bird in a gilded cage, that one, Reggie. You mark my words. One of these days some-one's going to release her.'

'I really don't think –'

'All right, keep your hair on. I'll do my best to mind my p's and q's. Besides, you know what I always say about the thrill of the chase. But I'll tell you this. It's not right that a young woman like that should be left on her own at night. George ought to take better care of her.'

'You'll be down there in the basement with him tomorrow evening,' I said. 'Why don't you tell him yourself?'

Tom sniggered. 'No fear. I'll be on my best behaviour, you can be sure of that. Don't want him suspecting anything, do we?'

'He isn't a fool,' I said slowly. 'You're playing with fire, Tom.'

He laughed out loud. 'Oh, don't you worry about me. I'll be fine.'

I shall never forget the way he smiled as he spoke. His words came back to me the following Wednesday morning, when my mother arrived unannounced at the solicitors' where I worked. As soon as Mr Pardoe, the senior partner, told me to see her in the spare room, I knew that something terrible had happened. Six months earlier she had turned up in just this way, to break the news that Ronald was missing, believed killed.

'It's your cousin Tom.' Like me, she seldom had much colour in her cheeks, but never had I seen her look so white. 'And your Uncle George.'

'What's the matter?' I demanded.

'They were firewatching together at your uncle's office yesterday. Just like you and he did the other night.'

I nodded, uncomprehending. 'But I thought there wasn't any bombing on that side of the city last night?'

'No, the place wasn't bombed. Or set on fire. Oh, it was worse, much worse than that.'

'What happened?'

'This morning, the two of them were found together in the basement.' She sniffed, struggling to contain her distress. 'Both of them were dead.'

I put my arm around her, my mind working furiously. 'How did . . .?'

'The place was full of fumes.' She dabbed at her eyes with a lace handkerchief. 'There's an old boiler down there, apparently. Something went wrong with it – they are saying that the flue was blocked. I don't know the details. No one seems to know how it happened, it's a bit of a mystery. Anyway, they were both suffocated. When the office was opened up this morning, they were found.'

Time is a healer, they say, but as the days and weeks have passed, I have never managed to rid my mind of the image my mother's words conjured up. I picture my uncle and my cousin in the murky squalor of the basement, slowly succumbing together to the poison in the air. Their deaths are no mystery, at least not to me. I'll never prove it – God knows, I don't want to prove it – but I can guess what happened. George put two and two together and made five. Tom had not succeeded in seducing Lucy, that I know for certain, but my uncle was sure that he'd been cuckolded by his own nephew. Faced with utter humiliation, half a year after losing his own boy, he saw only one way out. He found how to block that flue and end it all. But in his bitterness he decided to take Tom with him. I can see him in my mind's eye, telling Tom to take a nap, then lying down beside him and waiting for the boiler to do its deadly work. In my imagination, I can smell the fumes. That was not the only poison my uncle had in his system when he died.

I cannot rid my mind of the memory of the basement. Such a damp and dreadful place for life to end. I cannot help repeating to myself that it might have been my corpse they found there with him. And in the small hours after the all-clear, as I lie in bed warmed by Lucy's soft flesh and listen to her contented breathing, I torment myself with the knowledge that it should have been.

Jürgen Ehlers

The Crime Writers' Association is a British organisation, but it welcomes suitably qualified members from anywhere else in the world. Jürgen Ehlers, a successful writer of short stories in Germany, here provides us with a skilful crime story set in the United States of America. The Golden Gate has featured in crime stories before – and also, most memorably, in Hitchcock's *Vertigo*. Here again it plays a crucial part, with a soundtrack provided by Albert Hammond's most famous song.

GOLDEN GATE BRIDGE – A VIEW FROM BELOW

Jürgen Ehlers

'How nice to see you again!' Thus the reunion with my brother began with a lie. I had not been looking forward to seeing him for the first time in fifteen years. His telephone call the day before, and instantly it was all there again, everything I had tried to push out of my mind ever since. He had been giving a lecture at Hamburg University and wanted to call briefly before flying back. 'You look fine,' I said. And that was not a lie. He did not look his age. I wondered if he had dyed his hair.

He looked about my room. Of course, he spotted the photo at once. The only souvenir of my trip to California fifteen years ago. The photo that still kept its place in my study was a picture of the Golden Gate Bridge. No ordinary picture though. None of those you can buy at any souvenir shop in San Francisco. It just showed part of the steel construction of one of the piers. My brother had taken it. 'Just give me your camera!' he had demanded and then held it obliquely downward into the gap between footwalk and driveway, and pushed the button. 'Farewell to California, I would call the shot,' he had suggested. This being the ultimate view of the sun-kissed state for the several hundred suicides who had jumped off the bridge so far. That was typical of my brother. Always good for some bizarre action, clever, fast, unpredictable. The years spent together had never been sufficient for me to grasp more than half of his mind. In the meantime I had stopped trying to understand him.

'You should have thrown it away,' he said. He took the picture off the wall and tore it to pieces. As if that could make any difference.

Many people assume it would be a great advantage to have a big, strong brother. That is only half true. Certainly, I used to

69

admire and envy him not only for being ten years my senior but also for his intelligence. But at times I had also hated him, especially when he said things like 'You would not understand that!' in the arrogant manner which only big brothers are capable of. Naturally he had got that job in California, picked out of a crowd of over two hundred applicants, whereas I had to be glad to find any job at all.

My invitation to California had arrived when I had almost given up hoping for it. He had announced that he had quit his job and was about to do something different, somewhere else in the US, but before leaving San Francisco he intended to show me around. He couldn't spare much time, but an extended weekend would be fine. The plane tickets? It would be his pleasure. He had always been a show-off.

I might have forgotten some of the details if I had not kept a diary in those days. We had never been able to afford major trips. The flight to the US was the most exciting event of my life. I simply had to write it down. There I was, standing on the Golden Gate Bridge, together with my brother and Nick Mintford, his landlord, and with Parker, the guide dog. Mintford was about my brother's age. 'I am Nick,' he had introduced himself. We all called each other by our first names, which was completely new for me. I felt part of a big family.

'Over there, I think that is Fisherman's Wharf, and the tiny island in the middle of the Bay, that is Alcatraz.' Nick pointed exactly in the right direction. I was impressed. Of course, my brother had told me in advance that Nick was blind. Nick, the freelance journalist and landlord of a little apartment in the attic of his house in Oakland. I was impressed at how independently he could find his way around. Only after a closer look did I grasp that his seeming independence was carefully orches-trated. Part of his freedom of movement, of course, he owed to Parker. His ability to point out the tourist spots to us, however, he probably owed to the fact that he had not been blind all his life. Right now he was holding on to the railings for orientation. I was sure that he was not making this tour for the first time; he might well have rehearsed his act with his wife, Marie.

Nick was clearly proud to show me his town. To be honest,

I was pretty tired after the twelve-hour flight and would have preferred to get some sleep first. However, Nick's enthusiasm just carried me along.

Our sightseeing tour ended abruptly when all of a sudden a heavy shower of rain poured down upon us. I had seen the clouds well in advance, but my brother had swept away my concern saying, 'Not at this time of year!' Obviously, there were exceptions, and even my big brother did not know everything. We were completely drenched by the time we reached our car. Parker shook his coat and jumped on to the back seat. Nick took the seat next to his companion. My brother pushed back his wet hair and sat down behind the wheel. Probably only I could hear that he was humming under his breath: 'It never rains in California.'

Marie I did not meet before the evening. She was a nurse. We collected her at the hospital and drove to a small Afghan restaurant near the University to have a meal. After dinner we went to Nick and Marie's place.

The house was over in Oakland, half-way up the hill, and from the back you had an astounding view of San Francisco and the Bay. Nick moved about in his house like a seeing man. Without hesitating he found the right drawers, and I would not have been able to open a bottle of wine more expertly than him. We drank Californian red wine. Nick knew all about it. I liked the wine; we emptied several bottles.

We talked about all sorts of things. Of course I had to appreciate Nick's column that had appeared in the *New Yorker* a year ago. The central part was the description of a sunrise in San Francisco. Those guys over in New York apparently had been unaware that their author was blind.

Later I helped Marie with the washing up. 'That is one of the things Nick hates to do,' she said. 'He is afraid of breaking something. To be honest, he probably doesn't drop any more plates than I do. It doesn't bother me much. Just carelessness, nothing more. But he always blames it on his blindness.'

'I think he takes it marvellously,' I said.

Marie smiled. 'A lot of it is just façade. He tries to make it all

71

look light and easy, but really it bothers him a lot. You can see that from the fact that he drinks too much.'

I felt silent, because I had also drunk too much. Did that show? Did I talk too much? Was Marie's remark aimed at me rather? I watched her putting the glasses up on to the highest shelf. She was a beautiful woman, although she must have been well beyond thirty, which was old for me at the time. How lucky Nick had been to have found such a companion!

'Was Nick already blind when you first met?' I asked.

She nodded.

'Some kind of illness?' I asked. At that moment I sensed already that she did not want to talk about it.

She answered in a single word: 'Vietnam.'

I fell silent. What could I possibly say? All of a sudden I became fully aware of the wonderfully innocent country I was living in. Eternal peace all my life. Other people had been less lucky. But at least Nick was still alive, and he had found Marie. I envied him for Marie.

America is the land of firearms. Nick had one, too. He showed it to us the same evening, when we touched on the question of security. Him being in the house on his own most of the day, what if a burglar came?

Nick grinned. 'I would shoot him! Just like this!' He had jumped to his feet. His chair fell over. Two steps to the sideboard and he had pulled open the drawer and produced a gun which he now trained at us. Not just vaguely in our direction, but at every single one of us, one after the other.

We had all jumped up. I held my breath. After all, Nick had drunk a lot, and we had to assume that the gun was loaded. It seemed rather large and menacing, but I had never seen a gun before. Except on TV, of course.

For a few seconds we all stood as if frozen. I do not know why, but all of a sudden I felt the urge to test Nick. Very cautiously I slid sideways. Inaudibly, as it seemed to me. But not so for Nick. The muzzle followed my move.

'It's not easy to trick you,' I said. My voice sounded strange.

'No.' Nick put the gun down. 'And it is not advisable to try.'

He felt for the chair which he had pushed over. Uneasy silence.

'How about a cup of coffee?' asked Marie. The spell was broken.

It was well after midnight when we clambered up the stairs to my brother's flat. I was dog-tired. Right next to me the springs creaked when my brother flung himself on his bed. 'Nick is quite a character, isn't he? By the way, do you know how he became blind?'

'Vietnam,' I said. I had nearly been asleep.

My brother looked at me. 'Good joke!'

I hated it when he talked down to me like that. After all, I was almost twenty, and apart from that in this case I was pretty sure. 'Marie told me so.'

'All right, it had to do with Vietnam,' he conceded. And then he told me: Nick had not been wounded in the war, as I had assumed. He had not been to Vietnam at all. He had fired a bullet through his head when they had come to draft him.

'My God,' I said.

Again I thought of myself. How easy it had been to dodge the draft in Germany, even for me, who had only half believed in being a 'conscientious objector'. And the risk of ever having to go to war had appeared so remote that I had never considered it seriously.

Again my brother looked down at me. 'You think now that it's ever so cool to protest against war like that? Kill yourself in order to avoid killing others?'

Indeed I had thought along those lines. 'But – couldn't he have simply gone to Canada? I mean, others have done that, as far as I know.'

He had gone to Canada. Staying with friends near Ottawa. But then his mother had died and he had decided to go to her funeral. That was not in San Francisco but some place in the north, the name of which I have forgotten. Nick's father was the mayor. They say he had not agreed with his son's decision to flee to Canada. They say he hadn't known that he would come down for the funeral, just for the day. The family reunion took longer than he had expected, and eventually Nick was talked into staying overnight. And then, next morning, there were the police.

'Nick assumes that his father turned him in. That in the course of the night, all of a sudden, he realised that as mayor he had no choice but to enforce the law. And after all, everybody had seen that his son was back. Nick locked himself into his father's study. When the cops threatened to force the door open, he took the pistol out of his father's desk, put the muzzle to his temple and pulled the trigger.'

He had been lucky. The bullet had penetrated his skull too far to the front and caused no lasting brain damage. Only that he was blind. And so, of course, unsuitable for military service. He was lucky twice. At the hospital where he was nursed he met Marie. She was a young probationer then, and of course she was also fervently against the war. They got married three months later.

After breakfast my brother and I went out to explore. The University and Botanic Gardens. Nick did not want to join us. The sun was shining. Only too soon would I be on my way back home to Hamburg. To drizzling rain and 17 degrees Centigrade. I congratulated my brother on his wonderful life here in California. If I were him, I would never leave the place.

My brother looked at me. 'You wouldn't believe how lonely I felt over here for the first few months. Sure, all the people I met were nice and friendly, but most relationships are rather superficial. If it hadn't been for Nick and Marie, I would have despaired.' That was something he had never mentioned in his phone calls. But there had been frequent calls during the first months. Suspiciously frequent calls, I would say with hindsight. When the calls got less frequent, our mother concluded that he had found new friends. Or a friend rather.

'You have really been lucky with Nick and Marie,' I said. 'Such nice people. I think it's marvellous how compatible they are.'

My brother nodded. 'So it seems, doesn't it? But all the same they will split up later this year!'

I thought I couldn't trust my ears. 'What do you mean by that?'

'Marie will leave him,' he said.

I stared at him.

'You can't see it yet, can you? She's pregnant, into the fourth month. And not by Nick.'

No, I had not realised that. 'And she chose you to confess that to?' I could not get over it.

My brother nodded. 'Of course. It is my child, after all.'

'Your child!' I exploded. Oh yes, I could easily imagine how it had happened. My brother, the charming boy, the heartbreaker. Whenever he wanted a woman, he just had to look at her with his big dark eyes. Irresistible. At least that's how it seemed to me. He had once demonstrated this glance to me, just for fun, and I had spent hours in front of the mirror afterwards, practising. I had no chance. My eyes were lighter, smaller, and on top of that I lacked his maturity, as I know now, which gave him this air of superiority. Sure, he was a good-looking guy and an able scientist. Why else would they have called him to Berkeley?

I might have hit him. In fact, I should have done so, although it would have been futile because it would not have changed anything. And on top of that he was the stronger, so in the end I would have got a beating.

'You consider me a pig?'

I spared him my reply.

My brother lit a cigarette. He had never smoked back home. He was nervous. 'Dear little brother, you must know that it always takes two,' he said. 'To make love, I mean. And I can assure you, I didn't rape Marie.'

I said nothing. Not raped, but seduced, I thought. With your eyes. That was something poor Nick was unable to compete with.

'You're outraged, I can see that.' That didn't require much. I blush easily when I'm excited, and apart from that my lips get quite thin. My brother tried hard to explain that Marie would have left Nick anyway; it was just a matter of time. That their marriage had been a romantic mistake from the very beginning. Only later had it occurred to Marie that his attempted suicide had not been a heroic act at all – otherwise he would not have run away to Canada in the first place. Grabbing the gun had been nothing but a panic reaction.

And the relationship between my brother and Marie, that was no romantic mistake? Wasn't it perhaps just an easy escape from her unattractive everyday life with a cripple? Because a cripple he was, regardless of all his skills and his charm. But I didn't mention it, as it was too late anyway. The baby was on its way; the decision had been made. 'When are you going to tell him?' I queried.

My brother could not conceal a hint of uncertainty. 'In a few weeks, I think. At least, we didn't want to bring the issue up before your visit. We wanted to show you a little bit of California without any problems.'

The next few days passed like a dream. We rode the cable car, took a short and very cold bath in the Pacific and paid a visit to the sea lions at Fisherman's Wharf. In the evening, drinking wine in Nick's living-room, we talked and laughed a lot, and during all this I nearly forgot the dark clouds that were gathering over the three of them. When on the last evening late at night a hailstorm swept over the house, Nick and my brother sang loudly and rather out of tune: 'It never rains in California.' My brother shouted so loudly that Parker, the dog, looked at him reproachfully. I have no idea what became of Parker afterwards.

The last entry in my diary describes the flight back home. However, that was by no means the end of the story.

Three weeks later. The short note was on the last page of my newspaper, which I used to look at first, for the weather. Under the heading 'The world in brief' there was an entry saying that in San Francisco a blind man had shot his wife by mistake. The man's name was given as de Boer. No first names were mentioned. I was alarmed. Of course, Nick's and Marie's second name was Mintford, but de Boer sounded familiar, too. Marie's maiden name, perhaps? And the house was owned by her parents, as far as I knew. You couldn't trust a newspaper in such matters, and surely there could not be all that many blind men in San Francisco.

I rang up Nick. Or I tried. I let the telephone ring over twenty times, but nobody answered. I checked the time. Early morning in San Francisco. Nick and Marie would still be at home normally. I tried again, dialling with greater care, but to no avail. Nobody lifted the receiver.

The next day, when the original events were already two days old, the *Abendblatt* gave a more detailed report, and this time there could be no doubt. The names had been corrected. They said Nicholas Mintford had mistaken his home-coming wife for a burglar and shot at once. Marie had not realised the danger because the flat had been in total darkness. She was dead by the time the ambulance arrived. There was no mention of any unborn baby. A tragic accident.

Accident? I had my doubts. Had Nick not moved about in his flat in light and dark with absolute confidence and recognised every sound? Was it possible that he might have mistaken Marie for a burglar at any time of day? Was it not much more likely that Marie's intention of leaving him had triggered the same kind of panic as the cops had done with his suicide attempt? That he had knowingly shot at Marie? And, if so, wasn't then my brother in extreme danger, too? If Nick had killed his wife in anger, wouldn't he possibly or even most probably try to kill my brother as well? After all, he had caused Marie's decision.

I tried to call my brother at his job. In vain. Finally I got hold of the operator. The girl tried to put me through, but again with no result. The phone kept ringing in my brother's office. Then the girl's voice again: 'Mr Berger is not in his room; do you want me to leave him a message?'

I asked her to put a note on his desk, saying would he please ring me back at once. I did not leave the house for the next few hours. In vain. My brother did not call. Perhaps he spent the weekend with friends somewhere in the country. Perhaps he had hidden in some hole in mournful misery over the death of Marie and refused to hear or see anybody. Or he was dead already. I was helpless. I could only wait for him to call.

When he eventually called, very much later, everything was clear anyway, even without him admitting anything. We did not even touch on the issue, and police investigations had been closed some time since. Again I had not understood anything. One thing I know by now, however: Nick's revolver, of which I had been so afraid for my brother's sake, had been confiscated by the police, of course.

Hamburg, today. My big brother, nervously pacing the room. And me, just as nervous, watching him. 'I just had to come,' he said. 'You are the only person to whom I can talk about this.'

But, of course, I would not be able to help him, and he knew it. 'The airmail letter then,' I said, 'that came from you, right?' He nodded. The envelope had contained nothing but a newspaper clipping. The article said a blind man had jumped off the Golden Gate Bridge at dawn the previous morning. Suicide number 828. A passing coastguard vessel had eventually pulled the man out of the water, but he was dead by then. A probable cause for the suicide had been the death of his wife, whom the blind man – as reported yesterday – had accidentally shot dead.

'What did you think?' he asked.

I shrugged. To be honest, initially I had been relieved. Suicide. And my brother would not be in danger any more. But then I had my doubts. Suicide? Sure, Nick knew his way around the house perfectly well. He went everywhere and did anything he wanted. But the Golden Gate Bridge was at the other end of the town. It was much beyond Parker to take his master there. Even if Nick had taken a taxi it would have been difficult to get on the bridge without help.

'There is only one possible reason why you sent me that letter,' I said.

He avoided my eyes. 'Police investigations found no traces of foreign interference.'

'You didn't come all the way to tell me that,' I said.

My brother did not say anything for a while. Then, finally: 'He did not even put up a fight.' I looked up. He wept. My big, strong brother. My poor brother.

78

Lesley Grant-Adamson

Lesley Grant-Adamson rarely writes short stories, but when she does turn to the form, her work is as economical and varied as it is at novel length. This piece is a case in point. Lesley tells me that the theme of the scene of the crime caused her to reflect on 'inner city crime rates and the unrealistic fears they engender. As a matter of interest, it is based on a true story. The characters have changed but the set up, the actions of the police and the crime itself are true. I was the one who called the police . . .'

THE SCENE OF THE CRIME

Lesley Grant-Adamson

When we moved to the inner city the first thing we unpacked was our siege mentality. That's what Francesca said. She was our next-door neighbour, glinting at us through venetian blinds while we hovered on guard by the emptying removals van.

Once all was safely gathered in, she emerged offering welcome and a drink, satisfying her curiosity. If we had said yes, perhaps none of it would have happened.

Instead John said, 'Um . . .' doubtfully, and I said, 'Er . . .' more so. Then we both said together that while we'd love a cup of tea we felt we'd be unwise to leave the house unattended.

A smile quivered at the corners of Francesca's mouth. 'I'll bring the tea to you,' she said.

Francesca was a glossy blonde. The owner of a money-spinning clothes shop, she knew the right people, went to the right places, and skimmed the bright surface of city life.

We guessed she was in her late thirties, perhaps ten years younger than us. It seemed more and not only because of our premature greyness. Beside her I felt distinctly middle-aged in my tastes and attitudes. And I realised John felt the same when I heard him describe her as reckless and immature. He said it with a grin, mind, because she was one of those people who inspire affection even when they are at their most maddening.

Whether her ex-husband would agree with that I couldn't say. We didn't meet him. She lived alone except for a series of friends passing through London, stranded between flats or trying out freedom before leaving husbands. We grew used to the thrum of music and Francesca's high laughter in the garden.

And she grew accustomed to the clatter of chain and iron bar as John let himself out of the house to go to the office each morning. We had moved because of his work. The branch office was closing and he had to follow the job. Leaving our country town was a wrench but we'd decided to give London a try, in spite of our qualms that the inner city was tough, a young person's place. We could never be citywise as Francesca was.

Gently she teased us about the extra locks John fitted to our doors and windows, and the iron grille that decorated our rear glass doors.

He would bounce back with, 'Don't you know what the inner city crime rate is?'

But she laughed it off.

He grumbled to me: 'Just because she's been lucky so far . . . She's only got a Yale on that front door, you know. And it's on the catch half the time!'

'Her kitchen window's always open too,' I added.

We couldn't influence her any more than she could lure us into her careless ways. Each household regarded the other with amusement.

Shaking his head over her folly John would report to me: 'She's left the milk money on the doorstep again.'

And she mocked him with, 'Life's too short for that,' as he unclipped the car radio and carried it indoors each time he parked. I hung net curtains after reading that they discouraged thieves. John was poised to fit a burglar alarm until Francesca claimed they advertised there were good things to be had.

'It's best,' she said, 'to let the outside of the house appear a bit run down. If it's too smart, you arouse interest.'

Unfortunately our house had been painted by the previous owners to improve chances of a quick sale. Time and weather would tatty it but meanwhile we would have to be ultra-vigilant.

The local paper fed our fears. It was the sort that passes off the week's court cases as news. I gave up wearing necklaces because they were being plucked from the throats of women on buses. Actually, I didn't use buses but I reasoned that this plucking could as easily happen in the street or on the Underground.

I stitched pockets into my coats because handbags were being snatched. I sent John on errands to late-opening shops rather than venture myself after dark because rape was rife. We went as a pair to the bank cash machine because of muggers. And we always walked the longer well-lit way after dusk. After a while we gave up the local paper, it was too depressing.

And then Francesca announced a holiday. 'Tuscany for two weeks. You won't mind keeping an eye on the place for me, will you?'

I was aghast. 'Won't you have a house-sitter?'

Everybody had one, it was the only safe thing to do. Of course, once upon a time all you did was tell the police your house would be empty and they checked it on their rounds. But then there was that case of the policemen who, instead of checking, had . . .

Francesca shrugged. 'I was expecting a friend to stay but she's gone back to her husband. Anyway, with you two watchdogs next door I'll have nothing to fear.'

Seeing our faces, she threw back her head and laughed. 'Oh, don't look so worried. The house will be fine. It's been here two hundred years and it'll still be here in two weeks' time.'

Then John went away too, just an overnight business trip but the first occasion I'd been alone there. Before driving off he insisted, 'Keep doors and windows locked all the time, even if you're in the garden. That's when sneak thieves grab their chances.'

That night I did as he told me, double-checking I was locked in. In my mind I heard Francesca's ironic tone: 'Suppose you need to get out in a hurry? A fire, perhaps. Grilles keep you in as well as other people out. And I must say I wouldn't like to hunt for the key to a window lock in an emergency.'

The telephone rang. John, checking I'd checked. Then I went to bed.

The noises began around two o'clock. The scuff of a shoe on a step, then scraping. Without switching on a light I wriggled into my dressing-gown. One good thing about the city is that it's never truly dark. Street lamps and porch lights see to that.

A thud. The house vibrated.

I peered between curtains but window boxes limited my view. The sound seemed close yet I couldn't tell whether someone was outside my house or not, the thin-walled terrace communicated too easily.

I went downstairs. All was secure.

A rhythmic assault on wood. Someone was attempting to break in through Francesca's basement door.

Silence. During the lull I persuaded myself the burglar had failed and gone away. I decided to make a mug of cocoa.

Breaking glass.

I froze, my hand white-knuckled on the red cocoa tin. Then I was gliding to the sitting-room window. A small figure stood outside Francesca's basement door. I called the police.

They promised me a patrol car. Four came. Policemen milled around like lads at a dance, blue car lamps giving the street a disco light show.

I heard, 'All right, out you come.'

A woman answered, too loud. The police grew louder in reply. A disco light flickered off down the terrace. Radios chattered and another light was away.

Two constables leaned against my railings and smoked, their conversation depriving me of more interesting exchanges as the police and the woman made a jerky progression from suspicious question and truculent answer to jolly banter. Soon the burglar and several policemen were grouped on Francesca's doorstep and struggling with her front door.

My twitching curtain gave me away. One of the constables tossed his cigarette into the gutter and came to explain. 'Sorry about the disturbance. The young woman locked herself out and made a racket trying to get in. Someone sent for us.'

I felt the urge to confess. 'It was me.' Then, in mitigation of my foolishness: 'That isn't the woman who lives there. I've never seen her before.'

'Says she's a friend of the owner, looking after the place. Had a bit to drink, if you ask me.'

'But the owner was let down by her house-sitter. She asked me to keep an eye on it.'

'Then I'm sure she'll be very grateful.' He sounded a mite patronising and turned away.

A thought struck me. 'Who does she say the owner is?'

His smile was thin. Well, they'd thought of that one. Four car loads of policemen, of course they had. 'Francesca James, who's got that posh clothes shop in Upper Street.'

Locking up again, I almost forgot the chain and bar.

As I made my cocoa, I heard Francesca's door open to echoing thanks from the woman and cheers from her helpers. Moments later the last of the disco lights winked down the street.

Next evening I told John. 'I felt such a fool. Francesca's right, we have a siege mentality, you and I.'

When she returned, though, she was immediately screaming at us that she'd been burgled. 'Jewellery, paintings, silver, everything.'

The uproar had been concealed by those venetian blinds. Display cabinets were smashed open; pale patches on walls showed where pictures had hung; and contents of drawers had been hurled on floors.

Francesca was distraught. 'Are you sure you didn't hear anything?'

I said quietly, 'It was a woman. The police let her in through the front door.'

Beside me John murmured, 'Only a Yale lock . . .'

I thought that was heartless when she was so upset, but he broke off anyway because the police arrived. We went home.

Later Francesca called round, unhappy to be indoors on her own.

'They know who did it,' she said. 'A sales assistant I'd sacked for stealing from the shop. She was on bail after being charged with theft and she broke in to take her revenge.'

She seemed about to cry but, being Francesca, she managed her high laugh instead, saying, 'You know, it's almost funny.'

John opened his mouth to object but I stopped him with a look. I poured her a cup of tea. 'I'll come and help you tidy up,' I said.

John Hall

John Hall has come to the contemporary crime story via
Sherlockian pastiche. He is a regular contributor to an excellent
publication for crime fiction fans, *Sherlock Holmes: The Detective
Magazine*, and last year he made his debut in the CWA anthology
with a story featuring A. J. Raffles. Here he comes right up to
date with an entertaining mystery set in the academic world
which has, to my mind, a pleasing literary flourish.

IN THE RIGHT PLACE

John Hall

The phone rang, and Chief Superintendent Adler picked it up. 'Yes? Oh, yes, sir . . . Where? Yes, I see . . . No, of course I understand . . .' He frowned, thought. 'I think Cody's the best man for this – yes, sir, I know he's a piss artist – aren't they all? – but I must admit that he is on the same wavelength as these people . . . Right, sir.'

'Look at that!' DCI Cody nodded in disgust at the greengrocer's window next to the traffic lights.

'The mangoes, sir? They do look a bit mouldy.' DS Zajac, third generation exile (from the Nazis, the Communists, and then the Thatcherite free market economy), glanced at the shop without interest, then turned his gaze back to the lights.

'Not the mangoes! The sign, man! "Tomato's" with an apostrophe! To what possession of the tomato – singular – does it refer?'

'I expect he just doesn't know how to spell "Tomatoes", sir. Come to that, I'm never too sure myself if there's an "e" or not. I always have to think of "Potatoes", and that gives me the clue.' Zajac pulled away from the lights. 'Of course,' he added, with a sidelong glance at his superior, 'they may be Dutch.'

'The tomatoes?'

'Or the owners of the shop, sir. See, Dutch nouns that end in a vowel – because terminal vowels are long in Dutch, apart from "e" – normally form the plural with apostrophe "s", not to denote possession, but to indicate the omission of the repeated vowel, which would otherwise be necessary to maintain the length; because a single vowel followed by a consonant is short. Example: *paraplu* – umbrella – plural *paraplu's*. Of course, you have to see it written down to get the full effect,' he added.

'Are you taking the waz, Zaj?' demanded Cody, suspicious.

Zajac looked hurt. 'Not at all, sir. It's the wife; she's taking lessons in Dutch at night school. I must have heard that business about the vowels and what have you a couple of dozen times, that's why I know it off by heart. We plan to go to Belgium next year, take the kids. She already speaks a bit of French, but apparently they speak Dutch up north.'

'Flemish, actually. Although it is, despite what the Flemings might tell you, not much more or less than a dialect of Dutch.'

Zajac shrugged. 'All Greek to me, sir. My grandfather used to try to teach me Polish, but I never got the hang of it – apart from some of the swear words.'

'Here it is.' Cody nodded to the ancient college building. 'Better park over there, by the uniformed boys. What's the chap's name?'

Zajac was used to reading his superior's mind. 'Carter, sir. He's apparently the bloke who looks after these rooms.'

Cody nodded again. 'I'll bet he's the anxious bloke over there.'

The anxious bloke, elderly, balding, ran across as Zajac parked by the oak door. 'Police, is it?'

'It is.' Cody produced his identification. 'Mr Carter?'

'That's right. I found him – gave me a right turn, I can –'

'If you could just take us to the room, sir?'

Carter nodded. 'This way,' and he set off up the broad staircase.

'The dead man – Professor March, is it?'

'Doctor, sir, Dr March. Not a medical man, of course. English, that's his subject, sir. Was, I should say.' Carter stopped at a closed door, before which stood a uniformed PC, and nodded. 'In there, sir. Will you be needing me?'

'Later, perhaps. Did you shut the door?'

'I did, sir, but only after I'd opened it to go in, if you follow me. It was closed when I came here first. I'd meant to ask Dr March if he wanted a cup of tea. I knocked, the door wasn't locked, so it swung open, and I put my head round, to see if he was in. Well, as soon as I set eyes –'

'Yes, thank you, Mr Carter, that's very clear. And you shut the door again, and went to ring the police?'

'Yes, sir. Thought it best to leave things as much as they were.'

'You did very well. You have an office, or something?'

'My cubbyhole, sir. "Lodge", is the polite term. Anyone can tell you where it is.' And Carter nodded a last time, and went down the stairs.

Cody glanced at Zajac, then at the PC. 'Who's in there?'

'Pathologist, sir. And SOCO.'

Cody nodded. The PC opened the door, and Cody entered. The pathologist, Dr Curll – 'the abominable Curll,' as Cody, who had literary pretensions, called him – turned to greet them. 'Ah, Chief Inspector Cody!'

'Doctor. All finished here?' Cody asked the room at large. There was a general murmur of assent. 'Right, let's just take a quick look,' and Cody went over to the mahogany desk – a century old, no environmental concerns when that was put together! – and studied the body of the late Dr Henry March. He sniffed the air, shrugged, then nodded. 'Right, you can take him away.' To Curll, he said, 'Well?'

'At a guess, suicide.' He tapped the glass that stood on the table.

'Fingerprints done? Yes,' and Cody picked the glass up carefully with a handkerchief, sniffed it delicately, then waved it under Zajac's nose.

'Cyanide? Classic, isn't it, sir? Bitter almonds. Only ever smelled it once before, in chemistry lessons at school. Shouldn't have then, by rights, of course, but –'

'Where'd he get it?' asked Cody.

Curll shrugged. 'There is a whole wing devoted to chemistry and allied sciences. A couple of poison cupboards, I shouldn't wonder. And if they're as secure as they were when I was at university –' and another shrug finished the sentence.

'Hmm.' Cody pointed to the empty whisky bottle. 'Nerving himself up for it?'

Curll nodded. 'I can tell better later, obviously, but I'd say so. He reeks of it, as you no doubt noticed.'

'And the stuff dissolved in the last glassful?'

'Again, I need to do some tests, but, yes, unless we learn otherwise.'

'Time of death?'

'Oh, say between two twenty and two fifty.'

Cody frowned. 'Your precision amazes me.'

Curll grinned happily. 'He had lunch with a couple of colleagues, then had an interview with the Professor of English. That ended at two fifteen, more or less, and he was seen walking back here, say twenty past. The porter called at ten to three, to ask if he wanted a cuppa. OK?'

'OK. Who told you all this?'

'The porter, mostly. Couldn't get him to shut up. You could ask around yourself, verify it.'

'I will.' Cody nodded in the general direction of Zajac, who left the room.

Curll asked, 'Are you done with me? I'll get on with the PM, if so.'

'Yes, thanks. Oh, was there a note?'

'Was there!' Curll nodded at the litter on the desk.

Ten minutes later, Zajac returned, to find Cody in undisputed possession of the room. 'All checked out, sir. As the doctor said. One thing, sir – everybody I talked to says it wasn't suicide.'

'Oh?'

'No, sir. He had too much to live for.'

'Oh!'

'Really. He was divorced, right, but he planned to marry – remarry. And then he wasn't a professor here, but he'd had an offer from another place down the road, full professorship – chair, is it? He was to start there next term. And just had a book published; over the moon about that, by all accounts.'

'Is that so?' Cody picked up the note, enclosed in a plastic bag. 'Take a look at that.'

Zajac took the note, a strip torn from a sheet of ordinary writing paper, and read the sprawling handwriting:

> *I'm terribly sorry, but there's really*
> *nothing else I can do, despite the fact*
> *that I'm sure you'll say that its bad*

'Pretty clear, that, sir? I wonder who it's addressed to? Intended for, I mean,' Zajac added hastily, before Cody could correct him.

'The world at large, I wonder? Describe the note.'

'A piece cut from a sheet of notepaper, using a penknife, or perhaps this letter opener,' and Zajac tapped the silver blade as he spoke. 'Cut from the bottom of a sheet, I'd say, because the slightly ragged edge is at the top. Unless, of course, he cut it from the top of the sheet and turned it over.'

'Why would he do that?'

Zajac shrugged. 'Might not have known he *was* doing it, sir.' He gestured at the desk, which was covered with slips of paper, most of them bearing scribbled jottings. 'Most likely he'd cut the rest off to use as a bookmark or something – most of the books on the shelves have bits of paper stuck in them, you see – and this was the bit that was left. Just the first bit of paper he laid his hands on.'

'And the content of the note?'

'Pretty standard, apart from not being addressed to anyone specific. As you said, it was most likely intended for "who it may concern". Or is that "whom", I wonder?'

Cody ignored the grammatical challenge. 'I was reading a story the other day, and the detective in that would ask his sidekick to find errors in written evidence.'

'Oh, that? You mean "its" without a comma, when he meant "it is"?'

'Apostrophe. But, yes.' Cody threw back his head, and sniffed loudly. 'What d'you smell, Sergeant?'

Zajac sniffed delicately. 'Dust.'

'Learning, Sergeant! Learning!'

'Dust, sir,' amended Zajac confidently. 'The wife, she's very hot on dust.'

Cody made a derisive noise. 'Though it could do with a spring cleaning,' he conceded. 'No, Zajac, that's centuries of learning you can smell. Now, in these surroundings, sitting there facing a bust of Milton – if I'm not mistaken – and a portrait of Shakespeare, how could he make an elementary mistake like that?'

Zajac shrugged. 'Wasn't the first thing on his mind, perhaps, sir? Other things to think about?'

Cody shook his head. 'A man like that, death before dishonour, Sergeant.' He shook his head again, but this time to rid it of side issues. 'Now, to work. If he didn't kill himself, who did?'

'Ex-wife? New girlfriend? The fellows – that's "Fellows" with a capital "f",' he added for Cody's benefit, 'who didn't get the professor's job that he did?'

Cody nodded. 'Sounds a reasonable starting place. I wonder if he had a secretary, someone of that sort?'

Zajac consulted his notebook. 'A Miss Amersham, sir. Not "Ms" ', he added, 'she was insistent on that.'

'Fetch her in, would you?'

Miss – not Ms – Amersham was forty-odd, tall and thin with a cynical look in her eye. She had clearly been shaken by the death of Dr March, thought Cody, but she was not the sort to let that affect her. 'Sit down, please,' he said. 'You were Dr March's secretary, is that right?'

'Hardly. I'm more the departmental secretary. Professor Merriman's secretary, officially. We don't run to individual secretaries for every Fellow and tutor, so I take messages for all the department, try to keep them organised as best I can.'

'But you knew Dr March well?'

'Oh, yes.'

'You see,' said Cody, 'there's been a suggestion – a very disturbing suggestion – that it may not have been suicide.'

'Oh, it wasn't!' said Miss Amersham decisively.

'No?'

'No. Definitely not.'

'I see. Then,' said Cody, 'it must have been murder.'

'I rather think it must,' said Miss Amersham briskly.

'In that case, who can you think of who might have wanted to kill Dr March?'

'Nobody.'

'Ex-wife?'

Miss Amersham shook her head. 'No. Melissa had the money; oh, she took a few hundred from the divorce, on principle, but she had no need. Besides, she remarried, and now lives in the States. The new one, she's not the sort, and she was obviously smitten with him. And she's in Italy.'

'Oh?'

'She works for a publicity firm, and they're doing a TV commercial for deep-frozen pizzas. I tried to contact her, but there was some failure to communicate. I'll keep trying, though, because it will – I almost said it would be "better" coming from

92

me, but that's nonsense – but it will not be quite so impersonal. Unless you'd rather I didn't?'

Cody, who always had problems conveying bad news to relatives and friends, shook his head. 'No, better from you, as you say. What about business rivals, so to speak?'

'Another non-starter, I'm afraid. It may perhaps be that some of the junior staff members were envious of his post – he was a Senior Lecturer, did you know? – although frankly I doubt it; but if they had been, the post would be vacant anyway in a few weeks, at the end of the academic year, when Dr March left.'

'And the other candidates for the chair he was to take up?'

'There were only three candidates shortlisted. One is in the Midlands, one in Scotland, and I haven't seen either of them in these parts today.' Miss Amersham gestured at the telephone. 'I could check with their respective departments, if you can spare five minutes? I'll ring from my office, I have the names and numbers there.'

'If you would.'

Miss Amersham left the room. Cody stood up and wandered round, gazing at the books on the shelves. Zajac opened his notebook and studied it closely, wondering in a vague sort of way what Mrs Zajac would be preparing for his tea.

Five minutes after she had left, Miss Amersham returned, shaking her head. 'Both where they ought to be, and going about their legitimate concerns,' she said.

Cody, who had been thinking, said, 'What about students? Had Dr March failed any, thrown any out, threatened to do so?'

Miss Amersham managed a humourless smile. 'Rather the reverse. He'd been lenient, not wanting to spoil anyone's chances, not when he'd been so fortunate himself.'

'Hmm.' Cody shook his head. 'English, that was his subject? Was he hot on grammar, punctuation, style?'

'Oh, red hot! "Who" and "whom", and "can" and "may" and "might". You name it.'

'Hmm. So he wouldn't make elementary mistakes of that sort himself?'

'Certainly I never knew him do so.'

Cody studied the note again, then asked, 'What was he working on at the moment, do you know?'

93

Miss Amersham shook her head. 'Nothing special, as far as I know. His teaching duties, of course, and general admin, though he didn't have much to do in that line. He'd just published a book, and he may have been planning another, but I don't think so, I think he was waiting until he was settled in the new job so that his attention was focused.'

'A novel, was the book?'

'Hardly! No, it was on the influence of Nietzsche on post-modernist semiotics.'

'Ah.'

'No, it didn't mean a lot to me either,' said Miss Amersham frankly. 'But I am assured that it will make a considerable impression on the half-dozen people who are interested in these things.'

'Right. So it would be fair to say that he was ticking over, keeping his desk clear until he moved in a few weeks' time?'

Miss Amersham nodded. 'It would be fair to say that. Oh, he was writing a book review.'

'Was he a regular reviewer?'

'No, but he was occasionally asked to review things. You know how it is.'

'Indeed. Do you happen to know what it was he was reviewing?'

Miss Amersham glanced round the untidy room. 'Here it is. *Strangers from the Stars*, by Arnold Hampton.'

'The name doesn't ring a bell. What's it about?'

Miss Amersham studied the back cover. 'Astrology? Men from Mars who visited Earth and changed the course of human history, that sort of thing. Or so it would seem.'

Cody frowned. 'Was Dr March an expert in that field?'

'Not so far as I'm aware.'

'Odd that he should be asked to review a specialist work like that?'

'Specialist only in the sense that it's a narrow subject,' Miss Amersham pointed out. 'It is written in a popular way, or so it seems from a hasty glance. And remember that Dr March was an English lecturer; he could pass an opinion on the style, and what have you.'

'But not the content,' Cody said.

Miss Amersham frowned. 'No, that's true. In fact ...' She hesitated.

'Yes?'

'Well, the obvious choice would have been Dr Gresham. He's a historian, and I know he's made a study of some ancient myths, tried to relate them to some of the more bizarre "men from Mars" theories.'

'Does he believe in those theories?'

'Good Lord, no! He gets quite angry with them.'

'I see. Where can I find this Dr Gresham?'

'I'll ask him to step over, if you wish.'

'Thank you. Oh, one thing more – we've assumed that this note –' he waved the plastic bag – 'is in Dr March's handwriting. It certainly seems the same as the writing on these other bits of paper. But could you just confirm that it is his writing?'

Miss Amersham studied the note. 'Oh, yes. No doubt of that.'

'Thank you. If you could ask Dr Gresham to come along?'

Miss Amersham nodded, and left. Cody opened the book, and started to read. After a couple of minutes, he skipped a few pages, read on. Then he closed the book and clicked his tongue.

'Rubbish, is it, sir?' asked Zajac.

'No, it makes out a good case for thinking that the alien visitors theories are nonsense. But it's very badly written – the author is obviously trying to interest the popular reader, and failing miserably. Dumbing down, as they say. No sort of style at all. I fancy our Dr March would have rubbished it in his review.' He glanced around the desk. 'Can't see anything that looks like a review here, though.'

Zajac nodded at the computer that stood on a more modern desk under the window. 'Perhaps he used that, sir.'

'Well, it's no good looking at me,' complained Cody.

Zajac went over to the computer, switched it on. 'There's a floppy disk in there, sir.'

'Great!'

'It'll be what he was working on last,' explained Zajac. 'Hang on. Here's a file, "REV.DOC".'

'Even better!'

95

'It'll mean a document file – text – labelled "REV", see? I'll bet that means "review".'

'I see.'

Zajac hit the keys again. 'This is it, sir. Shall I print it out?' He did so, and brought two sheets of paper over to Cody.

Cody glanced at the opening paragraph. 'H'mm.' He turned to the second sheet, then back to the first. 'This is interesting. He liked it!'

'Well, if it's an interesting –'

'Oh, it's interesting, at least the few pages I read were, but it's badly written. And he never mentions that.'

'He may not have finished his review, though,' said Zajac. 'He may have been sweetening the pill, so to speak. Good points first, so as to seem fair and balanced, then the faults.'

'Possible. But it doesn't look that way, because he concludes by saying that he recommends the book. Odd that he doesn't mention the style even once.'

'Perhaps the subject seemed more important, sir? After all, if the style's brilliant, but the subject is boring, then the book's bad, isn't it?'

'But here, Zajac! Here, in his own study, where he did his own work, where he wrote his own books. And if he was so keen on style, on grammar?' Cody looked up as there was a tap at the door. 'Come in!'

A short, stout man entered the room. 'Inspector – Cody?'

'Chief Inspector, sir, but I'm Cody.'

'Ah.' The newcomer held out his hand. 'I'm Dr Gresham.' He glanced round the room, as if expecting to see March's body still there, and licked his lips. 'Dreadful business! Dreadful. But I'm sure I don't know –'

'It's what you could call a technical matter, sir. Your expertise might be very useful.'

'Oh. I see. Of course –'

'It's this book,' said Cody. '*Strangers from the Stars*. I don't know if you've come across it?'

'Indeed,' said Gresham, an odd expression on his face. 'It – it's something of a hobby of mine, you know.'

'So I understand. In fact, I'd have thought that you would have been the one to write a review, not Dr March.'

'Ah.' Gresham looked positively embarrassed by now. 'You see, the thing is . . .'

'Yes, sir?'

'I wrote the book. I'm Arnold Hampton. Obviously, the publishers wouldn't want me to review my own book,' he added.

Cody frowned. 'Why the pseudonym?'

Gresham relaxed, smiled. 'You obviously don't know the academic world, Chief Inspector! For anyone wanting to maintain a reputation as a serious scholar, to be associated with any sort of bizarre theory is the kiss of death. You'll not find any zoologist who will betray the least interest in the Loch Ness Monster, let us say.'

Cody frowned. 'But your book debunks the theories about alien visitors altering the course of human history!'

'True, up to a point.' Gresham studied Cody closely. 'You haven't read the book fully? No. Well, it was necessary to discuss the theories with what you might call a straight face; to appear to take them seriously. I assure you, that would be enough to damage the reputation I have built up in this particular field.'

'I see. The book is written in a popular style, though? Would it be read by your scientific colleagues? It isn't intended for the specialist – no offence.'

'Oh, none taken. But that's another thing; my publisher rejected the first draft, said it wasn't "sexy" enough! I ask you, "sexy"! How can you make a book like this seem sexy? It makes it sound like *Fanny Hill*, and even that isn't sexy in the least. If it came out that I'd written a book for a popular readership – well!'

Cody laughed. 'So that explains Dr March's being asked to do the review.' He looked at Gresham. 'Did you see his review?'

'Ah – no.' Gresham flushed.

Cody handed over the two sheets which Zajac had printed out.

Gresham glanced at the top sheet. 'He's – he was very kind.'

'You see, I find it odd that he discusses the arguments fully, and with obvious knowledge; but he never mentions the style,' said Cody.

Gresham stared at him for a long moment, then – to Cody's

mild surprise, and Zajac's complete astonishment – put his head in his hands.

'Take your time,' said Cody gently.

Gresham looked up, straightened his back. 'How did you know?'

'It was the note that did it.'

'The note?' Gresham was puzzled.

Cody turned the note round, pushed it towards Gresham.

'Ah,' said Gresham. He smiled. 'I never noticed that. Too preoccupied, of course. And it would have been so easy, you know – after all, an apostrophe isn't like a page of writing, is it? You'd never have noticed if I'd put one in.'

'What did the rest of the note say?' asked Cody.

'Oh, it was a covering note. With the review, of course. The first bit said, "Here's the review", or words to that effect, and that he was sorry that it was so destructive. And it really was, you know. It would have ruined me. And then the last bit, on the back of the sheet of paper, at the top – it didn't show when I cut it, of course – well, it went on, "I'm sure you'll say that its bad grammar and excruciatingly jocose style don't detract from its main theme". Something like that – I can't swear to the exact words, and I burned the rest of it.'

'You came across here to try to talk him out of it?'

Gresham nodded. 'To no avail, of course. It wouldn't have been so bad, but he had said who "Arnold Hampton" really was, and I couldn't have that.'

'The whisky?'

'Oh, he was civilised enough,' said Gresham vaguely. 'Offered me a drink, to soften the blow. He liked single malt, of course – who doesn't? Drank most of the bottle himself, possibly to blunt his conscience. And I put the cyanide in when he went over to the bookcase. That was after I'd tried to get him to change his mind, of course,' he explained, anxious lest there be any misunderstanding on this point.

'And you typed this – revised – review?'

Gresham nodded. 'I hoped that it would be found, and sent off to the magazine. If not, then I hadn't lost anything.'

'What about fingerprints?' asked the practical Zajac.

'Oh, I wore surgical gloves. I took them from the chemistry lab, at the same time as I took the cyanide.'

'Isn't there a poison cupboard?' asked Cody.

'Yes, but the Prof keeps the key on a hook in his office, and I waited until he went out to lunch.' Gresham stood up. 'I think you'd better have a word with him about that, don't you? I mean, it isn't exactly being an accessory, or anything like that – is it? But we wouldn't want it happening as a regular thing, would we?'

'No, sir, we wouldn't,' said Cody.

Edward D. Hoch

For many years, people have predicted the demise of the detective story with tedious regularity; just as often, their pessimism has been confounded. But even dyed-in-the wool fans of the traditional detective story must have been wondering, not so long ago, if that elaborate sub-genre, the impossible crime story, was finally played out. Ingenious locked room mysteries seemed, with a few honourable exceptions, to belong to the past. Suddenly, all that appears to have changed. The tremendous success of the BBC television series *Jonathan Creek* has proved that there is a large contemporary audience for the skilfully crafted impossible crime story and that tireless anthologist Mike Ashley, another CWA member, has compiled a new collection of impossible crime stories. In the meantime, Ed Hoch continues to produce some of the very best examples of this appealing type of detective story. 'Circus In The Sky' ranks with his finest achievements in this vein. A man is found dead on the seventeenth floor of a skyscraper and it seems 'as if a lion had appeared from nowhere, killed him, and then vanished.' Who could resist a set-up like that?

CIRCUS IN THE SKY

Edward D. Hoch

Her name was Carpathia, or at least that was her professional name on the posters for the Breen Brothers Circus. *The Beauteous Carpathia, Tamer of Lions and the Human Animal! Live! In Person!* I was a young man in my mid-twenties, working for a month as a computer programmer in an unfamiliar city far from my home office, staying in a drab hotel room for which the company paid. I hadn't seen a circus since my childhood in the midwest, and it seemed as good a way as any to pass another boring evening. After two weeks I'd exhausted all the downtown entertainment possibilities the city had to offer.

This was the end of the century and circuses no longer played in big tops set up along the railroad tracks in cities like Omaha and Des Moines. Now they were arena events, competing with rock stars and ice shows, hockey and wrestling for the best dates. The Breen Brothers Circus had come into the Memorial Arena during the third week in May, before children and their parents had time to scatter on their summer vacations. I went to the Wednesday evening performance, in an off-and-on drizzle, on a night when some of the city's prominent politicians and businessmen cavorted in clown make-up before the real thing came on.

But the true stars of the show for me weren't the clowns or bareback riders or high wire acts, but Carpathia and her lions. I sat there through the first twenty minutes waiting impatiently for her appearance in spangled tights and feathery headdress as shown on the poster. Surely no one could tame lions in such a Vegas-style costume, but when Carpathia made her spectacular entrance she was wearing just that, complete with high heels. She circled the arena once, heavily made up, waving and throwing trinkets to the crowd, then retreated briefly to change into

101

her working clothes. During her absence the roustabouts were busy erecting an animal cage in the centre ring. When she returned, wearing the traditional safari costume of khaki shorts, shirt and pith helmet, the crowd went wild. Even one of the amateur clowns ran up to her with a bouquet of flowers but she pushed him roughly aside.

She entered the cage as if it were just another day at the office, and almost at once three full-grown male lions were released into it. They growled convincingly, but were no match for Carpathia. Using a chair and whip she quickly cowed the beasts and placed them on their proper pedestals. The spectators cheered when one of the big cats jumped through a hoop at her command. Carpathia's quarter-hour act was far too short for me, and the remainder of the show seemed bland by comparison. As I left the arena, wanting more, I spotted her in a heated conversation with one of the clowns. They almost seemed to be arguing about something. Finally the clown turned away, abruptly ending the conversation.

There was a late-night restaurant across the river from the Memorial Arena, named Hale Eddy after a small natural whirlpool in the water at that point. As the circus crowds scattered to their cars I strolled over the bridge. I was working this month in one of the several office buildings grouped there, developing a new computer program for a company that installed security systems. Sometimes when I worked nights I grabbed a sandwich and beer at Hale Eddy to take back to the office. Since the circus crowd had been made up mainly of family groups there were few others in the place when I arrived. I ordered a drink and took it to a table by the window where I could watch the lights on the whirlpool below. It wasn't much but, as one of my co-workers had remarked, it was better than watching paint dry.

I'd been there about an hour, watching the eddy and nursing a second drink, when she came in. I recognised Carpathia at once, even though she was wearing a light summer raincoat with its collar turned up. She sat at the table next to me and ordered a glass of white wine. I thought she looked nervous, but perhaps that was her normal reaction every night after spending fifteen minutes in a cage with three lions.

It took me nearly that long to work up my courage and say, 'I enjoyed your performance tonight.'

She looked up, surprised that I'd spoken, and said, 'Thanks.'

'Is it still raining out?' I asked, figuring the weather was always a good ice-breaker.

'Just a little. Is this the rainy season here?'

I shrugged. 'I'm a visitor like yourself, in town for a month.'

She laughed, a pleasant, melodic sound. 'I wish I could stay somewhere for a month at a time. I wasn't cut out for circus life. Or not the travel, at least. I love the animals.'

We chatted about some of the other cities the circus had visited and finally I invited her to join me at my table. 'Could I buy you another glass of wine?'

Her hesitation was brief. 'Sure, just one more and I'm finished for the night.'

Close up, her face had a natural beauty that hardly needed the garish make-up she'd worn for her grand entrance. Seeing her like this, without the chair and the whip and the make-up, she seemed oddly defenceless. I had a young man's fantasy that I could say a few words and lead her out of there to my hotel room.

The drinks came and we were settling in for some casual conversation. 'How did you ever get to be a lion tamer?' I asked.

I could tell from the sudden gleam in her eye that she had a witty answer she'd used before, but I never got to hear it. At that moment two men wearing navy blue raincoats entered the Hale Eddy and made directly for our table. 'Miss Carpathia?' the taller one asked. He had thinning grey hair and a look of being in charge.

She raised her head slowly and peered at him. 'Yes?'

'I'm Detective Sergeant Frazier,' he said, showing his badge and ID. 'This is my partner, Detective Isaacs. We're investigating a suspicious death in the office building across the street. We'd like your help.'

Carpathia frowned, shaking her head. 'I don't understand. I don't know anyone in that building.'

'You visited an office on the seventeenth floor a half-hour ago and saw a lawyer named Richard Strong there.'

'You're mistaken,' she insisted. 'I've been here with this gentleman for the past hour.'

That was certainly no better than a half-truth, but I saw no reason to correct her just then. 'You'd better both come along,' the detective said. 'This is serious.'

I paid the check and we followed the two detectives across the street to the Granite Building. It was next to the one in which I'd been working for the past couple of weeks, but I'd never been inside. I saw now that a couple of police cars, a technical unit truck, and a morgue wagon were parked in front. Neither of us spoke as the detectives escorted us past the security guard and into the elevator.

On the seventeenth floor Sergeant Frazier led us past a police photographer and several others, through the reception room of a law firm and into a large corner office. A dead man in the remains of a business suit lay on the floor in the centre of the room. There was clown make-up on his face, and blood had obviously mingled with the wide red greasepaint lips. Both face and suit had been shredded by bloody claw marks, but there was little blood and no sign of a struggle.

It was as if a lion had appeared from nowhere, killed him, and then vanished.

'Do you wish to make a statement, Miss Carpathia?' Frazier asked after we'd had a chance to recover from the shock.

We were in one of the office conference rooms down the hall from the crime scene. She sighed, not looking my way, and said, 'Carpathia is my professional name. My real name is Mimi Gothery.'

'How well did you know the deceased?'

'Not at all. He was one of the businessmen acting as clowns at tonight's performance.' She made a disgusted face. 'He tried to push some flowers on me during the performance. Later he give me his business card and invited me up here for a drink.'

'The lobby security guard, Walt Nealy, says you went up in the elevator to see Strong and left shortly afterward. He watched you cross the street to the Hale Eddy. Then he decided to phone up to Strong's office to be sure everything was all right. When there was no answer he called us.'

'I went up to his office but the place was dark and the door was locked. I came right back down.' Her voice was nervous and defensive.

Sergeant Frazier was making notes. 'Why would you come here if you didn't know him?'

Carpathia (I still thought of her by that name) was drumming her nails on the conference table. 'I should tell you how these things work. When Breen Brothers goes into a city our advance man tries to line up prominent citizens to appear as clowns for one night's performance. Sometimes there's a charity tie-in. You'd be surprised how easy it is to recruit politicians and lawyers and businessmen. I guess everyone wants to be a clown. Even our boss, Charlie, puts on a polka-dot clown suit and make-up. He called on Strong and the others the day we got in, to line up their appearance tonight.'

The detective turned his attention to me. 'Is that your story too? You want to be a clown?'

I identified myself and explained that I'd seen Carpathia performing at the circus. 'When she sat down at the next table in Hale Eddy, naturally I spoke to her.'

'I'll want to interview you both separately,' he told us. 'But I have one more question for you now, miss. What was your reason for coming up here to Richard Strong's office tonight?'

'Charlie wanted us to be friendly with the amateur clowns. It's good for business. I pushed him away earlier when he tried to give me flowers, and when he invited me for a drink Charlie said I had to go.'

'Here in his office, late at night?'

'He said there'd be other people. When I saw there weren't, I took off fast.'

'Do you have any idea what could have caused those claw marks on his face and body?'

'No, except that it wasn't one of my cats. Or maybe you think I turn into a lion on nights when the moon is full?'

The detective closed his notebook. 'All right, Miss Carpathia, or Gothery. If you'll just wait in the next room, I want to take a statement from your friend here.'

When we were alone he said, 'I'll be frank with you, sir. I don't think you're directly involved in what happened here, but you're an important witness. I expect truthful answers to my questions

105

if you want to stay out of trouble. How long was that woman with you at the Hale Eddy?'

'Maybe twenty minutes,' I admitted. 'But she was sitting there at least ten minutes before I spoke to her. You can't think she had anything to do with his murder!'

'That's exactly what I think. She went there for some sort of assignation with the victim. Things got out of hand and she defended herself, perhaps with one of those clawed garden tools.'

'Which she just happened to have in her pocket? Be reasonable, Sergeant! If she'd killed him, why would she remain in the area, crossing the street to have a drink at the Hale Eddy?'

But Frazier had an answer for that too. 'Because she wanted to dispose of the murder weapon by throwing it into the whirlpool.'

'How could she have struggled with Strong and clawed him with that weapon without getting blood on her clothes? Or for that matter, without getting clown make-up on her?'

'She might have cleaned it off. We'll examine her clothes for blood and greasepaint. Meanwhile, will you be in town for the near future?'

'My work here ends in two weeks. I'll be here till then.'

'Good! We'll probably want to talk with you again.'

I waited downstairs for Carpathia, hoping they wouldn't bring her out in handcuffs. The lobby security guard had given up any attempt at keeping track of the police comings and goings. 'They've been in and out for the past hour,' he grumbled.

'Are you Walt Nealy, the man who phoned the police?'

'That's me, last time I looked.' He gave a little giggle. 'Usually nothing happens around here at night.'

'Did you see Richard Strong go up before the young woman arrived?'

'Yeah, about twenty minutes before, just after ten. He still had that clown make-up on, with those thick purple lips and white cheeks. I wouldn't have recognised him if he didn't show his ID. See?' He showed us his ledger. 'He went up at 10.05 and she came in at 10.22.'

'Was she alone?'

'Sure.'

'And she left alone? No one else left the building?'

'Just her,' he confirmed. 'I watched her walk across to the Hale Eddy.'

'She didn't have a lion with her?'

The security guard giggled again. 'What do you think?'

I was still waiting forty-five minutes later when Carpathia finally appeared. She seemed tired and nervous, surprised to see me there. 'How'd it go?' I asked.

'Terrible! They think I killed him! I'm lucky they didn't lock me up.'

'How about a drink across the street?'

'Isn't that where it all started?'

'We can't be that unlucky twice in one night.'

'One drink,' she agreed.

We took the same table overlooking the river, and the waiter remembered us. This time she ordered Scotch and water, and I did the same. 'I saw you talking to a clown after the performance,' I told her. 'Was that Strong?'

She shook her head. 'That was my boss, Charlie Craft. He loves being a clown, especially at shows when we have amateur clowns from the community. He always dresses up and joins them. He saw me push Strong's flowers away earlier and that upset him. He said I had to go have a drink with Strong after the show.'

'Why did you push the flowers away?'

'I could smell the liquor on his breath. I don't care what sort of a big deal he is. You don't get liquored up to entertain kids.'

'But you still agreed to go up to his office?'

She shrugged. 'There are some things you have to do if you want to keep your job. Even lion tamers can be replaced. I didn't waste any time when I saw the office was dark, though. I turned around and went right back down.'

'The guard said Strong went up ahead of you.'

'I don't know where he was hiding. The door was locked.' She finished her drink quickly and stood up. 'Thanks. I've really got to go now.'

I jotted down the number of my office phone on the back of a business card. 'Call me if I can help in any way.'

'Thanks. We'll be out of here after three nights and I hope that's the end of it.'

But it wasn't the end. The killing of Richard Strong was big news in the morning paper, and that afternoon Carpathia phoned me at the office. 'That detective just came by with bad news, impossible news! They've been here checking the claws of my lions! The official cause of death was a heart attack, but they say Gus was responsible for his death.'

'Gus?'

'One of the lions. They examined the claw marks on the body and found that one claw seemed broken. Gus has a broken claw just like it.'

'But that's crazy! Everyone knows you didn't walk across that bridge last night with a lion on a leash.'

'The office building has a freight elevator around back. Sergeant Frazier says I could have brought Gus in a van, parked him around back, and then entered the building and unlocked the back door.'

'Does he expect anyone to believe that?'

She was sounding desperate. 'I told him I wasn't in the building more than five minutes. In that time they think I opened the back door, took Gus up in the freight elevator, killed Strong, returned the lion to the van, and left the building. It's just impossible.'

'Have they actually arrested you yet?'

'Not yet, but I can't leave town with the show after Saturday's performance. I have to stay until their investigation is complete.'

I stared at the computer screen in front of me, trying to calculate how much longer my work would take. 'Where are you now?'

'At the arena. We have a matinée today.'

'I'll see you there in an hour. Try to be at the lions' cages.'

The afternoon show was still in progress when I walked across the bridge to the Memorial Arena, but I knew Carpathia's lion act would be finished. The acrobats and clowns had come and gone, and the bareback riders had almost finished the penultimate act. I made my way down the ramp to the lower level, where the animals were kept between performances. Carpathia was standing near one of the cages, looking sombre. 'This is Gus,' she told me. Reaching between the bars she gently lifted a paw and showed me his broken claw. 'That bastard Charlie wouldn't let me use him in the act tonight. Says he's a murder suspect.'

'Well, I suppose he is. If anything happened to you after Strong's killing, your boss would be in big trouble.'

She lowered her voice. 'This is him now.'

We were joined by a clown in full make-up, complete with fright wig and baggy polka-dot clown suit. 'Who's this?' he asked Carpathia, jabbing a finger in my direction.

She introduced me and then said, 'This is Charlie Craft. He runs the place – ringmaster, clown, part owner.'

'With the Breen Brothers?' I asked him.

'They sold the name years ago. I think they're in California now, running a winery.' He eyed me carefully as he removed his red plastic nose and started peeling off his wig. 'You a cop?'

'Hardly! I'm a computer programmer. I happened to be having a drink with Carpathia last night when the police found her at the Hale Eddy.'

'Ha! You're not the first one to try that! She's a lovely young lady.'

Carpathia seemed embarrassed by our talk. 'Look, I need a way out of this. You guys aren't helping.'

Charlie Craft was rubbing the purple greasepaint from his lips. 'If they try to arrest you, the case would be laughed out of court. Nobody walks along a city street with a full-grown lion without being seen, even at night.'

'That detective, Frazier, has it all worked out. I drove Gus there in the circus van and took him up in the freight elevator, returning him the same way after he killed Strong. They're checking the van for hairs now.'

Craft gave a snort. 'They won't find a thing.'

'Don't be too sure, Charlie. Remember the week before last when I took a lion to the parking lot of the children's hospital in Nashville? I used the van to do that.'

'Look here,' I said, trying to be logical about it. 'We need to draw up a timeline for last night, to prove you couldn't have done it.'

Craft finished wiping off the white greasepaint around his eyes and I had my first real look at a handsome man in his forties, of average height and build. The abandoned clown suit had given way to a sport shirt and trousers. He produced a pair of glasses from the shirt pocket. 'Clowns don't wear glasses,' he explained. 'We get batted around too much.' He picked up a clipboard and pencil, passing them to me. 'For your timeline.'

'All right. What time did the performance start?'

'Seven thirty. We don't like to keep the kiddies up too late.'

I started writing. 'Richard Strong and the other amateur clowns were here then?'

'Sure, for the opening parade.'

'Was Strong acting normal?'

'He was half in the bag,' Carpathia told me. 'That's why I pushed him away when he tried to give me the flowers. His breath almost floored me.'

'If I remember correctly, you came on in your feathers and spangles around ten to eight, then went off for a costume change while the roustabouts erected the cage.'

'She was in the cage from eight to eight fifteen,' Charlie Craft confirmed, wiping away the last of the white greasepaint from around his eyes. 'We have these things timed to the minute. We try to end the show by nine thirty.'

'I saw you two talking, or arguing, as I was leaving.'

Craft nodded, with a sideways glance at Carpathia. 'Strong had invited her to his office for a drink and I told her she should go. We need community support in cities like this. The amateur clowns are important to our box office.'

'I told him I wouldn't do it,' she said. 'I stormed out of there and walked the streets for about forty-five minutes. Finally I decided I had to show up if I wanted to keep my job. I just prayed he'd be gone. When I found the office dark, I went back downstairs.'

'You didn't try the door?'

'No, I – Well, it was unlocked but I wasn't going in there in the dark. I just figured he went home and forgot to lock up because he'd been drinking.'

'Frazier thinks she drove the lion to the back entrance by the freight elevator, entered through the front, brought Gus up in the elevator and let him kill Strong. Ever hear of anything so wild?'

'The timing doesn't seem possible,' I admitted. 'And there are lots easier ways of killing someone.'

'I'm ready to swear in court that Gus never left his cage last night. And I've got a witness.' He called to a sandy-haired young man who was cleaning the cages. 'Wayne, wasn't Gus in his cage after last night's performance?'

'Sure was, Mr Craft.'

'You were here every minute?' I asked.

'I was in and out,' Wayne answered, 'but one of us was around all the time.'

'Did Carpathia return after the performance?'

'I didn't see her.'

'What about the circus van?' I asked. 'Could she have taken it?'

'I have the only set of keys,' Charlie Craft said. 'Sometimes she borrows them, but not last night.'

'Maybe you drove the lion up there.'

Wayne laughed at that. 'Mr Craft wouldn't handle those cats for a million bucks! Besides, I just told you the lions never went anywhere last night.'

'All right,' I said finally, folding my timeline and slipping it into a pocket.

'What now?' Carpathia asked.

'I don't know.'

I thought about questioning the security guard, Nealy, again but there seemed little point to it. He might have followed Richard Strong upstairs and killed him, but he certainly couldn't have used Gus as a murder weapon. I told Carpathia I was going for a walk and headed back across the bridge to my office. When I was half-way across I was attracted again by Hale Eddy. The small whirlpool was the city's prime attraction, at least so far as I was concerned. I leaned on the railing and watched the water spinning around, forever spinning,

'You could watch it by the hour,' a voice behind me said. It was Sergeant Frazier.

'Yeah,' I agreed.

'This case was a lot simpler when I thought she'd tossed the murder weapon into the whirlpool.'

111

I guess that's when it came to me, watching that water spin around. 'They say whirlpools spin in the opposite direction south of the equator,' I told him.

'Yeah. I've heard that.'

'If you look at Richard Strong's death the other way around, it makes sense.'

He frowned at me. 'What other way around?'

'From the lion's viewpoint.'

We were back at the circus that evening, Frazier and I, with his partner Isaacs bringing up the rear. When Carpathia came off after the closing parade she hurried over. 'Is he here to arrest me?' she asked, motioning toward Frazier.

'We'll see.'

'What is it now?' Charlie Craft asked, strolling up in his clown outfit. 'More questions?'

'Some answers, I hope,' the sergeant told him. 'Mr Craft, before you remove your make-up I'd like you to meet Walt Nealy, the night security guard at the Granite Building.' Right on cue, Isaacs stepped forward with Nealy.

'What is this?' Craft asked, his voice a bit tense.

'Mr Nealy, take a good look at this clown. Could this have been the man who went up to Richard Strong's office at 10.05 last night?'

The guard stared at Craft. 'These clowns all look alike to me. He had Strong's ID card.'

'But they're not all alike,' I pointed out. 'Each one has a distinctive style and colouring of make-up. When I saw Strong's body last night his big clown lips were red, yet you told me the man you admitted had purple lips. I figured the light had been bad, but then this afternoon I watched Mr Craft remove his make-up and he had purple greasepaint on his lips.'

'Yeah, you're right,' Nealy decided, with a little giggle to hide his embarrassment. 'This is the guy.'

'But if Charlie went up there, what happened to him?' Carpathia asked. 'And how did Strong get up to his office?'

Sergeant Frazier smiled, pointing to me. 'Ask your friend here. He's an expert on the lion's viewpoint.'

'I think after last night's performance a somewhat inebriated

112

Strong wandered down to the lions' cages and decided he could tame them as easily as you, Carpathia. And we can guess how Gus reacted to that. Strong got clawed badly across the face and body for his trouble. That brought on a fatal heart attack. So Craft here was faced with a nightmare situation – one of the city's distinguished attorneys killed by a circus lion. He must have envisioned not only terrible publicity but million-dollar lawsuits as well. What to do? The only thing he could think of was to get the body away from here, back to Strong's office. You see, it wasn't the lion that came up in the freight elevator, it was Richard Strong's body.'

'It was his own damn fault. I didn't kill him,' Craft muttered, 'and neither did Gus.'

'But you loaded his body into the circus van, to which only you had the keys. Maybe Wayne or one of the other roustabouts helped you. You drove around the back of Strong's building, where you'd visited him earlier in the week, and parked the van by the freight elevator. Then you went through the lobby entrance, convincing Nealy you were Strong, and up in the elevator. You used Strong's key to unlock the office and then brought the body up on the freight elevator. The key and the ID card went back in his pocket. You turned out the office lights and returned to the van via the freight elevator. You couldn't lock the office door after you because the key was back in Strong's pocket.'

'What about Carpathia's part in all this?' Frazier's partner asked.

'She had nothing to do with it. She'd told Charlie she wouldn't go up there and he had no reason to think she'd change her mind. He certainly wasn't trying to frame her, even though it worked out that way. He figured Strong's death would be attributed to a burglar with a knife or some sharp tool.'

'What are you going to do to me?' Craft asked.

'The District Attorney will decide on the charges,' Frazier told him. 'You have the right to remain silent and to have a lawyer present.'

'I just want it wrapped up,' he said. 'All I did was move a body.'

'That was enough.'

113

Later, as they had a drink at the Hale Eddy, Carpathia asked, 'Did you know I was innocent all along?'

'Sure,' I answered gallantly. 'The timing just wasn't right for you to have done it. And when I got thinking about it, there was little blood and no signs of a struggle in the office. That's when I decided Strong was killed somewhere else, and where else but at the circus?'

'You should have been a detective. What will you do now?'

I signalled the waiter for another drink. 'Probably go to the circus every night until you leave town. Then I'll just sit here and stare at that damned whirlpool.'

Peter Lovesey

It is a particular pleasure to introduce a short story by Peter Lovesey in the year in which his outstanding career as a crime writer has been recognised by the award of the CWA Cartier Diamond Dagger. Peter is a gifted entertainer and his work, which has been filmed, televised and adapted for radio, has given pleasure to millions. His novels are deservedly popular, but his short stories are equally enjoyable, as a glance at collections such as *Butchers*, *The Crime of Miss Oyster Brown*, and *Do Not Exceed The Stated Dose* will confirm. But I think it can fairly be said that 'Interior, With Corpse' ranks as one of the very best short stories he has ever written.

INTERIOR, WITH CORPSE

Peter Lovesey

Her chestnut brown hair curved in an S shape across the carpet, around a gleaming pool of blood. She was wearing an old-fashioned petticoat, white with thin shoulder straps. The lace hem had been drawn up her thigh, exposing stocking-tops and suspenders. The stockings had seams. Her shoes, too, dated the incident; black suede, with Louis heels. One of them had fallen off and lay on its side, close to the edge of a stone fireplace. The hearthstones were streaked with crimson and a bloodstained poker had been dropped there.

But what really shocked was the location. Beyond any doubt, this was Wing Commander Ashton's living-room. Anyone who had been to the house would recognise the picture above the fireplace of a Spitfire shooting down a Messerschmitt over the fields of Kent in the sunshine of an August afternoon in 1940. They would spot the squadron insignia and medals mounted on black velvet in the glass display cabinet attached to the wall; the miniature aircraft carved in ebony and ranged along the mantel-piece. His favourite armchair stood in its usual place to the right of the hearth. Beside it, the old-fashioned standard lamp and the small rosewood table with his collection of family photographs. True, some things had altered; these days the carpet was not an Axminster, but some man-made fibre thing in dark blue, fitted wall-to-wall. And one or two bits of furniture had gone, notably a writing desk that would have been called a bureau, with a manual typewriter on it – an Imperial – and the paper and carbons under the platen. It was now replaced with a TV set and stand.

DI John Brandon stared at the scene in its gilt frame, vibrated his lips, stepped closer and peered at the detail. He had to act. Calls had been coming in all morning about the picture in the window of Mason's Fine Art Gallery. Some, outraged, wanted it removed. Others, more cautious, inquired if the police were aware of it.

They were now. Brandon understood why people were upset. He'd drunk sherry in the Wing Commander's house many times. This oil painting was a near-perfect rendering of the old fellow's living-room. Interior, with corpse.

Brandon wasn't sure how to deal with it. Defamation, possibly. But defamation is usually libel or slander. This was only a picture. Nothing defamatory had been said or written down.

He went into the gallery and showed his ID to Justin Mason, the owner, a mild, decent man with no more on his conscience than a liking for spotted bow-ties.

'That painting in the window, the one with the woman lying in a pool of blood.'

'The Davey Park? Strong subject, but one of his finest pieces.'

'Park? He's the artist?'

'Yes. Did you know him? Local man. Died at the end of last year. He had his studio in that barn behind the Esso station. When I say "studio", it was his home as well.'

'Did he give the picture a title?'

'I've no idea, Inspector. He wasn't very organised. It was left with a few others among his things. The executors decided to put them up for sale, and this was the only piece I cared for. The only finished piece, in fact.'

'How long ago was it painted?'

'Couldn't tell you. He kept no records. He had some postcards made of it. They're poor quality black and white jobs, 1950-ish, I'd say.'

'You realise what it shows?'

'A murder, obviously. You think it's too gory for the High Street? I was in two minds myself, and then I remembered that series of paintings by Walter Sickert on the subject of the Camden Town murder.'

'I wouldn't know about that,' Brandon admitted.

'I only mention them to show that it's not without precedent, murder as the subject of a painting, I mean.'

'This is a real location.'

'Is it? So was Sickert's, I believe.'

'It's Wing Commander Ashton's living-room.'

Mason twitched and turned pale.

'Take my word for it,' said Brandon. 'I've been there several times.'

'Oh, good Lord!'

'People have been phoning us.'

'I'll remove it right away. I had no idea. I'd hate to cause offence to Wing Commander Ashton. Why, if it weren't for men like him, none of us would be living in freedom.'

'I'll have to take possession of it. You can have a receipt. Tell me some more about the artist.'

'Park? A competent professional. Landscapes usually. Never a big seller, but rubbed along, as they do. Not an easy man to deal with. We expect some eccentricity in artists, don't we?'

'In what way?'

'He drank himself to death, so far as I can make out. Was well known in the Crown. Amusing up to a point, and then after a few more beers he would get loud-mouthed and abusive. He was more than once banned from the pub.'

'Doesn't sound like a chum of the Wing Commander's,' Brandon commented. The Battle of Britain veteran, not far short of his ninetieth birthday now, was eminently respectable, a school governor, ex-chairman of the parish council and founder of the Town Heritage Society. He'd written *Scramble, Chaps*, reputed to be the best personal account of the Battle of Britain.

'They knew each other, I believe, but they hadn't spoken for years. There must have been an incident, one of Davey's outbursts, I suppose. I couldn't tell you the details.'

'I wonder who can – apart from the Wing Commander?' Brandon left soon after with the painting well wrapped up. Back at the police station, he showed it to a couple of colleagues.

'Nasty,' said DS Makepeace.

'Who's the woman supposed to be?' said DC Hurst.

'A figment of the artist's imagination, I hope,' said Brandon. 'If not, the Wing Commander has some awkward questions to face.'

'Have you spoken to him?'

119

'Not yet. It's difficult. He's frail. I'd hate to trigger a heart attack.'

'You're going to have to ask him, Guv.'

'He's a war hero. A gentleman through and through. I've always respected him. I need more background before I take this on.'

'Try Henry at the Crown. He knew Davey Park better than anyone.'

Henry Chivers had been landlord for most of his life, and he was seventy now. He pulled a half of lager for the inspector and gave his take on Davey. 'I heard about the painting this morning. A bit of a change from poppy fields and views of the church. Weird. Davey never mentioned it in here. He'd witter on about most things, including his work. He had an exhibition in the old Corn Exchange a year or so before he died. Bloody good artist. None of that modern trash. It was outdoor scenes, mostly. I'm sure this one with the woman wasn't in the show. The whole town would have talked.'

'They're talking now. He must have been inside the Wing Commander's house, to paint it so accurately. It's remarkable, the detail.'

'In years past they knew each other well. I'm talking about the fifties, now, half a century ago. They had interests in common – cricket, I think, and sports cars. Then they fell out over something pretty serious. Davey wouldn't speak of it, and whenever the Wing Commander's name was mentioned in the bar, he'd look up at the beam overhead as if he was trying to read the names on the tankards. Davey had opinions on most subjects, but he wouldn't be drawn on the Wing Co.'

'Could it have been a woman?'

'The cause of the argument? Don't know. Davey had any number of affairs – relationships, you'd call them now. The artistic temperament, isn't it? A bit saucy for those days. But the Wing Co wasn't like that. He was married.'

'When?'

'In the war, to one of those WAAFs who worked in the control rooms pushing little wooden markers across a map.'

'A plotter.'

'Right.'

120

'She must have died some years ago, then. I don't remember her.'

'You wouldn't. They separated. It wasn't a happy marriage. He's a grand old guy, but between you and me, he wouldn't move on mentally. He was still locked into service life. Officially he was demobbed in 1945, and took a local job selling insurance, but he wouldn't let go. RAF Association, British Legion, showing little boys his medals at the Air Training Corps. And of course he was writing that book about the Battle of Britain. I think Helen was suffocated.'

'Suffocated?'

'Not literally.'

'What became of her, then?'

'Nobody knows. She quit sometime in the fifties, and no one has heard of her since.'

'That's surprising, isn't it?'

'Maybe she emigrated. Sweet young woman. Hope she had a good life.'

'Dark-haired, was she?' Brandon asked. 'Dark, long hair?'

'Now don't go up that route, Inspector. The old boy may have been a selfish husband, but he's no murderer.'

Brandon let that pass. 'You haven't answered my question.'

'All right, she was a brunette. Usually had it fastened at the back in a ponytail, but I've seen it loose.'

'You said Davey Park was a ladies' man. Did he ever make a pass at Helen Ashton?'

Chivers pulled a face. 'If he did, she wasn't the sort to respond. Very loyal, she was. Out of the top drawer.'

'That's nothing to go by,' said Brandon. 'So-called well-brought-up girls were the goers in those days.'

'Take my word for it. Helen wouldn't have given Davey the come-on, or anyone else.'

'She couldn't have been all that loyal, or she'd never have left the Wing Commander.'

'I bet it wasn't for another man,' said Chivers. 'You'll have to ask the old boy yourself, won't you?'

Brandon could see it looming. How do you tell a ninety-year-old pillar of the community that half the town suspects he may have murdered his wife? Back at the police station, he studied

121

that painting again, trying to decide if it represented a real incident, or was some morbid fantasy of the artist. The detail was so painstaking that you were tempted to think it *must* have been done from memory. The index and middle fingernails of the left hand, in the foreground, were torn, suggesting that the woman had put up a fight. The rest of the nails were finely manicured, making the contrast. Even the fingertips were smudged black from trying to protect herself from the sooty poker.

Yet clearly Davey Park couldn't have set up his easel at a murder scene. The background stuff, the Spitfire picture, aircraft models and so on, could have been done from memory if he was used to visiting the house. The dead woman – whoever she was – must have been out of his imagination, unless Park had *been there*. Was the picture a confession – the artist's way of owning up to a crime, deliberately left to be discovered after he died?

If so, how had the killing gone undetected? What had he done with the body?

The interview with the Wing Commander had to be faced. Brandon called at the house late in the afternoon.

'John, my dear fellow! What a happy surprise!' the old man innocently greeted him. 'Do come in.'

The moustache was white, the hair thin and the stance unsteady without a stick, but for an old man he was in good shape, still broad-shouldered and over six feet. Without any inkling of what was to follow, he shuffled into his living-room, with the inspector following.

The room was disturbingly familiar. Little had changed in fifty years.

'Please find somewhere to sit. I'll get the sherry.' He tottered out again.

Brandon didn't do as he was asked. This would be a precious interval of at least three minutes at the old man's shuffling rate of progress. With a penknife he started scraping at the dark strips of cement between the hearthstones. If any traces of dried blood had survived for half a century, this was the likely place. He spent some time scooping the samples of dust into a transparent bag and pocketed it when he heard the drag of the slippers across the carpet.

He was upright and admiring the dogfight picture over the fireplace when the Wing Commander came in with the tray.

'My, this is a work of art.'

'Don't know about that, but I value it,' said the old man. 'Takes me back, of course.'

'Did you ever meet the artist?'

'No, it's only a print. There are plenty of aviation artists selling to dotty old critters like me, nostalgic for the old days. We had a copy hanging in the officers' mess at Biggin Hill.'

'I suppose it comes down to what will sell, like anything else. There was an artist in the town called Park, who specialised in landscapes. Died recently.'

'So I heard,' said the Wing Commander with a distinct change in tone.

'You knew him, didn't you?'

'Years ago.' There was definitely an edge to the voice now.

'He painted a pretty accurate interior of this room. It was found among his canvases after he died.'

'Did he, by Jove? That's a liberty, don't you think? Abuse of friendship, I call that.'

'He didn't remain your friend, I heard.'

'We fell out.'

'Do you mind telling me why?'

'Actually, I do, John. It's a closed book.'

In other circumstances, Brandon would have put the screws on. 'But you must have been close friends for him to know this room so well.'

'I suppose he'd remember it. Used to drop in for a chat about cricket. We both played for the town team.' The Wing Commander poured the sherry and handed one to Brandon. 'Are you here in an official capacity?'

It had to be said. 'I'm afraid so. The picture I mentioned wasn't just an interior scene.' He hesitated. 'I wish I didn't have to tell you this. It had the figure of a woman in it, lying across the carpet, apparently dead of a head wound.'

'Good God!'

'There was a poker beside her. You don't seem to keep a set of fire irons any longer.'

'It's gas now.' The Wing Commander had turned quite crim-

123

son. 'Look here, since you've come to question me, I think I have a right to see this unpleasant picture. Where is it?'

'At the police station, undergoing tests. I can let you see it, certainly, later in the week. What bothers me is whether it has any foundation in real events.'

'Meaning what? That a woman was attacked here – in my living-room?'

Brandon had to admire the old man's composure. 'It seems absurd to me, too, but he was an accurate painter –'

'An alcoholic.'

'– and wasn't known to paint anything he hadn't seen for himself.'

'Don't know about that. Painters of that time used to use their dreams as inspiration. What do they call it – surrealism?'

'I have to ask this, Wing Commander. You separated from your wife in the 1950s.'

'Helen? She left me. We found out we were incompatible, as many others have done.'

'Did you ever divorce?'

'No need. I didn't want another marriage.'

'Didn't she?'

'Evidently not.'

'You're not in touch?'

'When it's over, it's over.'

He's lost none of his cricketing skills, thought Brandon. He could stonewall with the best.

The dust samples went to the Home Office forensic department for analysis. In three days they sent the result: significant traces of human blood had been found. Normally, he would have been excited by the discovery. This was a real downer.

So a gentle inquiry was transformed into a murder investigation. Wing Commander Ashton was brought in for questioning and a scene of crime team went through his house. More traces of dried blood were found, leaving no question that someone had sustained a serious injury in that living-room.

The Wing Commander faced the interrogation with the dignity of a veteran officer. He had lost contact with his wife in 1956 and made no effort to trace her. There had been no reason to stay in contact. They had no children. She had been comfortably off and so was he. No, her life had not been insured.

Brandon sensed that the old man held the truth in high regard. It was a point of honour not to lie. He wasn't likely to volunteer anything detrimental to himself, but he would answer with honesty.

When shown the painting that was the cause of all the fuss, he gave it a glance, no more, and said the woman on the floor didn't look much like his wife, what you could see of her. He was allowed to go home, only to find a team of policemen digging in his garden. He watched them with contempt.

A public appeal was made for the present address of Mrs Helen Ashton, aged seventy-nine. It was suggested that she might be using another name. This triggered massive coverage in the press. Davey Park's painting was reproduced in all the dailies with captions like: IS THIS A MURDER SCENE? and PROOF OF MURDER OR CRUEL HOAX?

The response was overwhelming and fruitless. Scores of old ladies, some very confused, were interviewed and found to have no connection with the case. It only fuelled the suspicion that Helen Ashton had been dead for years.

The investigation was running out of steam. Nothing had been found in the garden. There were no incriminating diaries, letters or documents in the house.

'What about the book?' someone asked. 'Did he have anything mean to say about his wife?'

Brandon had already skimmed through the book. Helen wasn't mentioned.

The answer to the mystery had to be in the picture. If the artist Davey Park knew a murder had been committed, and felt strongly enough to have made this visual record, he'd wanted the truth to come out. Then why hadn't he informed the police? Either he had killed Helen Ashton himself, or he felt under some obligation to keep the secret until he died. The picture was his one major work never to have been exhibited.

Either way, it suggested some personal involvement. He'd been known to have numerous affairs. Had Helen Ashton refused his advances and paid for it with her life?

Brandon stared at the picture once more, systematically studying each detail: the bloodstained fireplace, the pictures, the medals, the photos on the table, the armchair, the typewriter on the bureau, the dead woman, the blood on the carpet, her clothes, her damaged fingernails, her blackened fingertips. By sheer application he spotted something he'd missed before.

She wasn't wearing a wedding ring. The hand in the foreground was her left and the ring finger was bare.

'I deserve to be sacked,' he said aloud.

Park had been so careful over detail that he wouldn't have forgotten to paint in the ring. And in the fifties, most married women wore their rings at all times.

'You're joking, Guv,' said DS Makepeace when Brandon asked him to make a list of the women Davey Park had been out with in the 1950s.

'I'm not. There are people in the town who remember. It was hot gossip once.'

'Did he keep a diary, or something?'

'If he had, we'd have looked through it weeks ago. All he left behind were pictures and unpaid bills. Start with Henry Chivers, in the Crown.'

After another week of patiently assembling information, Brandon had the Wing Commander brought in for further questioning.

Sergeant Makepeace thought he should have waited longer, and didn't mind speaking out. 'I think he'll stall, Guv. You won't get anything out of him.'

'No,' said Brandon firmly. 'He's one of those rare witnesses you can rely on. A truth-teller. With his background it's a point of honour to give truthful answers. He won't mention anything that isn't asked, but he won't lie, either.'

'You admire him, don't you?'

'That's what makes it so painful.'

So the old man sat across the desk from Brandon in an interview room and the tape rolled and the formalities were gone through.

'Wing Commander Ashton, we now believe the woman who was attacked in your house was not your wife.'

A soft sigh escaped. 'Isn't that what I told you from the beginning?'

'The woman in the picture doesn't have a wedding ring. I should have looked for it earlier. I didn't.'

The only response was a slight shrug.

Brandon admitted, 'When I realised this, I was thrown. The victim could be anybody – any dark-haired young woman without a ring. There had to be some extra clue in the painting, and there is. She was the woman who typed your book. Her name was Angela Hamilton. Is that correct?'

He said stiffly, giving only as much as his moral code decreed, 'I had a typist of that name, yes.'

'She was murdered in your house in the manner shown in the painting. Davey Park saw the scene just after it happened and painted it from memory.'

The Wing Commander spread his hands. 'The existence of this painting was unknown to me until I saw it here a few days ago.'

'But you confirm that Miss Hamilton was the victim?'

'Yes.'

'I'm interpreting the picture now. It gives certain pointers to the crime.'

'Like the typewriter.'

'Just so. And the reason she was partially dressed is that you and she had been making love, probably in that room where she typed for you. Precisely where is not important. Your wife came home – she was supposed to be out for some considerable time – and caught you cheating on her.'

The Wing Commander didn't deny it. He looked down at his arthritic hands. The passions of fifty years ago seemed very remote.

Brandon continued: 'We think what happened is this. To use an old-fashioned phrase, Angela Hamilton was a fast woman, an ex-lover of the artist Davey Park. Park heard she'd been taken on by you as a part-time typist and found out that she didn't spend all her time in front of the machine. Perhaps she boasted to him that she'd seduced the famous Battle of Britain hero, or perhaps he played Peeping Tom at your window one afternoon. Anyway, he decided to tell your wife. He'd been trying to flirt with her, with no success. He thought if she found out you were two-timing, she might be encouraged to do the same. She didn't believe him, so he offered to prove it. They both turned up at your house when you and Angela were having sex. Is that a fair account?'

'They caught us in some embarrassment, yes,' said the Wing Commander.

'You were shocked, guilt-stricken and extremely angry. The worst part was seeing Park and realising he'd told your wife. Did you go after him?'

'I did, and caught him in the garden and let fly with my fists.' At last, the Wing Commander was willing to give more than the minimum of information. 'I was so incensed I might have injured him permanently.'

'What stopped you?'

There was an interval of silence, while the old man decided if at last he was free to speak of it. 'There was a scream from the house. I hear it now. Like no other scream I have ever heard. The fear in it. Horrible. We abandoned the fight and rushed inside.'

'Both of you?'

'Yes. He saw it too. Angela, dead on the floor, with blood seeping from her head and the poker beside her, just as it is in the picture. Helen had already run out through the back. Such ferocity. I never knew she had it in her.'

'What did you do?'

'With the body? Drove it to a place I know, a limestone quarry, and covered it with rubble. It has never been found. I blamed myself, you see. Helen had acted impulsively. She didn't deserve to be hanged, or locked up for life. You'll have to charge me with conspiracy.'

'I'll decide on the charge,' said Brandon. 'So you felt you owed it to your wife to cover up the crime. What did she do?'

'Packed up her things and left. She wanted no more to do with me, and I understood why. I behaved like a louse and got what I deserved.'

'You truly didn't hear from her again?'

'I have a high regard for the truth.'

'Then you won't know the rest of the story. Your wife took another name and moved, first to Scotland, and then Suffolk.

Davey Park, always scratching around for a living, saw a chance of extorting money.'

'Blackmail?'

'He set out to find her, and succeeded. We've looked at a building society account he had. Regular six-monthly deposits of a thousand pounds were made at a branch in Stowmarket, Suffolk, for over twenty years.'

'The fiend.'

'He painted the picture as a threat. Had some postcards made of it. Each year, as a kind of invoice, he would send her one – until she died in 1977.'

'I had no idea,' said the Wing Commander. 'He was living in my village extorting sums of money from my own wife. It's vile.'

'I agree. Perhaps if you'd made contact with her, she would have told you.'

He shook his head. 'Too proud. She was too proud ever to speak to me again.' His eyes had reddened. He took out a handkerchief. 'You'd better charge me before I make an exhibition of myself.'

Brandon shook his head. 'I won't be charging you, sir.'

'I want no favours, just because I'm old.'

'It would serve no purpose. You'd be given a suspended sentence at the very worst. There's no point. But I have a request. Would you show us where Angela Hamilton was buried?'

The remains were recovered and given a Christian burial a month later. Brandon, Sergeant Makepeace and Wing Commander Ashton were the only mourners.

On the drive back, Makepeace said, 'One thing I've been meaning to ask you, sir.'

'Ask away.'

'That picture contained all the clues, you said. Davey Park made sure.'

'So he did.'

'Well, how did you know Angela Hamilton was the victim?'

'She was on your list of Park's girlfriends.'

'It was a long list.'

'She was the only one who temped as a typist. The typewriter was in the picture. A big clue.'

'Yes, I know, but –'

'You're not old enough to have used an ancient manual type-writer,' Brandon added. 'If you remember, her fingertips were smudged black. At first I assumed it was soot, from the poker, but the marks were very precise. In those days when you wanted more than one copy of what you typed, you used carbon paper. However careful you were, the damned stuff got on the tips of your fingers.'

Phil Lovesey

As the son of Peter Lovesey, Phil has a lot to live up to in the crime writing field. His career in the genre has, however, got off to a flying start with dynamic novels and skilfully composed short stories. Until now no anthology has contained a story by both father and son and the time has certainly come to put that right. The story-telling flair of the two Loveseys is such that I am sure that their work will appear side-by-side in many future collections. 'One Bad Apple' is very different from 'Interior, With Corpse', but it offers the same marriage of sharp characterisation with pleasing plot.

ONE BAD APPLE

Phil Lovesey

'Here's a little teaser for you, Detective Constable,' said the portly man eating crisps in the passenger seat. 'Scene of the crime. Care to tell me where every crime in criminal history has been committed?'

'Why don't you piss off, and stop littering my Guv'nor's car with your half-eaten crap?' DC Colin Taylor wanted to reply. But didn't. He flicked the windscreen wipers on instead, listening to the soft rhythmical pattern, watching the rubber blades smash and blur the rain outside. 'No idea, sir,' he eventually settled for.

The older man worked another fistful of crisps into his mouth, pausing to chew loudly. 'I'm talking about every crime, Detective Constable. The scene of every crime, from a sick stateside serial killer to a little old lady in Chelmsford half-inching a Fray-Bentos chicken and mushroom pie.'

'Really, I've no idea, sir,' Taylor replied, wishing the journey away. How much longer until they reached their mysterious destination? He'd never known the M11 as bad, four lanes of near total congestion, thirty-second bursts of twenty miles an hour, then back to standstill. For the last three-quarters of an hour.

He thought of his Guv'nor, DI Melling, sunning himself no doubt, somewhere idyllic on the Algarve. Lucky, lucky bastard. Still, the Guv'nor deserved it. Can't have been easy forking out for and organising the wedding. Taylor remembered how drained he'd looked at the reception, father of the bride, leaning against the marquee bar, tie askew, nursing a pint he'd held for the previous forty minutes. Shattered. Still, it was a blinding do.

And then to come back on Monday to DI Adams. Two weeks

of the fat, self-opinionated lump until the Guv'nor returned. Major downer.

Adams shifted slightly in the seat, reaching down under the sensitive police equipment in front of the dash, pulling out a Mars Bar. His third since leaving New Street. 'Come on, young Taylor, think, man! Scene of every crime, ever.'

Taylor felt forced to hazard some kind of guess, if only to shut the bloke up. 'Planet Earth?' he replied, silently determining to book the same holiday time as the Guv'nor next year.

Detective Inspector Adams stubbed a short, plump forefinger into the side of his fleshy temple. 'The human mind, Taylor,' he said, milking it. 'Every crime always starts in the darkest recesses of a three-pound lump of knobbly mush upstairs.' Then punctuated the revelation with a large lump of knobbly Mars Bar.

'Very interesting, sir,' Taylor wearily replied, tired of the journey, the endless stream of De Bono-type mind-games, and the ever-increasing stench of cheese and onion. He looked over, found the source. Adams, helping himself to another bag, a confectioner's graveyard of old wrappers at his feet. No wonder the others on the squad had taken the piss when he'd learnt the identity of his temporary partner.

He'd smiled back, bemused at first, new to CID, unaware of the routine when other squad members went on holiday. On most occasions, he was told, the squad made do. But then sometimes, 'this fat bloke from Romford gets sent over. Adams, his name is. Adams Apple, we call him – on account of the fact that his is forever bobbing up and down as he stuffs his fat face. Old-timer, mid-fifties, never made it above DI. And that's after serving nearly thirty. Good collar record, though. Fingered a fair few nut-jobs over the years. But don't worry, son. Chances are, we'll all just muck in together until DI Melling gets back.'

Twenty minutes later Taylor stood in DCI Shrimp's spartan office, the normally spacious room made chaotic and smaller by the round smiling man wedged into a creaking wooden chair.

'Taylor,' Shrimp said simply. 'This is DI David Adams. He's with you for the next fourteen. Answer his questions, do as he says. He leads, you follow. Got it?'

Taylor nodded, walked to the seated man, took the proffered podgy hand.

'Thanks,' Adams replied. 'They call me Apple. Just answer me this, will you?'

'What, sir?'

'That corner shop up the road still open?'

An hour later, they were stuck in driving rain and idling traffic on the M11. Taylor wondered what Adams' agenda was – beyond stuffing his fat face. The paperwork back at New Street nick was no nearer to getting done, and from what he'd gathered over the police radio, most of the rest of the squad were now occupied with a possible armed suspect holding a woman hostage on a car-park roof. Bloody typical, the young DC thought. A big one goes down, and he's playing chauffeur to Billy Bunter's dad.

Adams sucked at his fingers, savouring the last of the damp orange Cheesy Wotsit powder. 'Care to tell me about Liz London?' he asked jovially.

A brief nauseating image of a girl's body stuck with a hunting knife crashed into Taylor's mind. Liz London. 'Fast' Liz London. But utterly still, stopped by death and the blade lying by her side. The raw DC's first murder case, him and the Guv'nor turning it round, bringing charges, wrapping it up. 'Junkie, speedball.' Taylor replied. 'Topped by her boyfriend . . .'

'Jamie Harrington?'

'Right.' But why the sudden interest? Taylor wondered. The case was closed, Harrington sent down for life three weeks before the Guv'nor's daughter's wedding. Old news, Fast Liz London. 'Routine domestic,' he went on. 'She was the speed-freak, he mainlined any shit he could get his hands on. Tripping off his face, he was, when me and the Guv'nor arrived.'

'He made the 999?'

Taylor nodded, tried to ignore the strangely uncomfortable tone in Adams' voice. No cryptic puzzles now, no lateral brain-teasers, just simple questions. He felt almost as if he was being interrogated.

'And then,' Adams continued, 'you and DI Melling answered the call, went round to the address?'

'S'right.'

An uncomfortable silence. Just the radio crackling. The

135

woman on the car-park roof had been saved, gunman talked down. Taylor saw the others in his mind's eye, driving back to the nick, motors bursting with grinning CID men chuffed the business had ended before opening time. Armed siege – worth a long lunch that one, my lad, Melling would've said, propelling Taylor towards the bar.

Back to the past – Fast Liz London. 'Point is, Colin,' Adams managed over a poorly suppressed belch, 'Harrington's brief looks set to appeal against the sentence.'

'Standard for life, though, isn't it?' Taylor replied.

'Absolutely, Colin. Normally just a legal formality. Chance for the wig-wearers to bung another few thousand in the overseas account. However, in this case . . .'

'What?'

'Your mainlining, knife-wielding, tripping, murdering junkie could have grounds.'

A horn from behind. Taylor came to, saw the thirty-yard gap in front of him, slowly pulled away. Grounds, he thought, what bloody grounds?

There was a squeaking somewhere close.

Adams opened a bright red bag of Skittles. 'You can turn the wipers off, Colin. It's stopped raining. Take the next exit, we're off to the rugby club.'

Quarter of an hour later they pulled up outside Royston Royals Rugby clubhouse, a two-storey affair with changing rooms and showers downstairs, bar and small function room above.

Adams hauled himself from the car, stretched the heavy frame, and turned to a sky fighting against low dark clouds to reveal scant patches of weak blue above.

Taylor was struck with how much smaller the place looked in daylight. Granted, he'd been three sheets to the wind when he'd last stumbled out of there, head spinning, reeking of stale cigarettes, whisky and beer, but somehow the place had just seemed bigger.

'Recognise it, do you?' Adams asked as they made their way to the entrance.

'Guv'nor's new son-in-law plays for the Royals,' Taylor

replied cautiously. 'Had his stag do in here a couple of weeks back.'

'A predictably well-behaved, dignified and solemn affair, no doubt,' Adams said, waiting for Taylor to open the heavy swing doors.

'Not really, sir. No.'

'You surprise me.'

Inside they were met by a thick-set balding man in his early fifties, dressed in a Royals track-suit, chewing gum, and staring suspiciously back.

Adams flashed the ID. 'Mr Bennett?'

'Same.'

'Thanks for coming down.'

'No choice, did I? Old Bill ring up, and I can't do nothing else.'

When, Taylor wondered? When did Adams ring the man? This morning, before they left? Couldn't have. Which only left a call from DCI Shrimp's office, before Taylor had been summoned to meet his new partner – the one who he'd been ordered to follow, 'answer the questions, do as he says'.

They followed Bennett upstairs into the shabby bar area, again smaller than the night he remembered it, home to sixty leering, jeering men, three strippers and a crap comic called Dudley. Plus the Guv'nor, and him.

They sat at a small table, Adams fishing through his vast jacket for a photo he placed before the gum-chewing rugby man. 'Recognise the girl?'

Taylor could, even from upside down.

Bennett nodded, looked up at the pair of them.

'Well?' Adams pressed.

'S'Fast Liz, poor kid,' he replied. 'Or was. Done in, wasn't she?'

Adams nodded. 'Played a lot of rugby, did she?'

Bennett smiled. 'She tended to play the field, really.'

'Groupie of the uprights? Follow a lot of the home games, did she?'

Bennett squinted, eyes fixed on the younger man, trying to place him. 'We have a few gentlemen's evenings,' he said slowly.

'Stag dos,' Adams obliged.

137

'Liz used to come down, do a little number. The boys loved it.' He clicked his fingers, pointed at Taylor. 'You was down here a couple of weeks back, weren't you? Paul Canyon's piss-u . . . party.'

Taylor nodded, flushed.

'Bugger me. The Old Bill crashing a stag do. I mean, I knew he was marrying a copper's daughter, but I didn't think he'd invite half the force down for his final night of freedom.' The eyes looked suddenly panicked. 'But I mean, this is a private club. All the girls get paid. Nothing illegal's . . .'

Adams held up a fleshy silencing hand. 'This isn't about a few after-show "extras" in the changing rooms, Mr Bennett. It's concerning the murder of Liz London.'

Bennett looked slightly relieved, set back to renewed chewing, nodding his head like a compliant dog. 'Sure. How can I help?'

'So,' said Adams as he and Taylor drew away from the club-house. 'What do we have, Colin?'

'I really don't know, sir,' Taylor replied, feeling edgy. 'I really don't know what any of this is about.'

'Well, let's start from scratch, shall we?'

Taylor said nothing, waiting.

'For starters we now know Liz London used to do a turn at the Royals. Shouldn't really surprise us, she was attractive, had an expensive habit and a fast reputation.'

'How did you know?' Taylor asked suddenly. 'How did you know she used to go there?'

'Fast Liz didn't always confine her nocturnal employment to the Royston area, Detective. I may look like a barrage balloon, but a few years ago I held up the Romford Rascals scrum on Saturday afternoons. I saw her routine half a dozen times in various seedy club houses across the county.'

Taylor didn't know which was harder to accept, the image of Adams on a rugby field, or the pathetically slain girl doubling as a stripper.

'When Tony . . . DCI Shrimp called me over to your manor and told me of the impending appeal, I took a look through the case file, recognised the deceased's photo.' Adams suddenly tapped the passenger window. 'Pull over, Colin,' he ordered, pointing to a newsagents. 'Time to replenish supplies.'

Three minutes and two pounds seventy-five pence later, Adams hauled himself carefully back down into the car. 'He pleaded guilty, didn't he, Jamie Harrington?' he said without ceremony.

Taylor nodded, wondered what was coming next.

'Didn't strike you as odd, at all?'

A shake of the head.

'Your first murder inquiry, right?'

'Yeah.'

'Explains it,' Adams replied, opening an economy pack of custard creams and offering one across. 'Want one?'

'No thanks.'

'Don't worry about the mess, Colin. You know as well as I do, squad motors are cleaned inside and out whenever you need it. Simply fill out the paperwork, put in the request, and – bingo – this time tomorrow, you'll never know I was sat in this old jalopy.'

'Right, sir.'

'And it's "Apple", Colin, please.'

'Right, Apple.'

Fifteen minutes later they were back on the M11, southbound, forty minutes from New Street nick.

'Know why a lot of junkies will plead guilty to murdering their own grannies if needs be, Colin?' Adams asked eventually.

Another stupid bloody question. He'd had enough. The tight-lipped reply betrayed his annoyance. 'No. Apple.'

'Treatment,' Adams replied. 'Contrary to what you might think, life inside has its compensations for druggies. It's warm, dry, and if you act out enough, you'll qualify for daily methadone, virtually as good as the real thing. All at the taxpayers' expense.' He attacked another custard cream. 'Course, it's a very different outlook if you plead innocent, and are then found guilty. Judges frown on it. Entrance on to rehab programmes

139

becomes harder, your name drops straight to the bottom of the pile.'

'So what are you saying?' Taylor asked.

'Guess.'

'That Jamie Harrington pleaded guilty, when he wasn't?'

'Wasn't that difficult, was it?'

'Bollocks, is what it is.' Taylor finally broke. 'He was messed up, out of his head. He stabbed the girl, hallucinated she was some sort of monster. I know, Apple. I was there when the Guv'nor and I interviewed the smackhead back at the nick. His prints on the knife, the lot.' He took his eyes off the road, shot them to the passenger side. 'Look, what the hell is it with this Liz London thing, anyway?'

Adams didn't react, absorbed in rebuilding the shattered biscuit. 'DCI Shrimp just wants to make sure everything's on the level. We're looking into things, that's all.'

'But there's nothing to see!' Taylor insisted.

'And the autopsy report?'

The DC cast his mind back. 'She was pregnant.'

'But not by him.'

Taylor almost lost his grip on the wheel. The son of a bitch was smiling at him, enjoying the wind-up! 'You what?'

Adams licked his fingers. 'Jamie Harrington wasn't the father of the unfortunate foetus, Colin. He said he was. He said a lot of things to get on rehab while on remand. But now he's straightened out a bit, he's having second thoughts.'

'This is a joke, right?'

A can of Coke popped suddenly, spilling on the upholstery. 'Sorry about that, Colin. Works will dry-clean it. No, it's not a joke. Harrington didn't get her pregnant, because, as he's now revealed to his brief, he's a jaffa.'

'A what?'

'Seedless – he had the snip five years ago.'

'A vasectomy?'

Adams smiled, nodded.

Taylor thought for a moment. 'So he wasn't the father. So what? The girl was a slut. Anyone could've . . .' He stopped, mind ticking over.

'Yes, Colin?' Adams teased.

Taylor wouldn't be drawn, regardless of the vague scenario which was beginning to surface.

Adams yawned. 'Just a notion, you understand, Colin. But maybe your Guv'nor's new son-in-law could've banged her up, eh?'

'Him and any number of other guys,' Taylor replied. 'Could've been you. You said you used to go and see her shows.'

Adams chuckled. 'Years ago, Colin. And believe me, the only way I'd have fallen victim to Liz London's charms was if she'd dressed herself in a five-foot wrapper saying Mars Bar.'

They turned off the motorway, began heading past Stanstead Airport towards Great Dunmow.

'Be amazing if it *was* him though, wouldn't it?' Adams continued a little later. 'And Liz, far from being the slut you imagine, would've been over the bloody moon.'

'I don't see how,' Taylor truthfully replied.

'Girls like that, they're canny. Born survivors. Street tough. Suppose the lad had got her up the stick. Don't think for one minute Liz wouldn't have been smart enough to sniff the opportunity.'

'Which was what?'

'Come on, man. A well-to-do lad like that, common knowledge that he was engaged to a copper's daughter, exposed as a two-timing rat who got a stripper pregnant?'

'Blackmail?'

'One possibility, isn't it?' Adams replied, reaching into a pocket and retrieving an earlier opened pack of M and Ms. 'Maybe she told him. Confronted the lad. Told him her price for silence. Chances are he was sweating buckets. One piece of loose talk from her, and the wedding's off.'

Taylor tried to concentrate on the road. 'Nah, not him. No way. Saw him at the stag do, the wedding. Cool as a cucumber, happiest man on earth. Not a care in the world.'

Adams said, 'True. But that was two months after the girl died. Four days after Harrington had been sent down for murdering her.'

Taylor saw the lay-by ahead, pulled in sharply, switched off the engine, turned to the chocolate-scoffing man. 'Apple, please. Can we drop the speculation?'

'Not with the appeal coming up, no.'

141

'So all this is because some murdering junkie's straightened out inside, and now wants to finger some other innocent sod for the crime?'

'No. It's more than that.'

'Tell me.'

'Fast Liz London used to be one of the best grasses I had.'

A long silence.

Adams sighed. 'When I heard she'd been topped, well, let's just say I took more than a little interest in the case. I'd lost a valuable asset. When Liz worked my manor, she helped me bang up any number of villains.'

Taylor sat, watching passing traffic, head spinning.

'I knew Liz, and I knew her idiot boyfriend, too. Not by association, just what she told me. He needed her, her brains, her suss. She was the smart one of the pair, sorting the money, organising the scams, scoring the dope.' Adams turned to the young DC. 'Believe me, Colin, Jamie Harrington would never have killed his woman. She was his supply. Last thing in the world he wanted was to be left to fend for himself.'

Taylor shook his head, desperately trying to recall events, memories already blurring, fading in the claustrophobic confines of the car. 'He was off his face that night. Path lab put the time of death sometime earlier that afternoon. He reckoned he must have had some bad gear. Stabbed her. Came to wandering around Chelmsford market a few hours later. Wandered back home, saw what he'd done. Called us. End of story. It's nothing to do with the Guv'nor's son-in-law!'

But Adams wasn't listening. 'I contacted DCI Shrimp, asked him if I could have a root around. Didn't want any more egg on the force's face. He sanctioned it. Then I discovered the payments.'

Taylor needed a good neck massage, feeling rock stiff with the tension, revelations. OK, so he was a relative newcomer to CID, but what the bloody hell was going on? Adams, from another division, snooping around the case? And with DCI Shrimp's blessing?

'It happens sometimes, believe me,' Adams said, reading the confusion.

'What payments?' Taylor barely managed.

'Five hundred a month for three months before she died. All

cash, paid in every third Wednesday into Liz London's building society account. She'd never been richer in her miserable life than on the day she died.'

Taylor struggled to get back to what he knew. 'So, she was a good-time girl, probably on the game, maybe had a regular client, rich bloke, easy pickings . . .'

'Colin,' Adams said slowly. 'DCI Shrimp gave me a back-stage pass. Access All Areas. I talked to the anti-corruption boys. They pushed some buttons on their computers. In those same three months, your Guv'nor's account showed a regular withdrawal of five hundred. Cash, every third Wednesday of the month.'

They stopped off in Great Dunmow, found a café, left the car parked outside.

Adams tucked into a weary slice of strawberry gâteau, while Taylor watched over a coffee, trying to ignore the one mental image which wouldn't go away – his Guv'nor's face at the wedding, exhausted, yet relieved, so very relieved.

'The day before the murder,' Adams pressed. 'What shift were you working?'

'C,' Taylor replied. 'Two till ten.'

'Anything stand out in the memory?'

He thought back. 'Fairly routine. Bit of a punch-up outside one of the clubs. We attended.'

'Not Uniform?'

'One of them was a bail absconder. We got the call to run him back in. Bastard puked in the back of the car.'

Adams pulled a face. 'Happens, Colin. So you filled in a docket, got Works to clean it up, right?'

'Guv'nor said he'd do it. Said he needed the wheels the following morning, had to organise a photographer for the wedding.'

'Why not use his own car?'

'In for an MOT.'

Adams smiled to himself. 'That old chestnut. So he takes a sick-stinking car back to his place for the night, then drives it round to a wedding photographer's the next day? Come on, Colin.'

Taylor tried to swallow the growing anger with another sip of coffee. What was the fat bastard saying now, that his Guv'nor had lied to him, done the girl in? What? 'I think this is getting out of hand,' he said quietly.

'Want to know what I think?' Adams quickly replied, leaning in close.

'Not really.'

'I think your Guv'nor was paying Fast Liz off.'

'Crap!'

'I think she sussed him good and proper. Got herself up the duff with the son-in-law, then sought out the proud father of the bride-to-be, and made a little hush-money arrangement –'

'He's not like that!'

'He's her dad, for Christ's sake!' Adams replied. 'And she's the apple of his eye. The wedding – her big day. What kind of father's going to take the risk of a junkie-stripper turning up and ruining the damn lot? Think of the money, the shame. He had to do something. Knew Liz London wouldn't let up –'

'You're off your head –'

'So when you get a puker in the back of the car the night before, he sees his chance –'

'Jamie Harrington killed her!'

'No. He *found* her. She'd been dead for hours, remember? Dumped back in the flat is my guess.'

The whole scenario was as ludicrous as it was comic. Any other situation and Taylor would have dismissed it utterly. But having Adams so close, so insistent, pinned him down. He fought to calm himself, not get sucked in. It was as if the big man could somehow eat him, ingest him in the same casual manner as he had the chocolate and crisps. Taylor felt hunted, cornered, shocked vermin about to be consumed by a fat cat. 'I want to speak to my Guv'nor about this,' he croaked, cursing his naïvety, inexperience, feeling a traitor the moment he opened his mouth.

'You're not the only one, Colin,' Adams replied.

They were back in the car, heading back towards New Street once more.

'Answer me this,' Adams suddenly announced. 'When did DI Melling have Works clean this car?'

144

Taylor was beginning to sweat. 'I . . . can't remember.'

Adams reached into a pocket, pulled out a folded docket, brushing off crisp-crumbs as he laid it on the vinyl dash. 'On the afternoon she died, it says here. Just before you started the shift. Had the whole motor cleaned down.'

'Because it stank of puke!' Taylor insisted.

'Chances are there was something else in your car, too. Forensic traces, Colin –'

'This is crap!'

'I reckon he murdered Liz London, right here, on the back seats of this car.'

Taylor laughed out loud, looking around, mouth agape. 'It's insane!'

Adams' voice was cold and sombre. 'He met with her, told her to get in the car, maybe promised her a final payment to keep quiet. She gets in. He stabs her. Drives her round to the flat. Lets himself in with her keys. Dumps the body inside. Drives back to Chelmsford, has Works clean everything up. It still stinks of sick, so no one's going to pay too much attention to a few spare hairs, urine, saliva.'

'Bollocks!' Taylor shot back. 'Christ's sake! If he stabbed her in here, there'd have been blood everywhere!'

'Only if he took the knife out, Colin,' Adams replied. 'And he didn't do that. Jamie Harrington did.'

'This is so much –'

'Harrington came back wrecked. Saw the body, the knife sticking out of the love of his life, so he goes over, pulls it out, the blood begins to seep out, his prints are on the handle.'

'No way.'

'Then he calls the police. You and DI Melling attend. He's brought in, off his face. A little pressure from the pair of you and he confesses, knows he doesn't stand a dog's chance fighting it. So he takes the only option. Prison, chance to straighten out, start again, maybe.'

'He murdered her,' Taylor replied, nauseous in the cramped car, trying to concentrate, feeling the metal, plastic and glass close in on, trap him. As he'd been trapped, conned by this grinning slug of a man.

Maybe they had gone in hard on Harrington. So what? The man was a useless murdering druggie – bang to rights. The

Guv'nor doing it? It was laughable ... yet ... this Adams, this apple, this one bad apple would see to it that the whole damned inquiry would be reopened. What then?

Taylor's thoughts swirled and collided wildly.

His throat dried.

Again, the image of his Guv'nor – so very relieved.

And all the time Adams waffling on ... and on ...

Scene of the crime, he'd said. It all starts in the mind, every crime ...

Taylor looked down to the left, saw the fat slob hadn't even put his seat-belt on ...

There'd be an inquiry. Careers would be ruined ...

Something exploded in his head.

He suddenly accelerated, closed both eyes, and spun the wheel sharply to the left ...

Gradually it came into focus. Pockets of distant colour, blending to form clouds, lines, images. Then the pain. He screamed. Sounds. Voices. Something sharp in his arm. Then white. A face.

The Guv'nor.

Taylor managed a brief smile.

DI Melling stared back at the broken body in the hospital bed. 'Typical,' he said. 'I leave you for a fortnight, and you spend the time lying around in hospital.'

Taylor stared at the tanned face. 'Am I all right?'

Doctors and nurses worked all around, pushing, prodding, poking.

'Few breaks here and there,' one answered. 'You were damned lucky. But you'll be in here for another month at least.'

'And the other bloke,' Taylor asked groggily. 'Adams?'

'No seat-belt,' came the quick reply. 'DOA, I'm afraid.'

Taylor fought to find Melling's face, waiting until the other had gone before speaking. 'What happened?'

Melling sat, looked awkward, flushed, couldn't meet Taylor's inquiring eyes. 'Car's a write-off. Steering column snapped, possibly. Thing was a bloody death-trap.'

'Not the car. Liz London.'

146

Melling froze, took a moment to compose a reply. 'She died. We nailed the murderer.'

'He's planning to appeal.'

'They always do.'

'Adams thought . . .' Taylor closed his eyes, memories of the last journey coming back. '. . . he had a chance, Guv.'

'Not any more,' Melling murmured. Then stood. 'You're lucky to be alive, Colin.'

'I know. Like you said, that car was a bloody death-trap, wasn't it?'

For a long time, Melling hesitated at the end of the bed. Then turned and walked quickly away.

Catherine Morrell

Catherine Morrell is perhaps better known to mystery enthusiasts under her pen-name of Gaynor Coules, which she uses for her thoughtful articles and reviews. 'Lover Come Back To Me', however, demonstrates that she is also herself a crime writer of considerable talent. So far, she has only published fiction infrequently, but I hope that, despite the demands of her day job – she works for the Authors' Licensing and Copyright Society – she will be tempted to spend more time writing stories as strong as this.

LOVER COME BACK TO ME

Catherine Morrell

10.47 a.m.

Her head was in a plastic bag. Williams was glad: it hid her face. Others had been there before him. He needn't look too closely. Dr Cullen was the doctor on duty, having his customary cosy monologue with the corpse.

'Considerate, you are, my girl. How kind.'

Williams found the doctor's grave-side manner offensive and usually tuned it out. This time, he couldn't. 'What are you on about?'

'Temper, temper! This woman is – was – considerate.' The doctor made no pause in his examination, carefully feeling the upper limbs, pressing the cold fingers. 'She knew there'd be mess, so spread the chair with plastic sheeting. Left us in no doubt what she'd taken.' A brown prescription phial and a bottle of Jamaican rum, both empty, sat on a small table under the window. 'Wanted to make it easy for us.'

'Yes.' Williams swallowed. 'Any note?'

'Not in this room. Only that pile of books.'

Williams reluctantly moved his head to peer at them. The rest of his body refused to follow. There were indeed three books on the windowsill. A greyness about them showed they'd been dusted already. A square of yellow paper stuck on the top one begged him to 'please read'. The handwriting was almost unrecognisable. The titles meant nothing to him: he'd no time for novels. DC Crane could have them: she enjoyed a good book.

Williams had never intended to fall in love, certainly not on a wet Friday night in October. There'd been a fight in a pub down The Lanes, probably because some villain smelt the undercover men there on a drugs bust. Detective Sergeant Morgan, piling in as usual, was rather asking for the pint of lager which went down his imitation Armani suit. He went home to get changed, *en route* to the next incident. His Detective Chief Inspector came with him for the ride.

'I'm back! Got the boss with me!' Morgan threw open the door. It hit the wall with a crash and bounced back on him. He swore. 'Where the hell is the bitch?'

Anna Morgan was in the kitchen, ironing to Radio 4. A pile of clothes waited their turn in a wicker basket on the kitchen table. The washing-machine hummed to itself in the corner, witness to the unending chore. Clothes already ironed hung on the door of a cupboard. Morgan walked straight past them, knocking them to the floor. Anna quietly picked them up and smiled a hello at Williams. Her eyes were nearly on a level with his: a woman in her early forties, dark hair tied back, the roots needing a touch up. Her pleasant face was flushed from the heat. Leggings and a loose shirt. Plump. Too tall, too old, too fat, too plain and not blonde. Yet he felt his stomach churn in the old familiar way. Perhaps the smell of hot linen and fabric conditioner had unknown aphrodisiac qualities.

Morgan showed no hesitation in shedding his soiled clothes. He dropped them on the floor and grabbed vest, shirt and jeans from the ironing pile. Stripped, he looked a mess. He shoved his choice at his wife, wordlessly. She, equally wordlessly, handed him ready-ironed clothes from the door.

'I want these.' He flourished the clothes in her face.

'The iron's on low for the delicates.'

'Hard bloody luck.'

'It's on the blink. Takes ages to heat up and cool again. Have these.' Her voice was low, soft and strained. She looked tired out.

'Get dressed, Morgan. We have to get a move on.' There were some advantages to being the boss.

'Sir? A cuppa first?'

'No time. Let's go.'

'I'm going for a slash. Don't do anything I wouldn't do.' Morgan scooped up the clothes Anna held out to him, dropping the unironed ones on the floor, and left.

'I don't mind making tea. But thanks.'

'We really do have to go.'

Her eyes blinked rapidly. Poor cow, he thought. What has he done to you? Sometimes Williams wished he'd never attended that course on body language. However useful it was in reading a suspect – or a victim – it made his non-professional life difficult. Anna was obviously starved for appreciation. Even that tiny bit of consideration he'd shown, mere politeness, had been taken at ten times its value. He thought hard for something to say to dilute its effect.

'Are you coming to the dance?'

'What dance?'

Great! He'd put his foot in it again. He'd forgotten Morgan's parade of young, extra-marital dancing partners.

'There's a Sixties Disco next week. Wives welcome.'

'For a change?' There was a twinkle in her eye, or was it a tear?

He grinned. 'I'd better book my dance now.' A smile lit up her face. He saw the girl of twenty years before.

'Oh, shite,' he said under his breath.

Don't you dare let her down, warned a voice inside him.

10.57 a.m.

The body and the doctor hadn't gone away.

'What else can you tell me?'

'Undoubted suicide. Pills, alcohol, a plastic bag tied over her head. She used knitting yarn. Knot consistent with being tied by the victim. She's vomited inside the bag and may have choked on that. Won't take the bag off now.' Williams nodded in agreement. The atmosphere was already touched with the sweet and sour smells of voided excreta: any addition would be unwelcome. And he'd see her face.

'Time of death?'

'Anywhere between midnight and 6 a.m. Depends how quickly her system absorbed the drug. Body temperature suggests the midnight end. She meant to do it.'

Their first time. She ran her fingers down his breastbone, over his belly-button, along that part she had temporarily tamed, and

151

on to his thigh. It tickled. Forty minutes before, they'd met in the Shopping City and he offered her a lift. They ended up in his flat.

'You don't do things by half, do you?' he said. It was three in the afternoon and a dealer in stolen videos was getting away with it. So, there was always tomorrow.

'Half-measures are useless. Put your whole heart into something or don't bother.'

'Keep that up and there'll be no half-measures.'

'Good. That's what I hoped.' And she smiled with all her being.

11.25 a.m.

Williams left the room whilst the body was prepared for removal. He joined his team who were looking for non-specific evidence or, as Crane put it, being nosy.

'It's Morgan's wife, isn't it?' asked a young constable.

'So tragic,' sighed a uniformed sergeant, on her way through to the front room. One of those Morgan hadn't got round to bedding and then discarding, Williams concluded.

'Thought she'd be glad to see the back of the bastard,' said DC Crane, voicing the unspeakable as usual.

Williams winced.

'You don't think so, sir? I do. Life should've been getting better for her, not worse. A man'll be at the bottom of this.'

'Not a woman?' Crane was gay, one of the few outed lesbians in the force. It helped if your father was a Chief Constable. Sometimes.

'Not her.' The subject was closed.

He was late for the dance. Not his fault, duty had called, but he still cursed himself. The room heaved, the noise a touch away from unbearable. He circled the edge of the maelstrom, looking for Anna. She'd laid a claim on him, or a spell. DC Crane met him by the bar. Crane: blonde, skinny but with breasts that added bounce, a head shorter than him, a pretty oval-shaped face. Everything he liked in a woman, except her sexuality.

'Hello, sir!'

152

'Not "sir" tonight.' He smiled: she'd be plugged into the gossip.

'Hello, Clive, then.' She grinned.

'Don't sound so surprised. Emma.'

'My God, you actually read my personnel file! Anyway, I've a right to be surprised. You've not been to one of these things in ages, Clive.'

'Want a drink?'

'No, thanks. Got one. On my way back from the loo.'

'All the team here?'

'Yes. You'll never guess: Morgan brought his wife.'

He could always rely on Crane. 'Really? Then, in honour of the occasion, I'll ask her to dance.'

'Good. The poor cow's been stuck in a corner all night. Not one bastard's been near her.'

'Why? She that bad?'

'No. She's made an effort. Looks quite good for her age.'

All the arrogance of youth.

'Hair's been cut. The dress is OK – three seasons old Marks & Spencer. Make-up could be a bit more daring . . .' She shrugged. 'I could fancy her if I was into mother-substitutes. No, the men're all afraid of Morgan.'

Williams drained his drink. 'Well, he can't do anything to me. I'm the boss.'

11.56 a.m.

The body passed through the hall on its way out. Williams followed it to the door and watched until it disappeared behind the ambulance doors. He turned and went back upstairs.

Anna was sitting in a corner, pretending she didn't mind not dancing. He could see the movement of her throat as she swallowed, fighting back the tears. She caught sight of him coming towards her and nearly lost control. Her eyes glittered with tears and relief.

'Hello. Sorry I'm late.'

She couldn't answer. He sat next to her and carried on chatting. Slowly, she recovered enough to answer.

'You don't talk much.'

She laughed. 'I'm afraid I'll say something idiotic. I shouldn't have come. No one's talked to me all night, except a couple of other wives. They only wanted to pry.'

'You've not been dancing?'

She laughed again. 'I don't get asked to dance. Too many prettier and younger women.'

Williams accepted the rebuke in retrospect, conscious of the many times he'd preferred younger meat himself. 'Your husband?'

'He's been dancing all night. Somewhere out there.' She waved her hand at the dance-floor. She'd varnished her nails. For some reason this tore him up inside.

'He doesn't like to dance with me. I make him look less cool.' She gasped, momentarily appalled at herself.

Running your husband down in front of his boss, Williams thought. Naughty, naughty! 'Less cool? It's time someone showed him how wrong he is.'

Williams' dancing style was more swing than sixties but it meant their hands kept touching. Her hands were warm and dry, a miracle in that atmosphere. She followed his lead, laughing at some of the moves he made. He began enjoying himself.

They ran into Morgan with his partner, the girl's face buried in his chest, moulded to him. Morgan bristled with anger when he saw his wife dancing, then relaxed when he saw who Anna was with. Morgan winked broadly before lowering his mouth back into the girl's curls. He only saw the boss doing a duty-dance. Williams felt Anna stiffen. She'd followed Morgan's line of thought and accepted the conclusion. All her gaiety vanished.

The music changed gear, slowing down, ready for the final smooch. Anna hesitated, unsure what to do, and moved away. The lights dimmed. He pulled her close.

'Don't worry. No one will think anything of it. Unless I tell them to.' They were cheek to cheek. There was a hint of a citrony perfume. She was soft and warm. His body responded. 'Your husband's a fool,' he whispered.

As long as it was dark enough, they stayed close. He managed to plant a kiss near her ear before they separated. Then came the goodbyes, the false brightness, a secret pressure of the hand as he gallantly saluted it. Her laughter at him. A promise given by one pair of eyes. The not-expecting-anything-to-come-of-it clouding the other.

12.03 p.m.

She died in the smallest bedroom of the house. It overlooked the garden and a municipal park. Crowded together were a sofa-bed, a small table, a chest of drawers and the armchair in which she waited for death. Williams stood and took it all in. He'd never been in this room. DC Crane entered behind him.

'Nice. This would make a great nursery.'

'They hadn't any children.'

'That doesn't stop it being true.' Crane knelt by the chair and looked through the window. 'Ideal place to sit while breast-feeding. Sunrise in the morning. View of trees and sky. I presume this was what she wanted to see last.'

'At night?'

'The stars?' She frowned. 'No. It was cloudy.' She noticed the books. 'What're those?'

'Cullen thinks that's her suicide note,' he said, passing off his own belief.

'Can we touch them?'

'The jackets've been dusted. One set of prints, probably hers. There's no foul play suspected. Look at them, if you want, but be careful. I'd like your opinion.'

He wandered off into the front bedroom. He glanced around it and sat on the bed.

It was their only time in the marital bed. The extra excitement wasn't worth the risk. They'd spent the evening sitting together on an organised group outing to the theatre, forced to behave casually; a touch of the knee here, a pressure from a foot there, a build-up of tension.

'Have you a lift home?'

'I'm getting a taxi.'

'Nonsense. Morgan'll have a fit if we leave you here. Look, I'm dropping Crane off on the way.'

Emma Crane had brought her partner, a dark, serious woman who insisted on sitting in the front because of motion-sickness. Crane and Anna had chatted amiably in the back about the play.

'Come in for a coffee, sir.' Crane had lots of energy left. Williams shot a glance at Crane's friend. She was scowling.

'No, thanks. Mrs Morgan is almost asleep. I'd better take her home. Bed is the best place for all of us.' Crane's friend looked at him and, unexpectedly, giggled.

Williams made it to the house in record blues-and-twos time.

In bed at last, he reached for his wallet which he'd dropped on the floor.

'No.' She straddled him and reached out to her husband's bedside cabinet. Hair tickled his stomach. She opened a drawer. 'Use his.' She held up a condom in a fancy packet.

'He doesn't even bother to hide them? Oh, my love.'

'They're fruit-flavoured.' There was contempt in her voice. 'This is tangerine.' She took another look in the drawer. 'I wonder who got the strawberry?'

He stroked her arms, wondering how to ease that pain.

'At least there'll be one less for him.' Her triumph sounded bitter.

'Two. Three!'

She giggled. 'Hello, Superman.'

12.15 p.m.

He found himself stroking the duvet cover. He calmed himself, then opened the bedside drawer. The condoms were gone. In fact, it was completely empty. He crossed to the wardrobe. There were no male clothes, no sign of a man anywhere. He closed the door and went back to Crane.

The books were hardbacks. Williams couldn't remember seeing any books in the house, though he knew Anna loved reading, and was always going to the library. Crane waved the first at him.

'It's a new copy, sir. Her own.'

'Considerate.'

156

'What, sir?'

'Cullen said she was considerate. No problems for us with library fines.'

Crane looked puzzled but didn't comment.

'You've read it before?' he asked.

'Yes. *Missing Joseph*, Elizabeth George. It's about the death and loss of children, of the gap they leave, those who want them, those who don't, all the combinations.'

'What about the next?'

'Hmm. Simon Brett. *Singled Out*. He writes crime fiction but I've not read this one.'

'Look at it now.'

'Wouldn't you like to, sir?'

'No. I need a woman's view on this.'

'Even a gay one's?'

Williams glared at her and left the room. He wandered downstairs this time.

When Anna was in his kitchen, she was not allowed to cook. She sat at the table watching him prepare food for, and with, love. Simple pastas with seafood, sloppy sandwiches, slices of chocolate gâteau which often ended up being licked from imaginative places. That night, the sandwiches were particularly gooey and designed to dribble down chin and chest. Anna was wrapped in a huge bath-towel, he wore his dressing-gown; they'd showered.

'Anna. Have you never thought of leaving him?'

'Hush, love. Don't start. Where would I go? And that wasn't a hint.'

He knew it was. 'I've been married.'

'I know. Was it as bad as mine?'

'In its way. We had a daughter.'

'You didn't say!'

'She's mostly with her mother or at school. I take her on holiday. The point is, I like the life I have.'

'I understand. Give me what you can.'

That was little enough. He knew she wanted more. But she never complained.

Crane came to find him. She looked impressed at his ability to navigate a strange kitchen. He didn't own up to his prior knowledge. He was pouring boiling water into a cafetière.

'There's a pattern emerging, sir. The first one, the George, opens with a woman who's desperate to have a child.' She held up the Brett. 'Then this one's about a woman who picks up a man in a bar to father her child.'

His grip on the kettle slipped and some water splashed over the counter.

Anna looked at him as though he was mad. He'd just asked if she'd wanted children.

'Of course! It was years before he told me about the vasectomy. He enjoyed taunting me. Told me it was my fault I wasn't pregnant. Said it was proof I was frigid.'

Williams kissed her stomach. 'That's demonstrably not true.'

'But I believed him. Not having an orgasm was apparently my fault, not his.'

'Bastard!' His head moved lower down.

'When he finally told me about his little operation, he dared me to find someone else. To try out my pulling-power. In terms of what he fancied, of course. Back when I believed he knew what attractive was! Can you imagine me in a tight dress, bosom uplifted, high heels and too much make-up, perched on a barstool? I'd empty the place! Don't stop!'

'Sorry! I was thinking about it. It's working for me . . .'

'Idiot!'

He knew laughter was the only way she could cope. He'd keep her laughing: he couldn't deal with tears.

The laughter stopped.

'What, sir?'

Christ, he'd spoken out loud! 'Go on to the next one.'

Crane went back upstairs. He sat in the kitchen, trying not to remember.

*   *   *

She insisted he use a condom more often than he liked. 'Why do we have to be so careful? I'm no risk.'

'It's not that.'

'Why?' He felt childish for sulking.

'Love . . .' She talked to him so gently. 'If I fell pregnant, he'd kill me.'

'There's that.' His sulk was receding.

'There's also this bloody enormous conscience I have. Childhood conditioning.'

'Catholic?'

'No, worse: Chapel Methodist. It's all so bloody confusing. I know, I've broken the conditioning partly or I wouldn't be here with you. He betrayed me first.'

'You know that?'

'Took me a while to catch on. The big giveaway was when he replaced all his knickers before the elastic went.'

'Not the aftershave? No lipstick on his collar?'

'Don't laugh! He never wears aftershave, probably for that reason. And all his shirts are dark.'

'So what are your limits of deception? You protecting his image?'

'Don't be bloody stupid. It's you I care for. I won't do anything to embarrass you . . .' She kissed his brow. 'Or compromise you . . .' She kissed his chin. 'Or put you at risk.' She kissed his chest.

'I know you won't.' He hugged her to him. 'I only wish there was something more I could do.'

'Oh, my love. You give me hope. That's all I need.'

01.10 p.m.

When Williams rejoined Crane upstairs, he got a shock.

Firstly, she was sitting in the dead woman's chair.

Secondly, she was crying.

He'd brought coffee with him. He handed her a cup and waited. She drank and battled to regain control.

'The final book's *Wasted Years*, John Harvey. The clue's in the title as well as the text. The detective had a bad, childless marriage.' She got out a man-sized linen handkerchief and blew her nose. 'There's a room in his house, I remember. It's certainly in the other books. The room he'd earmarked as the nursery. A man dies there . . .' She took a gulp of coffee. 'That's not relevant.'

Like hell, he thought.

The tears were flowing again. 'Sir, she must've been so lonely. All she wanted was a child. All she had was bloody Morgan. He died. She got her life back. Perhaps she couldn't cope with the guilt.' Tears ran down her face again.

'Guilt?'

'Of being happy he was dead. Because there was hope.'

He took her cup and went to make more coffee.

The kitchen was where he broke the news of Morgan's death. There'd been a high-speed chase on the motorway, ending in a pile-up. He'd insisted that telling the widow was his job and Crane was left outside in the car.

Anna had gone on washing up, the task he'd interrupted. She wouldn't let him touch her. After a few moments, she wiped her hands on a tea-cloth and made some tea.

'It's expected. A mourning ritual,' she said.

They drank it.

'Will you come over later?'

'We must be careful, Anna.'

She bowed her head. Her hands grasped her cup, white with force. 'How long?'

'Months, a year.'

She looked up again. 'A year? I can't wait a year.'

'You may have to.'

She sipped her tea. 'This is the beginning of the end, isn't it?'

He didn't answer.

'You'd better go. I won't contact you unless it's an emergency. Don't worry. I'll not do anything stupid. I love you.'

And he'd left. A coward. Relieved she let him off so lightly.

Crane was back in the kitchen, though he didn't notice her till she began to speak.

'I found this in the book. From her doctor.' Crane handed him a piece of paper. 'It was stuck inside the front cover. The last straw.' She sat down at the table and rested her head on her arms, watching him.

Williams stared at the letter, the words not making sense.

'It's dated the day before yesterday, sir. She must have got it this morning.'

A morning spent frantically trying to get in touch. An unsuccessful morning, her cries for help ignored, her messages torn up and thrown into waste-paper baskets. The final realisation that the only person she might turn to, didn't want to know.

He'd done that to her.

'What does this mean?' He knew but wanted to hear it.

'Menopause. No longer a potential mother. She'd've been a good one, too. Remember Mason's baby?'

'Hooray, the bloody cavalry's arrived.'

A neighbour of the Masons leaned against her front door-frame, fag in mouth, belligerence in her eyes. Williams had driven up with sirens, lights and a screech of brakes.

. . . the fuck you'll take my kid you walked out you have no right I have every fucking right and I'll take him now over my dead body keep away fuck that hurt I was always a better shot go now before I do some real damage keep away I won't come bloody well anywhere near you keep away from my kids I only want Ben you can't have him it's all your fault . . .

'What happened?'

'Use your bloody ears. He wants the boy. She won't let him near. Wish he'd come for the baby, bloody thing's driving the whole street mad.'

Williams entered Mason's house. Kiddies' things in the hallway. A smell of fried meat. It was Saturday afternoon and football hooligans were rampaging through the Shopping City. But Mason was one of their own.

. . . you're no bloody help with the kids it's me got up in the night what cleaned up the shit and piss and not all of it was the kids' you make me sick the way you behave I make you sick that's bloody fantastic you touch me and I'll scream you don't do a hand's turn around here you just sit and fart and eat and shag then bugger off to the pub with your mates well I'm sick of it all I'm glad I left I'm glad you left . . .

The children were crying, the two-year-old sobbing out heart-wrenching pleas to stop, the baby giving out a thin, piercing wail. Williams' sympathy was with the neighbours.

. . . it's your fault the baby's like this nothing wrong the fucking doctors say she'll grow out of it but she doesn't Ben never sounded like that Ben had a father came home at night you wanted me to go plain clothes as much as me you didn't have to live there when I got home there was no bloody peace I fell asleep all the time you think you were tired I had to stay here and fucking well cope you didn't fall asleep on duty and miss promotion it was all your fault you're a failure as a mother I'm taking the boy and you can keep the other . . .

The row was happening in the back room. Crane was stuck in a corner not able to do much. Williams hesitated on the threshold, checking all potential missiles had been thrown. Mason and his wife were yelling at each other from either side of a sofa on which the two-year-old Ben was jumping up and down. He was crying, 'Stop, stop' in between the sobs. The baby was in a carry-cot behind Crane, safely out of the line of fire but not earshot.

Morgan turned up with his wife in tow. They'd been shopping when the call came. Anna elbowed her way past Williams, a Fury on behalf of the children. She stamped on Mason's foot and got him to move over. His attention was locked on his wife and he hardly noticed. She reached behind Crane, picked up the baby and clamped it against her left shoulder. She swept the boy off the sofa with her right arm and on to her hip. She swept past Williams again.

Williams and Morgan were now free to tackle Mason. They dragged him into the front room. Crane stayed with the mother. The cajoling and reasoning started, attempts to lower the temperature. Attempts that failed.

In the same split second, Mason and his wife stopped shouting. Everyone was deafened by the silence. Blessed silence. Williams left Mason with Morgan. Crane popped her head out of the back room door. From behind her, Mrs Mason said, 'How'd she do that?'

In the kitchen, Anna Morgan had made toast and jam for the boy. He was happily crunching away, tears still marking his face but passion apparently spent. The baby was in Anna's arms, raptly watching the face above her, mouth crammed with fingers, sucking. Anna was singing very softly in Welsh. Williams hadn't realised she was Welsh. No accent.

'Oh, shit!' said Morgan, from somewhere behind Williams.

Anna looked up, her eyes shining with contentment. Williams smiled back.

'Go away, Clive. Send the mother in. I have to give a singing lesson.'

01.25 p.m.

Crane was crying again. Williams made no move to comfort her.

'Why didn't she talk to someone? Why suffer alone?' A thought struck her. 'Perhaps someone did know. Someone who let her down. These books could be a coded message.'

'But how could she guarantee he'd see it?'

'It's one of us, sir.'

Oh, very good, Crane. Can you take that further?

'She was having an affair with a copper? Never heard the slightest bit of gossip about her. Did you?'

'About her husband, yes.' She looked confused. Her grapevine had failed her.

'I think your instinct's probably right.'

Crane smiled uncertainly. 'We'd better keep our wits about us, sir.'

'Yes, we will.'

He saw her speculative gaze rest on him and held his breath. Then her focus changed: she'd dismissed him as a candidate. He was disappointed. He thought her more perceptive than that. Or perhaps six-foot, skinny, middle-aged men with thinning hair and the beginnings of a pot-belly didn't have affairs in her universe.

He took the book from her; the last message from his despairing love. It fell open at a poem about wasted tears. Mourning. To have time to mourn! He closed the book.

Crime fiction. He never read it.

Amy Myers

One of the reasons why the historical crime story has become so popular in recent years is that it offers readers the chance to enjoy the unravelling of a mystery while at the same time learning something about a very different society. Here, Amy Myers offers a rich confection. Tom Wasp and his side-kick Ned are a truly distinctive detective team; we smell the old Fleet Ditch as the events unfold; and the insight into a particularly grim aspect of Victorian society is shocking. Yet at the end of the story, there is both hope for the future and realism. All in all, this is an example of the short historical mystery at its best.

TOM WASP AND ANYBODY'S CHILD

Amy Myers

My name is Tom Wasp, master chimney sweeper, and at your service. You wouldn't believe that in Her Majesty's Reign this year of 1861 a humble chimney sweep could do better than the best pigmen in London in discovering where poor Lady Harkness was done to death. Not that I can claim all the credit, for that belongs to my chummy, my apprentice Ned, who, to my way of thinking, must have been an anybody's child himself before the Walworth Terror indentured him for his climbing boy.

Those wicked days may soon be over for ever, and may the Good Lord bless Lord Shaftesbury for making our government see that little children aren't put upon this earth to crawl up nine-inch flues with a raging fire beneath them and a black mass of soot above them to choke them or make them die of the canker. Having been a climbing boy in my youth, a career I began when I was about five years old, very glad I am of Ned's young energy to help with the brushes and our Smart's cleaning machine, for my legs are bowed and my back bent.

'Sweepie, sweepie!'

Ned was piping like a songbird on the river front. We had set out early that May morning, afore the rich folk were up and their servants bustling about their work to keep the great wheels of their houses moving down below. Not that there are riches to spare round here, for we were near the stone bridge at Blackfriars, intending to try our fortunes at the Apothecaries' Hall in Water Lane. We never reached it.

'Guv, that's a kid yelling.'

There was nothing new about screaming on the river bank, for the usual group of vultures and mudlarks was gathered round the Fleet Ditch outflow into the embracing arms of Father

Thames. In the half light, it was hard to pick out figures, for they were as grey and brown in their rags as the river mud itself. Ned, being only about ten himself, has a fellow feeling for young 'uns, so he went running across the mud as best he could, for his boots are more uppers than lowers and not much of either. I hobbled after him as fast as my legs would carry me.

'Stop, lad, the flood will be a-coming,' I roared.

I could see Ned perched atop one of the huge iron grilles across the crumbling brick arches of the sewer, but he took no notice, and plunged down into the murky scum the other side. No one tried to prevent him, for they'd seen it all before. Mudlarks, the young ones at least, seek to make their fortune by wading into the Ditch itself. The danger of being drowned by an unexpected onrush of flood water, or by the Thames high tide reaching too greedily into the outflow, adds spice to their hard days. Mudlarks are scroungers, and who can blame them, whether they are the outcast young, the forgotten old, or those who can find no other means to survive? Of them, there were many after this last bitter winter.

'Guv!'

Ned appeared over the top of the grille, hauling a mudlark of maybe six years old. Both of them were as white as a January frost with eyes like burnt saucepans, black with terror.

'The rats got him.' Ned pushed his charge into now willing arms. 'He couldn't find the way out. He'd be a dead 'un if the tide hadn't turned and the rats left.'

Many had died that way before him, I knew that.

'So what ain't you telling me, Ned?' I asked gently, and it all burst out. Ned keeps things close as a rule, so I knew it must be bad.

'There was a dead cove right up against the gate, all soft and the rats had been – oh, Guv!'

'There, lad, whoever it was, he's safe with his Maker now.' I was troubled, for living where we do between the Nichol rookery and the docks Ned ain't no stranger to dead bodies or to rats. 'A suicide, most like,' I said comfortingly, 'who's where he wants to be.'

There was no use prodding Ned like a brush up a chimney. The soot of a man's life gets stuck so fast it will come off in its own good time, not yours. All we could do was hunt for a pigman, and at dawn on a morning like this they was as rare as good meat in a penny pie. When we found one, Constable Peters of the City Police, he had to summon the River Police, this being a Thames job, and the constable escorted us back to the Fleet Ditch outflow to make sure we weren't joking. Two minutes later the men arrived to open the grilles, as was the routine at high tide. In addition there had been heavy rains last night, and the Fleet Ditch is a cantankerous beast. Its source rises in the Hampstead Hills, and rains can bring such a monstrous flood that its rush through bricked-in sewers must not be impeded even by grilles at such times. Constable Peters made them wait.

''Ere, where do you think you're going?' Constable Peters shouted, as he spotted Ned and me creeping away.

'Work, Constable.'

'You stay here,' commanded the nervous arm of the law.

It took some time for the River Police to arrive from Wapping, and we bade farewell to our threepences from the Apothecaries' Hall. Our meal tonight would have to come from the jar we keep our savings in. Most of the mudlarks had wandered off by now, for dead bodies are too common to give up the chance of meagre pickings elsewhere.

The mudlark Ned had saved had vanished. He too had a living to make. Most likely he'd been an anybody's child, fostered or sold by his loving parents and growing up in a rookery tenement. Everybody in a court like that loves anybody's children – that's until they get to four or five and need their schooling and clothes. Then anybody's child becomes nobody's child and is left to fend for himself. That's how they land up as mudlarks or climbing boys, if they don't fetch up even worse.

A small group of vultures who seemed to know one another kept us company though, and crowded round eagerly when the River Police arrived, who looked more like matelots than pigmen. The vultures weren't interested in dead bodies to my mind. They were after something that was being held back by that grille. They flexed their wings as the River Police ordered the grille to be opened, and Old Father Thames received an extra heavy onrush of combined London sewage and flood water.

169

'Get that dead meat out,' yelled the head matelot, and his sergeant and constable hoisted it out with boathooks.

The old vulture by my side crossed herself. 'The old Ditch burst its banks last night. It was the high river swept it down, poor soul.'

'It's a judy,' the sergeant cried. The pigmen must have wished they'd been more respectful after they realised what they'd got. This was no fallen woman for whom life was too much to endure, or an aged mudlark who'd missed her footing. This, for all the terrible rat bites and discoloration from bruising as the body had bumped its way along with the flood, was a lady judging by her clothes, although she'd been tied into some kind of coarse muslin sacking. A lot of the clothes and the sacking were gone, but what was left showed she'd been dressed like a queen. What's more, she seemed young, and it was far too soon for her to be summoned to her next life in the sky.

'You know who I think this is?' the pigman sergeant continued excitedly. Not to me, of course, but to his chief.

'Lady Harkness,' breathed the head pigman.

Even I had heard of her, thanks to Ritchie the patterer, whose pitch was outside the Paddy Goose pub last evening. Lord Harkness's wife had been abducted on Monday by a Chinese gang as vengeance for the destruction of the Summer Palace in Peking, his lordship having spoken in Parliament about what Lord Elgin did out there in China.

'Strangled,' pronounced the chief, with lugubrious satisfaction.

I inched a bit closer, and allowed myself a look. I considered he was probably right, and I also saw she hadn't been in the water that long, judging by her hands which weren't wrinkled in the way corpses get after being in water too long.

'Took all her jewellery, too.' The sergeant was busting his buttons to show off his brains. Except for the wedding ring, there were no rings or necklaces like you'd expect from a lady of fashion, and that was odd too. Why leave a nice gold ring?

'What you doing here?' Chief Pigman realised I was listening to his weighty deliberations.

'It's her wedding you should have been at, not her death.' The sergeant grinned at his own wit, it being a popular superstition that a chimney sweep brings luck if present at nuptials.

170

'He and the boy found the body, sir,' Constable Peters put in helpfully. It got him nowhere.

'You keep out of this. We're in charge here,' head pigman announced. Then he eyed us. 'Search 'em, Sergeant. That's where you'll find the rings.'

It wasn't too thorough a search, as chimney sweeps have that smell about them that would never go away even were we to bathe once a month. I didn't take to this sergeant *or* to the head pigman, but nevertheless they should know about a nugget of coal in my mind. London is a big city, and it pays to store up information about it, like lumps of coal against a rainy day. It was certain to me that her ladyship's body hadn't been thrown over the grille but been swept along by the flood. And I knew just where this crime could have taken place.

'Begging your pardon, sir –'

'Get out of here, sweepie.' Chief Pigman wasn't interested in my nuggets of information. 'Be about your proper business.'

To my mind, part of man's proper business is to help look after all the Lord's children whether they live in palaces or tenements, but try as I might I could not get those pigmen to hear me out. The river is what this force knows about, not the filthy rookeries and dens which empty themselves into the sewers that end up in their domain. Ned and I decided to join the vultures who were already wading into the river in search of drowned treasure, but then I heard the pigmen talking knowledgeably about how the Fleet Ditch rises in Hampstead, and how when it reaches Pentonville it passes all manner of houses of the gentry.

'That's where the deed was done,' Head Pigman said grandly. 'And where deeds are done, there'll you'll find the doer.'

'Wasn't it scum from Limehouse did this, sir, not swells?' asks the sergeant.

'No, Sergeant.' Chief Pigman swelled with pride. 'Scum maybe after she was dead to get rid of the body, and that's who took her jewellery. But Lady Harkness isn't going to go willingly with scum, is she? To abduct her ladyship, they had to get her on her own and they'd have to be seemingly respectable folk, one of those Chinese secret societies.'

'If you please, sir.' I tried once more. 'You might be mistaken about where her ladyship was killed.'

His lordship was pleased to chortle with mirth. 'So, you've got important information, have you? Scram, sweepie. Get that smell out of here. You're worse than the Ditch.'

I wasn't going to argue, for the only smells St Peter recognises at the Gates of Heaven are those of good and evil. I watched the vultures while the three matelots conferred. I made up my mind that those River pigmen would rue the day they scorned an honest chimney sweep, and I had a feeling young Constable Peters wasn't too happy with them either.

The vultures were busy making a pile of broken furniture on the shore, the fruits of their excavations in the river. There are three kinds of scavengers on the Thames: the coal-finders who scavenge for scraps of coal from the barges in the river, and the bone-grubbers who take whatever they can find to sell for grinding into manure. The third kind, rarer, were what I suspected this small group was: claimers of their rightful goods. Besides the old woman, now wading out of the river with an old chair, there was a young man of twenty or so, a thin man, older than me, forty maybe, crafty-looking, as though planning how to get the better of St Peter when his time came, and a beefy jolly-looking chap of about the same age. He had the most meagre haul, a washing dolly and a broken footstool.

The three men were making their way to a cart at the roadside, but the old woman was not so lucky. Determined not to let her precious chair from her hand, she attracted Constable Peters' attention, who decided it was time he started showing the matelots he was a pigman too.

'What are you doing with that?' he asked sternly.

'That's my chair,' the old woman shrieked at the constable.

'I can't let you take it.'

'But I'd know it anywhere.' The wail was pitiful as well as indignant, and Constable Peters, after shooting a glance at me, relented.

'Would I be right in thinking, ma'am, that you dwell in Clerkenwell?' I asked the old lady, as she staggered across the mud. Ned, reading my mind like his Bible at the Ragged School, took the chair from her to carry to the cart.

'I do. You may think I'm over-careful,' the old woman eyed

172

her chair hungrily as if Ned might make off with it, 'but with there being no work at the docks, we nigh starved to death.'

'And many did, ma'am,' I said soberly. With fourteen or fifteen degrees of frost most days in January, outside work had been impossible, and there had been bread riots in Bethnal Green. Men had dropped dead of starvation in the street, and though Clerkenwell was a working area, a cut above the Nichol, the lack of work had struck as deep there as anywhere. Poor old Tom Wasp would have starved to death too if it hadn't been for Ned going out on his own to sweep chimneys.

'How did you know we come from Clerkenwell?' The old eyes fixed on me suspiciously. So I told her what the pigmen couldn't be bothered to listen to.

'This furniture, ma'am. I've heard tell that when the Ditch bursts its banks with the rains as last night, it floods through certain tenement cellars there – a court on Turnmill Street, is it? – and carries all manner of things with it, down into the sewer.'

The Fleet Ditch is used as a sewer all its length now, but it's only totally enclosed by brick arches from Holborn Bridge down to the outflow in Blackfriars. Where Clerkenwell lies, it still runs open, as great a menace for sickness and disease as it once was treasured for its life-giving water. The patterer tells of how this will shortly change, for the Metropolitan Railway is carving its way towards Farringdon Street, and the Board of Works is anxious to quiet anxieties about the Fleet Ditch, after it flooded its banks twice and smashed the railway workings.

'That's why you were standing at the outflow this morning?' I continued.

'Yes, sir. It always happens when the old Ditch rises so sudden. If you don't or can't move, all your goods gets swept from the cellars. Our court is flooded ten foot deep at times, and we know if we lose anything where it will fetch up.'

'Tables, chairs – or a body maybe.'

'Body?' she screeched at us. 'We're respectable folk in Cherry Court.'

'You are, ma'am. I wonder if all your neighbours are.'

Tenements in such courts housing seven or eight to a room are a shifting population, some honest traders, others not.

173

'Ask 'em yourself,' she retorted. 'There they are: the young 'un's Widow Lake's son, he repairs clocks, Mr Oxney, the big one, works at Smithfield, and supports his family, Mr Smith is a businessman, and his family breeds dogs. Honest working folk, all of us.' She glared at me as though I was going to contradict her.

'And sure I am of that,' I said heartily. 'So sure I'd like to clean all the chimneys in Cherry Court free one day, as a neighbourly act seeing as how you've been hit by the floods.'

'Guv,' Ned screeched in protest.

'Shush, Ned.'

I lifted my stove hat to her. She flushed like a girl, and her step, it seemed to me, was a little lighter, as she wedged her chair on the cart and climbed in after it.

'Ned,' I said, 'it's my opinion we've found where this terrible deed was done. Poor Lady Harkness's body was in one of those Cherry Court cellars, and got swept out accidentally, before it could be got rid of properly. Can you see any reason a Pentonville swell would risk dropping it in so close to home? Even with the rains it might have been spotted higher up the Ditch. And why bother to truss it up in that sacking?'

'Don't know, Guv.' Ned was getting bored, but I'd got my mind set on the problem. The body was being removed now, and the constable, ignored by the matelots, was hanging around like a spare chimney brush.

'Ned,' I says, 'we've all got our own chimney in life to climb and that young constable deserves a hoist to clean air above.' So I went over to him. 'It seems to me,' I said, 'that our jobs are much the same, sir. I clear up the black remains of man's path through life and so do you. That's where the satisfaction of my job comes in. When you see those brushes come out on top of the chimney, you know you've won over the evil lurking down below.'

He went as red as a glowing ember, but I'd made my point.

'Constable Peters,' – best to keep matters formal – 'all the patterer gave out was that Lady Harkness was taken by the Chinese. You being in the know could tell me what's the reason for the police to think that, if this ain't revealing any secrets.'

The constable was glad enough to speak. 'No secret that

I know of. It's been in all the newspapers. When Lord Harkness arrived home Monday evening, his wife weren't there, and the servants said there'd been no callers. She had left the house alone, so her maid said, and we think they were waiting for her in a cab nearby.'

'And I suppose none of her clothes had been taken?'

'You're right, sweepie.'

'And what about her jewellery? Any missing?'

'I was wondering about that myself, sir.' (Sir? Constable Peters was getting over-excited.) 'Neither Lord Harkness nor her ladyship's maid thought anything was missing.'

'That's very satisfying.' It helped clear the flue I was inching my way along.

Constable Peters looked at me as though remembering who I was, so I said to him hastily, 'I didn't take to those matelot policemen, and I've got a few ideas of how this murder was done. Now if I find out anything, I'll let you know because you strike me as an able young chap.'

He blushed – you don't often see that in a pigman. I doubt if he believed I could find out the time of day, but he was pleased, and that was the important thing.

'Ned,' I said, as we got on our way, 'if you was Lady Harkness and you had a mission in Clerkenwell, what would you do?'

'Change me mind,' Ned obliged promptly.

'Very good, lad. To my way of thinking though, her ladyship *did* go there.'

'Then I wager that Mr Smith runs a jerryshop,' said Ned, with his knowledgeable man of the world expression.

'A pawnbroker, for a ladyship? No, moneylender perhaps.'

'Guv, we're only sweeps. How are we going to find out how her ladyship died?'

'The Lord provides brushes to clean His chimneys, and He gave us a brain to think things out.'

He didn't speed it up for us though. The days passed and even the patterer grew rich reporting on the rumours and hunt for the notorious Yellow Hand, a society so secret not one Chinaman in Limehouse could I find who'd ever heard of it.

One evening, as I bought us two stale mutton pies from our

coffee stall, they being a halfpenny instead of a penny for the fresh 'uns, I harked back to the vexing problem.

'Ned, suppose Lady Harkness did have a reason to visit Cherry Court. How did she get there? She wouldn't use her own carriage if it was somewhere she didn't tell her husband she was going to. My belief is she wore a plain mantle over her dress, and took off her jewellery save her wedding ring, so she wouldn't attract attention, and took a four-wheeler.'

'We could ask the cabbies,' Ned volunteered.

The advantage of being an outcast from society is that folks want to be rid of you because of the smell, so they tend to oblige by telling you immediately whatever you want. What's more, trades stick together. In the sweeps' fraternity I'm highly respected both by sweeps who go calling in the streets and those cautious gents who prefer to have their own regular trade. On 1st May each year we have a sweeps' festival to mark the fellow feeling with our brother sweeps. Why I say brother I don't know, since there are more than a few women in the trade, having done a climbing boy's job in their youth. Anyway, all I had to do was spread the word that I'd be much obliged to know of a jarvy who took a lady in his cab from Mayfair to Clerkenwell Monday afternoon. A *lady* I emphasised, not just any judy who'd been walking the pavements up West, poor soul. My request would be with all the coffee stalls in London within the day.

Meanwhile I had a word with the regular sweep for Curzon Street, where Lord Harkness lived, and arranged to take over the sweeping business there in return for nine-tenths of the divvy going to him. He said he fancied a day at Margate, wherever that may be, so he was glad enough, though I had to pay him in advance from the special jam jar fund.

Although sweeps have the run of the house (with a footman keeping a stern eye on the silver) they can't count on getting on chatting terms with the likes of Lord Harkness, so I planned my scheme another way. Most housekeepers are kind enough to provide you with sustenance, though they don't care for you eating it inside and messing up their spotless kitchens. My Ned has a pair of appealing eyes, though, that most cooks find hard to resist, all too ready to believe I treat him badly.

'I can see his lordship wants for nothing here, madam.'

I cleared my throat after a mug of beer and a maid of honour cake in the scullery. 'You must be a tower of strength to him in this time of trouble.'

'A house in mourning, sweepie, that's what we are.' The housekeeper's plump black-bombazined figure shook with emotion, as she wiped her eyes. 'To think of her ladyship dead at the hands of those nasty foreign garotters.'

'A nice lady, was she?'

'Couldn't have had a nicer mistress, and her only married a year.'

'A charitable lady, was she? Good works in the East End, that sort of thing?'

She stared at me as if I'd suggested Lady Harkness was in the habit of dropping into an opium den from time to time. Her voice was as stiff as a lamplighter's pole when she replied, 'Her ladyship took an interest in the plight of women forced into sweated labour, but visiting the East End on her own, if that's what you're getting at, no, sweepie. She knew her place. Besides, her ladyship's chest was delicate. She'd spent a year in foreign parts to get it right before she married, so she's not likely to put it wrong again by going to nasty damp hovels, is she?'

'Indeed not, madam,' I said warmly, as though shocked at the thought of dwellings much like my own. 'Doubly sad, then, to meet her tragic death with no worries on her mind.'

'I wouldn't say that.' She sniffed, and Ned sneaked a second cake.

'A happy household, you said?' I asked delicately.

'Lord Harkness was devoted to her, but there was poor Mr Dickens.'

'The author, ma'am?' This *was* a surprise.

'The dog.'

This took even more delicacy to unscramble, since it had been under the housekeeper's own eagle eye that her late mistress's little spaniel had disappeared during its evening walk in Berkeley Square some days before Lady Harkness disappeared.

'Very upset, she was, about Mr Dickens. It wasn't my fault. It's my belief he was took.'

'The Lord giveth, madam, and He taketh away.' I deliberately misunderstood her, but I knew well what wicked trade she referred to.

I pondered some more upon the tragedy of Lady Harkness over the next few days, which were busy ones for Ned and me as we strove to bring up the level of our pennies in the jar to their former glory of four shillings and nine pence.

'There's dosh and there's vengeance, Ned, and to my mind dosh is always the one that pulls harder. If that Yellow Hand Society took her ladyship, why didn't it make Lord Harkness *pay* for his wife's return, just like the –' I stopped, for suddenly I understood, as clear as daylight through the chimneypot, at least one reason why Lady Harkness might have gone to Clerkenwell, and maybe two.

The hue and cry over her murder had died down, and I was just on the point of putting the murder from my mind when I got a message from the Sweeps Evening (that being the grand name for the gathering at the Two Eagles each week) that a cabbie at a coffee stall had reported that a fare had told him to take her to Cowcross Street. She was a lady fare (if you'll excuse the pun) and that was why it had stuck in his memory for Cowcross Street wasn't the sort of place where ladies from up West went alone. I had a notion that wasn't far from Cherry Court.

'Shall we tell the pigman, Guv?' Ned was excited, maybe seeing fame and fortune coming our way, but he'll learn the world don't do things that simply.

'No, lad, we need more to show the pigmen that Cherry Court is where the crime took place.' All the same I took careful note of the cabbie's name. 'It's time to get chimney sweeping in Cherry Court.' Fortunately, soot visits poor folks' chimneys just the same as rich folks' flues.

Clerkenwell is much like the rest of London (save for big rookeries like the Nichol which are different hellholes). Here the swells' houses line the main streets, upon which their owners look from their front windows. If they ever glanced down at the back they'd see slums as bad as any in London. Cowcross Street wasn't too bad itself (not judging by Rosemary Lane near us, anyway) but when we reached Turnmill Street, and the enclosed alley to Cherry Court, the smell hit us. Sweepies smell of good clean soot, but this was the smell of the Nichol and well we

178

knew it. Garbage, excrement, everything bad and unwanted swirls along the Fleet Ditch and in the gutters of the court, making the houses islands surrounded by filth. With one privy serving maybe eighty people, it ain't surprising. Despair smothers hopes of cleanliness and hygiene.

There was no doubting Cherry Court backed on to the open Fleet Ditch. I knew the smell that had built up there ever since the times of merry old King Charles II, when he took time off from dalliance with his Nell to pay some attention to rebuilding London after the Great Fire and changed the old river into a dock. He called it, so I heard, the New Canal, but it didn't deserve that fresh name for long.

The houses in Cherry Court weren't the usual three- or four-storey tenements; there were six along here, all two-storey, low terraced houses that had given up all hope of light from the sky, huddled as they were down by the Ditch. Their walls were crumbling, and their roofs holed. You could smell where the flood had been in the court, but even so a dozen or so small children were playing hopscotch in there. They'd hardly a pair of boots among them, and more to be seen of skin than rags on their backs. These were anybody's children, no doubt about it.

'Guv.' Ned was pulling at my sleeve. 'I don't like it here.'

I looked down at his frightened face, astonished, for Ned had seen far worse than this. He works with me in the Paddy Goose, the most notorious pub in the East, without flinching.

'Come, Ned,' I said bracingly, 'a few minutes and we'll be off for our supper. How do you fancy eel pie?' This was a joke between us, for such luxury came but once a month, and that day was two weeks off yet. 'You stay here, and –'

'I'm coming with yer,' Ned yelled, clutching my hand so hard I felt his nails digging in.

It didn't take long to find our chair lady's house and she was willing enough to show us to her cellars, when I gave her a threepence for her trouble, and cleaned her chimney for nothing. When I say cellar, I don't mean those comfortable places stocked with wine like I've seen at swells' houses. These were crumbled ruins without windows or doors, open to the elements – including the Fleet Ditch.

'I take in weaving work, but it's too damp down here so I let it, sir, when I can, but not with them floods. I lost everything but my old chair.' She looked mournfully round her barren paradise.

Even the Union workhouse was better than this, so I knew her customers were beggars and vagrants, the 'undeserving poor' as the Relieving Officer calls them, thereby meaning they were able-bodied and able to work and thus not deserving of outdoor relief.

I couldn't see Lady Harkness coming to see a weaving lady here, so I asked her whether her neighbours accepted my kind offer. They had, not too much to my surprise. No one suspects a sweep, for we're too poor to risk being magsmen.

The first two homes had cellars that were in reasonable condition. The flood water had been here, no doubt about that, but there was no way a body could have been swept away.

Widow Lake's was a different kettle of stinking fish, enough of it open to God's elements to make it possible. The cellar was packed with wet boxes, some displaying lengths of soggy wool and silk.

'You lead a hard life, madam.'

'My Joe does his best.' She fired up in defence of her son. ''E tries to get work, but I has to keep him going, don't I?'

I did not ask why keep the boxes here, for I knew what the answer would be. In their one living-room there was no space for two adults and four younger children *and* boxes. She would work from 8 a.m. to 10 p.m., and be blind long before those kiddies could support her.

'Those children in the yard are yours?'

'Maybe. Or maybe Mrs Oxney's. Or others.' She made a hopeless gesture. 'They're all anybody's children round these parts.'

Ned whimpered at my side, tugging at me to come away, so I moved on to our next chimney. Next door was Mr Oxney, a big man as she said, who worked nights, only he was off sick. Just the downstairs flue, he told me, owing to their not keeping a fire upstairs.

I wasn't surprised at that, for it seemed to me, not wishing to be indelicate, that he kept enough warmth up there all by himself, as Mrs Oxney in the living-room had five little 'uns at her feet. I wanted a look at that cellar, so making an excuse I went into the scullery and peered down at it as I went. It was in a worse state than Widow Lake's and seemed to be full of boxes and cartons, and had certainly been flooded. I went back to find Ned gone, so making my adieux and gathering the brushes which Ned had left behind – to my surprise – I went out after him into the court.

Mr Oxney was beaming as he showed me out. Work with meat must be a happy job. Ned came running up to me, shivering, although the sun was up above, even if it didn't condescend to reach down to the court below. He didn't say a word, but I knew what he wanted.

'One more, lad, and then we're plodding home.'

He gulped and clung to my hand, as I banged on the door of Mr Smith, businessman and dog lover. Mr Smith, a most impolite individual, had no interest in us other than saving himself threepence for the sweeping of his chimney. No need for me to peer into that cellar. I'd heard all I needed. Barking dogs. There's a nasty racket where 'businessmen' like Mr Smith organise gangs to steal the dogs of the rich and ransom them for money. Very profitable, but most of the dogs land up dead.

'What line of business are you in, sir?' I asked cheerily, placing the bag over the hearth so as not one speck of dirt would sully this smelly, dog-haired, filthy room.

'Trading.' He answered me less cheerily.

'In dogs?' I asked brightly, as I finished my work, and a large fist in my face provided a powerful argument for leaving quickly.

'Ned,' I said quietly, 'we've got our man.'

'Let's go home, Guv.' There were tears in his eyes.

'Why, Ned?' I said, very puzzled now.

'I don't like this place.'

Not good with words is Ned, where he himself is concerned. 'Was you one of them once, Ned? Do you remember now?'

His eyes shot open wide. 'I don't like them,' he screeched. 'I don't. I know this place, Guv.'

I knew then that I was right. 'Ned,' I said gently, 'I know who done poor Lady Harkness to death and why. We'll be moving now. You've earned your eel pie, and we'll come back with the pigmen tomorrow.'

Our jam jar level was ebbing like the high tide, and we emptied it still further for our eel pies and porter.

Next day I persuaded Constable Peters to come back with us, and to notify the Clerkenwell Police. He didn't want to, but when I explained a bit further, his eyes shot open and he clasped his truncheon lovingly. I had to talk even harder to Ned to get him to return to Cherry Court, but when I told him how much he'd be helping, he agreed.

'Ned,' I asked when we got to the court where the kids were playing, 'are you brave enough to stay alone out here and cause a bit of a rumpus?'

He gulped. 'Yes, Guv. But not long, *please.*'

'Brave lad.' I told him what I wanted him to do.

I banged on the door I wanted, as Ned, like magic, began a prize fight among the anybody's children, himself in the centre. 'I'm going to the pigmen,' he yelled, over and over. 'I'll tell them what's going on here.'

As the devil Oxney rushed out to collar Ned, I hobbled in quick as a flash, with Constable Peters on my heels. This time I went upstairs; even I quailed. Inside was the silence of living death. A dozen or so toddlers and babies, all dull-eyed, yellow-faced and little more than skeletons, those that were too young to be anybody's children yet, lay limply on straw in one corner. Drugged, of course. Wouldn't do to make too much noise and upset the neighbours. They wouldn't all die for too many deaths would be inconvenient, but some would. As had Lady Harkness's baby no doubt. I was down those stairs as quick as a man with two new legs, following Constable Peters, with Mrs Oxney now screaming her head off. Oxney had laid hands on Ned, but the privilege was returned when Constable Peters blew his whistle and clamped handcuffs on him.

Constable Peters is a sergeant now, and transferred to Scotland Yard to become one of those detective policemen. The baby-farmers, for that's the heinous path the Oxneys followed, were convicted for killing several babies, and the sad story of Lady Harkness never came out. Baby-farmers are the sewers of humanity, advertising in respectable newspapers to foster babies and children. Working mothers and the gentry use them alike, but many of these children die, for their mothers never ask to see them again. Poor Lady Harkness did. I had thought what if she'd been away that year to have a little baby, not for her health. Being unmarried, she'd have been forced to have it adopted while she was abroad. Wanting to see it again, she paid an unexpected visit to the Oxneys; she'd found no baby and realised it was a baby farm. The Oxneys couldn't let her go, so they strangled her and put her in the cellar, not knowing the old Fleet Ditch was going to play its part in bringing their terrible crime to light. The spot where a murder takes place can sing the truth louder than a tub-thumper.

'And how did you guess, Guv?' Ned asked me, trying to be brave. I never inquired, but it's my belief Ned had been an anybody's child right there in Cherry Court, thrown out by the Oxneys, and then sold to the Walworth Terror. The horrors of that gentleman had blotted out memories of Cherry Court, and unknowingly I'd brought it all back to him.

'It had to be one of those two, Ned, if you rule out Joe Lake. I thought it was Mr Smith at first, what with her ladyship's dog being taken. Whether it was Mr Smith took Mr Dickens I can't say, but it's certain that's his trade. Then I guessed it wasn't him.'

'How?'

'Because, lad, to visit him or Joe or the Widow Lake, Lady Harkness would have taken her maid or husband, or even the police with her. This was something she had to do on her own, that she didn't want anyone, let alone her husband, to know about.'

'That's clever, guv.' Ned's eyes were shining in admiration and I felt the guiltier for what I'd put him through.

'And there was the jewellery. If she'd been killed for dosh, they'd have taken her wedding ring, as well as anything else in the jewellery line. A nice bit of gold never came amiss. So it had to be someone who killed her for some other reason. And then there's that muslin sacking she was wrapped in. Where do you find that, I ask? Butchers and meat markets. Smithfield, see? No doubt he was going to put her into storage, poor lady, and ship her out with other carcasses, only the floods came too quick.'

'Oh, Guv, you're clever.'

'Only thanks to you, Ned.' My anybody's child. 'I'll make it up to you,' I vowed. 'You'll never go in fear again!'

He looked at me with adult eyes. 'Not even you can promise that, Guv.'

I sighed. 'That's true. This city has a thousand windows to the light, but more than ten thousand dark holes which few ever see. No one can guard you against all of them. Take Windsor Castle now, underneath it has sewers just like everywhere else, and who knows what goes on in them?'

'No matter, Guv. I'll have another pie instead.'

I laughed. 'At the top of the chimney is the everlasting light. We'll get there. You'll do, Ned, you and me together.'

Ian Rankin

The last time Ian Rankin kindly submitted to me a story for the
CWA Anthology – 'Herbert In Motion', which appeared in *Perfectly Criminal* – it won the CWA/The Macallan Dagger for the
best crime short story of the year. In introducing the story, I said
that Rankin was destined to become a major force in the genre.
Four years on, it is a prediction that has been amply fulfilled, but
in truth it was always a safe bet. Rankin's economic, seemingly
effortless ability to delineate character and plot to devastating
effect is perfectly illustrated in 'The Slab Boys'. And the scene of
the crime itself is uniquely appropriate.

THE SLAB BOYS

Ian Rankin

The mortuary attendant's name was Derek. He walked into the staff room still wearing his white coat and wellingtons, bringing with him the clinging odour of meat.

'They're outside,' he said. By this, he didn't mean that the two CID detectives were out in the open air, but that they were in the body of the building – the storage area with its metal doors, each one concealing a sliding tray six and a half feet in length. One time the mortuary had had to deal with a seven-footer, a giant of a man. Lorraine seemed to remember that they'd resorted to leaving his door open, head poking out. She nodded now, holding the mug of tea to her face. Two more gulps and her cheeks were covered in a fine film of condensation. She got to her feet.

'Good luck,' Derek said.

But the detectives had moved on. They were in the lab area next to the autopsy suite, peering at the contents of the rows of specimen jars.

'Ah, Lorraine,' the woman said. Her name was Nelson. Her colleague just nodded. His name was Gilfillan. 'How's the head?'

'Fine. How's yours?'

'I wasn't drinking, remember?'

Lorraine remembered. She leant against the worktop and folded her arms.

'The Prof's car was still in its garage,' Gilfillan said, tapping one of the jars like a kid at an aquarium.

'Expect it to start moving?' his colleague asked. He turned away, got out his notebook.

'Now, Lorraine,' Nelson said, 'when we spoke to you last night, you were telling us what the Prof had said.'

'What's the problem?'

'Problem is, sweetheart,' Gilfillan interrupted, 'he's been reported missing by his missus.' He smiled at his own pun. Neither woman joined him. They were too busy staring at one another. 'So this time we need to know *exactly* what it was he told you . . .'

'Tell me he's not dead.'

Lorraine looked around, eyeballs aching from the stark whiteness of the mortuary's tiled walls.

'Tell me,' she said. All this whiteness, she saw it suddenly as an avalanche and willed it to smother her. Then she blinked and was where she'd always been: on her knees, with the body of a man lying in front of her. Derek leaned down, stuck two fingers into the warm, still-yielding flesh of the prone corpse's neck.

'No pulse,' he said, his voice thick with alcohol. His breath smelt tainted, as though he'd been gargling formalin.

'Oh hell,' Lorraine said. 'Not *here*.'

Derek started helping her to her feet. 'I'm trying to think what the opposite of ladykiller is. Mankiller? Never thought you had it in you, Lorraine.'

He started giggling, and she punched him hard in the chest. The paper crown she'd been wearing was falling over one eye, and she slid it back up her forehead, then, realising what she was doing, tore it off and let it flutter to the ground.

Derek tutted. 'Scene of the crime, Lor. Don't want to leave trace evidence.'

'Think you're so smart,' she said. But after a moment she crouched and picked the crown up. It was pink crepe paper with jagged edges and a gold star on the front. It had come from her cracker, along with a plastic bracelet that wouldn't fit round her wrist and a joke she couldn't remember. That had been back in the Chinese restaurant, a dozen of them around the table. Her boss, the Prof, had been telling her that pathologists couldn't drink, they were on call twenty-four/seven. But the fruit punch Derek kept bringing to the table was laced with absinthe, she later learned, and after two glasses, the Prof had accepted 'one small glass of wine', and that had been that.

'It's your fault anyway,' Derek was saying now. 'Romance in the workplace: didn't you warn me off?'

She glared at him again. Her head was pounding and her eyes seemed to focus only with every other blink. She remembered: Derek trying the come-on from her first day at the mortuary. Telling her she'd mucked things up; before she'd arrived, they'd all called themselves 'the slab boys'. Now, with a girl in their midst, they'd have to think again. Maybe they should discuss it over a drink. But over time she'd become 'one of the lads': the 'slab boys' they remained.

'I wasn't the one feeding him bloody absinthe,' she muttered, holding a hand to her head. She looked down again at the Prof. He'd removed his jacket and tie, unbuttoned the top two buttons of his shirt. His shirt-tail was hanging out, too. She'd done that, running her hand inside to stroke his stomach . . .

'What are we going to do?' she groaned.

Derek sniffed, glanced at his watch. 'Don't know about you, but I'm off home.' He waited for a reaction, then said he was only joking. 'First thing is to do his belt up again and zip the fly back up.'

'Then what?'

'Leave him for the cleaners to find.'

'Don't be wet, Derek. Everybody saw us at the restaurant.'

'No, Lorraine, everybody saw you and *him* at the restaurant.'

She had a flashback: snogging on the way to the door, a couple of the CID guys cheering. The Christmas party: mortuary staff and some of the cops they'd dealt with and liked through the year. Her and the Prof . . .

'He's married,' she said, her voice breaking.

Derek had finished making the corpse look presentable.

'When he's found,' Lorraine went on, 'they'll do an autopsy.'

Derek was standing up, weaving slightly. She looked at him.

'They'll find the absinthe,' she said. 'It wasn't for sale at the restaurant. They'll wonder where it came from. The Prof didn't drink, remember?'

Derek was nodding. 'We're for the boot,' he concluded, 'the pair of us.'

She was still looking at him. 'I wasn't the one did the poisoning.'

'It was his heart,' Derek argued, 'Plain as the nose on your face. Gave out on him due to exertions with a certain party.'

Her look became a glare. Derek had done some time inside, seven, eight years back. Been homeless for a while, too. There were crude tattoos on his forearms, needle and ink jobs. His jacket was off, sleeves rolled up. He'd been in the office, necking a tin of beer, while she'd been back here necking with the now deceased. All these polished chrome doors surrounding them; she tried to think how many bodies were in the place tonight. Four or five, two of them the usual yuletide suicides. She could see Derek turning things over, his mind fighting the effects of the drink. He crouched down beside her.

'He had about a half-bottle in the end,' he said.

'Poison to a non-drinker.'

A tic had appeared below his left eye; he seemed not to've noticed. 'Manslaughter,' he said quietly.

She shrugged. She was thinking of other things, trying not to let them show. The Prof and her ... twice before in his car, parked down by the docks far from any street-lights. Her hands under his shirt, hairy chest and back. She couldn't know what would come out at a trial. The CID guys, they were sharp, some of them. She imagined the autopsy scene. Dr Mullan was the city's other pathologist. He'd be making incisions into his friend, his colleague. He'd want to know what had happened. And the detectives, too, standing around, smelling alcohol – not just wine – as the incisions were made, and remembering the restaurant, the unruly 'slab boys': Derek and his fruit punch, while she got so drunk she started pawing the Prof, didn't care who saw it. They were lovers after all, weren't they?

The distraught widow ... the loving husband who would never leave her.

Revenge: they'd be looking for a motive, and that's the one they'd think they'd found. Lorraine and Derek, poisoning the Professor in the mortuary. It sounded like something out of Cluedo, but it wasn't.

It was real.

'I can't go back inside,' Derek said, shaking his head. 'Last time was enough. It was this job got me straight.'

'Well, we have to do *something*.'

'Let me think.' Derek slapped his cheeks with his hands, trying to sober up. There was a sound from out front, a door opening and closing. They looked at one another, eyes widening in horror.

'Anybody home?'

Gilfillan laughed at what he'd just said. 'Any *bodies*, I meant to say.'

His companion didn't laugh. Her name was Nelson and she was a rank above him. 'Hello?' she called.

They were in the long narrow corridor with doors off left and right. Left led you to the loading bay. Right took you into the staff room.

'It's like the *Marie Celeste*,' Gilfillan said, pushing open the door to the staff room. 'Maybe they've gone home already.'

'Must be someone here,' Nelson persisted. 'Wouldn't have left the door unlocked and the lights blazing.' She pointed into the room. 'Four cans on the table, and only one of them open.'

'Well spotted.' Gilfillan weaved inside, shook the open can. 'Some still left.' He lifted it to his ear. 'Plenty of fizz, therefore recently opened.'

She nodded. Gilfillan took another can, tugged on the ringpull and started guzzling. He made the offer, but she shook her head. A sound echoed at the end of the corridor: metal on metal. Then music, sudden and incongruous. They walked to the far door and pushed it open.

The two mortuary assistants were dancing a sort of reel. The music was seventies disco from a portable radio. One of the storage bays had been opened and its tray slid out. The radio sat on the tray.

Nelson cleared her throat. The slab boys stopped dancing, grinned at the newcomers.

'Thought you lot had headed home,' Derek said.

Gilfillan shrugged. 'Police club was boring, and you'd mentioned a booze-up here.' He raised his can.

'Well, you found the drink anyway.'

'Just beer?' Gilfillan sounded disappointed. Lorraine switched the radio off, wiped sweat from her forehead.

'Where's the Prof?' Nelson asked.

'Gone home,' Derek said.

'He seemed keen enough earlier.' Nelson gave Lorraine a look.

Derek took a step forward, squeezed Lorraine's shoulder. 'Best man won,' he said, making to plant a kiss in her hair. She dodged away.

'Prof's married anyway,' Gilfillan added, exhaling a burp. 'Twenty-odd years. What's his wife's name? Helen? Something like that . . .'

'Married men are the worst, though,' Nelson said, winking towards Lorraine. But it was Derek who laughed agreement.

'Who've you got in tonight?' Gilfillan said, clanging his can against one of the drawers.

'Nobody special,' Lorraine said, suddenly animated. 'We could go sit in the lab.'

Gilfillan tried one of the drawers, pulled it open. The tray was empty. He stuck his head into the space. 'Grim place to end up.'

'We like it,' Derek said, rubbing hard at his eyeballs with thumb and forefinger. The four of them went to the lab.

There were two rooms: one where the autopsies were performed, and the other where specimens were stored and sorted out. Several stained wooden shelves held a variety of cloudy jars, their labels faded. Gilfillan studied some of them.

'Ever been to the Black Museum?' He meant the medical faculty's collection of rare, strange and exotic specimens. The attendants shook their heads. 'I had a teacher at school, used to nip into the Physics store and come out with meths on his breath.' He shook the can again. 'Anything stronger than this on the premises?'

'Formalin?' Lorraine suggested.

Nelson read aloud from a sign on the wall. ' "To make twenty litres of ten per cent formalin, take two litres formaldehyde and add eighteen litres water." ' She didn't read out the sign's final two words – 'for brains' – which were underlined three times.

Gilfillan had wandered through to the autopsy suite. 'Gives me the heebies, this place,' he said. He lifted the lid from a large ceramic brain jar, then replaced it and made for the sink.

'Good meal, wasn't it?' Derek said. He had his arms folded and was leaning against the door jamb.

'Chinese.' Gilfillan wrinkled his nose. 'Puts a thirst on you.' He unhooked one of the green gowns and slipped it over his head. 'Go on then, Nelson, up on the slab and I'll give you an examination you'll never forget.'

Nelson looked at Lorraine and rolled her eyes.

'What about you, Lorraine?' Gilfillan went on. 'Can I interest you in my bedside manner?'

'Careful, Gillie,' Nelson said, 'you might have a challenger.'

The CID man looked Derek up and down. 'You think so? Seriously?' He made a slashing motion, Zorro style, then his shoulders slumped. 'Christ, this place is deader than the police club.'

'We were thinking the same,' Lorraine said.

'Give the pair of you a lift?' Nelson asked.

'I've got my car,' Derek said quickly.

Nelson looked at him. 'Amount I saw you put away, you better be careful.'

'I'm walking,' Lorraine said. 'Clear the cobwebs.'

Gilfillan had moved back through to the lab. Now he was watching from the window as headlights played across the ceiling.

'Looks like another customer for you,' he observed. 'Still, they never mind waiting, do they?'

Derek crossed to the window. It was the grey Leyland van, Chick and Donny in the front. They'd pulled to a halt in front of the loading bay doors.

'Hell,' he said, looking at Lorraine.

'Not your call, is it?' Nelson said. 'Pair of you are off duty.'

'They might need a hand,' Lorraine said. She was backing towards the door.

'Derek's just worried they'll nick his booze,' Gilfillan said.

'Hadn't thought of that,' Derek said. Then he was gone.

Lorraine turned to face the detectives. 'Funny about the Prof,' she said. 'He was sort of rambling, not making sense.'

'Can't hold his drink,' Gilfillan said. 'Three glasses of the house plonk and he was all over the show.'

'What was he saying?' Nelson asked. Her eyes were bright

and inquisitive, and Lorraine remembered that she'd been made fun of during the meal for sticking to Diet Coke.

'About his wife, Aileen . . .'

Gilfillan clicked his fingers. 'That's her name. Not Helen, Aileen.'

'What about her?'

Lorraine looked at Nelson. 'Just stupid stuff . . . how they needed time to think about things. Clean break, fresh start.'

'The drink talking,' Gilfillan muttered.

Nelson's eyes were still on Lorraine. 'Or wishful thinking . . .?'

Lorraine grabbed Derek's arm.

'It's all right,' he hissed, trying to keep his voice down. 'Old lady, sitting in her living-room a week before neighbours noticed the smell. So they've put her in the decomposing room.'

Lorraine closed her eyes in relief. The decomposing room was kept separate from the rest of the drawers. It was where the bad ones ended up. She kept her eyes closed while she spoke.

'I told those two the Prof had been talking of leaving his wife.'

'Why?'

'We get his car, drive the body somewhere far away. He's found slouched behind the wheel.'

Derek gnawed his bottom lip. 'Risky as hell,' he said.

'Riskier than what exactly? Just leave him in a drawer and hope he's never found?'

'This is a mortuary, Lor. Can you think of a better place to hide a body?'

'Are you serious?'

Derek was nodding. 'Never more so,' he said. And she knew he had a plan.

When Dr Mullan appeared next morning, he found the autopsy suite ready for him, and the two attendants hard at work.

'Thought the pair of you would be for the long lie today,' he commented, making for the shower. He was the only pathologist they'd ever met who showered *before* work. 'Mind you, you don't look like you got much sleep.'

194

They laughed at his observation, then went back to their chores. Lorraine was wiping down the deep stainless-steel sinks. Derek was sorting out the jars of chemicals. When Mullan came back, he asked about the previous evening.

'So-so,' was Derek's opinion. 'Meal was decent enough.'

Mullan was checking his watch. 'Prof's late,' he said.

'Bit too much to drink,' Lorraine explained. Mullan stared at her.

'Drinking? The Prof?'

She shrugged and watched him walk back through to the lab.

'Everything all right, Derek?' he asked.

'Fine, sir. Bit of indigestion, but apart from that . . .'

Mullan was looking at the shelves. 'Been moving the specimen jars?'

'Bit of a dust, that's all,' Derek said breezily. 'Ship-shape for the New Year.'

Mullan nodded. 'Only I don't remember there being so many of them.'

'Pulled a few out of storage, Doctor. Thought they improved the display.'

Mullan looked at him. 'It's not as if we're open to the public, Derek.'

The attendant laughed. His colleague, standing in the doorway, joined in. And eventually even Dr Mullan had to laugh, too, though he felt he'd missed the joke. When he crossed to the worktop to check the day's autopsy schedule, he happened to glance out of the window at another dull winter's day.

'CID car arriving,' he told the attendants. He glanced at his watch again. 'I get the feeling it's going to be one of those mornings . . .'

Ruth Rendell

There are some scenes of crime which attain a special place in the public consciousness. One thinks of addresses such as 10 Rillington Place and 22 Cromwell Street, Gloucester, while the scenes of the Whitechapel murders are now stopping-off points for tourists with a macabre mind-set. Does a sense of evil cling to these places? It is a subject that was tackled by Lesley Grant-Adamson not long ago, in her novel *Evil Acts*. Here Ruth Rendell deals with similar concerns in her customary evocative manner.

HARE'S HOUSE

Ruth Rendell

A murderer had lived in the house, the estate agent told Norman. The murder had in fact been committed there, he said. Norman thought it very open and honest of him.

'The neighbours would have mentioned it if I hadn't,' said the estate agent.

Now Norman understood why the house was going cheap. It was what they called a town house, though Norman didn't know why they did as he had seen plenty like it in the country. There were three floors and an open-tread staircase going up the centre. About fifteen years old, the estate agent said, and for twelve of those no one had lived in it.

'I'm afraid I can't give you any details of the case.'

'I wouldn't want to know,' said Norman. 'I'd rather not know.' He put his head round the door of the downstairs bathroom. He had never thought it possible he might own a house with more than one bathroom. Did he seriously consider owning this one then? The price was so absurdly low! 'What was his name?'

'The murderer? Oh, Hare. Raymond Hare.'

Rather to his relief, Norman couldn't remember any Hare murder case. 'Where is he now?'

'He died in prison. The house belongs to a nephew.'

'I like the house,' Norman said cautiously. 'I'll have to see what my wife says.'

The area his job obliged him to move into was a more prestigious one than where they now lived. A terraced cottage like the ones in Inverness Street was the best he had thought they could run to. He would never find another bargain like this one. If he hadn't been sure Rita would find out about the murder he would have avoided telling her.

'Why is it so cheap?' she said.

197

He told her.

She was a small thickset woman with brown hair and brown eyes and a rather large pointed face. She had a way of extending her neck and thrusting her face forward. It had once occurred to Norman that she looked like a mole, though moles of course could be attractive creatures. She thrust her head forward now.

'Is there something horrible you're not telling me?'

'I've told you everything I know. I don't know any details.' Norman was a patient and easy-going man, if inclined to be sullen. He was rather good-looking with a boyish open face and brown curly hair. 'We could both go and see it tomorrow.'

Rita would have preferred a terraced cottage in Inverness Street with a big garden and not so many stairs. But Norman had set his heart on the town house and was capable of sulking for months if he didn't get his own way. Besides, there was nothing to *show* Hare had lived there. Rather foolishly perhaps, Rita now thought, she had been expecting bloodstains or even a locked room.

'I've no recollection of this Hare at all, have you?'

'Let's keep it that way,' said Norman. 'You said yourself it's better not to know. I'll make Mr Hare the nephew an offer, shall I?'

The offer was accepted and Norman and Rita moved in at the end of September. The neighbours on one side had lived there eight years and the neighbours on the other six. They had never known Raymond Hare. A family called Lawrence who had lived in their large old house surrounded by garden for more than twenty years must have known him, at least by sight, but Norman and Rita had never spoken to them save to pass the time of day.

They had builders in to paint the house and they had new carpets. There were only two drawbacks and one of those was the stairs. You found yourself always running up and down to fetch things you had forgotten. The other drawback was the bathroom window, or more specifically, the catch on the bathroom window.

Sometimes, especially when Norman was at work and she was alone, Rita would wonder exactly where the murder had taken place. She would stand still, holding her duster, and look about

198

her and think maybe it was in that room or that one or in their bedroom. And then she would go into the bedroom, thrusting her head forward and peering. Her mother used to say she had a 'funny feeling' in the corners of some houses, she said she was psychic. Rita would have liked to have inherited this gift but she had to admit she experienced no funny feelings in any part of this house.

She and Norman never spoke about Raymond Hare. They tended to avoid the very subject of murder. Rita had once enjoyed detective stories but somehow she didn't read them any more. It seemed better not to. Her next-door neighbour Dorothy, the one who had lived there eight years, tried one day to talk to her about the Hare case but Rita said she'd rather not discuss it.

'I quite understand,' Dorothy said. 'I think you're very wise.'

It was a warm house. The central heating was efficient and the windows were double glazed except for the one in the upstairs bathroom. This bathroom had a very high ceiling and the window was about ten feet up. It was in the middle of the house and therefore had no outside wall so the architect had made the roof of the bathroom just above the main roof, thus affording room for a window. It was a nuisance not being able to open it except by means of the pole with the hook on the end of it that stood against the bathroom wall, but the autumn was a dull wet one and the winter cold so for a long time there was no need to open the bathroom window at all.

Norman thought he would have a go at re-tiling the downstairs bathroom himself and went to the library to look for a do-it-yourself decorating manual. The library, a small branch, wasn't far away, being between his house and the Tube station. Unable at first to find Skills and Crafts, his eye wandered down through Horticulture, Botany, Biology, General Science, Social Sciences, Crime . . .

Generally speaking, Norman had nothing to do with crime these days. He and Rita had even stopped watching thriller serials on television. His impulse was to turn his eyes sharply away from these accounts of trials and reconstructions of murders and turn them away he did but not before he had caught the name Hare on the spine of one of the books.

Norman turned his back. By a happy chance he was facing the section labelled 'Interior Decoration'. He found the book he wanted. Then he stood holding it and thinking. Should he look again? It might be that the author's name was Hare and had nothing at all to do with his Hare. Norman didn't really believe this. His stomach began to feel queasy and he was conscious of being rather excited too. He turned round and quickly took the book off the shelf. Its title was *Murder in the Sixties*, the author was someone called H. L. Robinson and the cases examined were listed on the jacket: Renzini and Boyce, The Oasthouse Mystery, Hare, The Pop Group Murders.

Norman opened it at random. He found he had opened it in the middle of the Hare case. A page or two further on were two photographs, the top one of a man with a blank characterless face and half-closed eyes, the other of a smiling fair-haired woman. The caption said that above was Raymond Henry Montagu Hare and below Diana Margaret Hare, née Kentwell. Norman closed the book and replaced it on the shelf. His heart was beating curiously hard. When his do-it-yourself book had been stamped he had to stop himself actually running out of the library. What a way to behave! he thought. I must get a grip on myself. Either I am going to put Hare entirely out of my mind and never think of him again or else I am going to act like a rational man, read up the case, make myself conversant with the facts and learn to live with them.

He did neither. He didn't visit the library again. When his book had taught him all it could about tiling he asked Rita to return it for him. He tried to put Hare out of his mind but this was too difficult. Where had he committed the murder was one of the questions he often asked himself and then he began to wonder whom he had killed and by what means. The answers were in a book on a shelf not a quarter of a mile away. Norman had to pass the library on his way to the station each morning and on his way back each night. He took to walking on the other side of the street. Sometimes there came into his mind that remark of Rita's that there might be something horrible he wasn't telling her.

Spring came early and there were some warm days in March. Rita tried to open the bathroom window, using the pole with the hook on the end, but the catch wouldn't budge. When Norman came home she got him to borrow a ladder from Dorothy's husband Roy and climb up and see what was wrong with the catch.

Norman thought Roy gave him rather a funny look when he said what he wanted the ladder for. He hesitated before saying Norman could have it.

'It's quite OK if you'd rather not,' Norman said. 'I expect I can manage with the steps if I can find a foothold somewhere.'

'No, no, you're welcome to the ladder,' said Roy and he showed Norman the bathroom in his own house which was identical with the next-door's except that the window had been changed for a blank sheet of glass with an extractor fan.

'Very nice,' said Norman, 'but just the same I'd rather have a window I can open.'

That brought another funny look from Roy. Norman propped the ladder against the wall and climbed up to the window and saw why it wouldn't open. The two parts of the catch, a vertical bolt and a slot for it to be driven up into, had been wired together. Norman supposed that the builders doing the painting had wired up the window catch, though he couldn't imagine why. He undid the wire, slid down the bolt and let the window fall open to its maximum capacity of about seventy-five degrees.

On 1st April the temperature dropped to just on freezing and it snowed. Rita closed the bathroom window. She took hold of the pole, reached up and inserted the hook in the ring on the bottom of the bolt, lifted the window, closed it, pushed up the bolt into the slot and gave it a twist. When she came out of the bathroom on to the landing she stood looking about her and wondering where Hare had committed the murder. For a moment she fancied she had a funny feeling about that but it passed. Rita went down to the kitchen and made herself a cup of tea. She looked out into the tiny square of garden on to which fluffy snow was falling and melting when it touched the grass. There would have been room in the garden in Inverness Street to plant bulbs, daffodils and narcissi. Rita sighed. She poured out the tea and was stirring sugar into her cup when there came a loud crash from upstairs. Rita nearly jumped out of her skin.

201

She ran up the two flights of stairs, wondering what on earth had got broken. There was nothing. Nothing was out of place or changed. She had heard of haunted houses where loud crashes were due to poltergeist activity. Her mother had always been able to sense the presence of a poltergeist. She felt afraid and sweat broke out on her rather large pointed face. Then she noticed the bathroom door was closed. Had it been that door closing she had heard? Surely not. Rita opened the bathroom door and saw that the window had fallen open. So that was all it was. She got the pole and inserted the hook in the ring on the bolt, slid the bolt upwards into the slot and gave it a twist.

It had been rather windy but the wind had dropped. Next day the weather began to warm up again. Norman opened the bathroom window and it remained open until rain started. Rita closed it.

'That window's not the problem I thought it might be once you get the hang of using the pole,' said Norman.

He was trying to be cheerful and to act as if nothing had happened. The man called Lawrence who lived opposite had got into conversation with him on his way home. They had found themselves sitting next to each other in the Tube train.

'It's good to see someone living in your place at last. An empty house always gets a run-down look.'

Norman just smiled. He had started to feel uneasy.

'My wife knew Mrs Hare quite well, you know.'

'Really?' said Norman.

'A nice woman. There was no reason for what he did as far as anyone could tell. But I imagine you've read it all up and come to terms with it. Well, you'd have to, wouldn't you?'

'Oh, yes,' said Norman.

Because he had his neighbour with him he couldn't cross the street to avoid passing the library. Outside its gates he had an almost intolerable urge to go in and take that book from the shelf. One thing he knew now, whether he wanted to or not, was that it was his wife Hare had murdered.

Some little while after midnight he was awakened by a crash. He sat up in bed.

'What was that?'

'The bathroom window, I expect,' said Rita, half-asleep.

Norman got up. He took the pole, inserted the hook into the

ring on the bolt, slid up the bolt and gave it a firm clockwise twist. The rest of the night passed undisturbed. Rita opened the window two or three days later because it had turned warm. She went into their bedroom and changed the sheets and thought, for no reason as far as she could tell, I wonder if it was his wife he murdered? I expect it was his wife. Then she thought how terrible it would be if he had murdered her in bed. Hare's bed must have stood in the same place as their own. It must have because of the position of the electric points. Perhaps he had come home one night and murdered her in bed.

A wind that was more like a gale started to make the house cold. Rita closed the bathroom window. About an hour after Norman got home it blew open with a crash.

'It comes open,' said Norman after he had shut it, 'because when you close it you don't give the bolt a hard enough twist.'

'It comes open because of the wind,' said Rita.

'The wind wouldn't affect it if you shut it properly.' Norman's handsome face wore its petulant look and he sulked rather for the rest of the evening.

Next time the window was opened petals from fruit tree blossom blew in all over the dark blue carpet. Rita closed it an hour or so before Norman came home. Dorothy was downstairs having a cup of tea with her.

'I'd have that window wired up if I were you,' said Dorothy, and she added oddly, 'To be on the safe side.'

'It gets so hot in there.'

'Leave it open then and keep the door shut.'

The crash of the window opening awoke Norman at two in the morning. He was furious. He made a lot of noise about closing it in order to wake Rita.

'I told you that window wouldn't come open if you gave the bolt a hard enough twist. That crashing scares the hell out of me. My nerves can't stand it.'

'What's wrong with your nerves?'

Norman didn't answer. 'I don't know why you can't master a simple knack like that.'

'It isn't me, it's the wind.'

'Nonsense. Don't talk such nonsense. There is no wind.'

Rita opened the window in order to practise closing it. She

spent about an hour opening and closing the window and giving the bolt a firm clockwise twist. While she was doing this she had a funny feeling. She had the feeling someone was standing behind and watching what she did. Of course there was no one there. Rita meant to leave the window open as it was a dry sunny day but she had closed it for perhaps the tenth time when the phone rang. The window therefore remained closed and Rita forgot about it.

She was pulling up weeds in the tiny strip of front garden when a woman who lived next door to the Lawrences came across the road, rattled a tin at her and asked for a donation for Cancer Research.

'I hope you don't mind my telling you how much I like your bedroom curtains.'

'Thank you very much,' said Rita.

'Mrs Hare had white net. Of course that was a few years back. You don't mind sleeping in that bedroom then? Or do you use one of the back rooms?'

Rita's knees felt weak. She was speechless.

'I suppose it isn't as if he actually did the deed in the bedroom. More just outside on the landing, wasn't it?'

Rita gave her a pound to get rid of her. She went upstairs and stood on the landing and felt very funny indeed. Should she tell Norman? How could she tell him, how could she begin, when they had never once mentioned the subject since they moved in? Norman never thought about it anyway, she was sure of that. She watched him eating his supper as if he hadn't a care in the world. The window crashed open just as he was starting on his pudding. He jumped up with an angry shout.

'You're going to come with me into that bathroom and I'm going to teach you how to shut that window if it's the last thing I do!'

He stood behind her while she took the pole and inserted the hook into the ring on the bolt, pushed the bolt up and gave it a firm twist.

'There, you see, you've turned it the wrong way. I said clockwise. Don't you know what clockwise means?'

Norman opened the window and made Rita close it again. This time she twisted the bolt to the right. The window crashed open before they had reached the foot of the stairs.

'It's not me, you see, it's the wind,' Rita cried.

Norman's voice shook with rage. 'The wind couldn't blow it open if you closed it properly. It doesn't blow it open when I close it.'

'You close it then and see. Go on, you do it.'

Norman closed it. The crash awakened him at three in the morning. He got up, cursing, and went into the bathroom. Rita woke up and jumped out of bed and followed him. Norman came out of the bathroom with the pole in his hand, his face red and his eyes bulging. He shouted at Rita:

'You got up after I was asleep and opened that window and closed it your way, didn't you?'

'I did *what*?'

'Don't deny it. You're trying to drive me mad with that window. You won't get the chance to do it again.'

He raised the pole and brought it down with a crash on the side of Rita's head. She gave a dreadful hoarse cry and put up her hands to try and ward off the rain of blows. Norman struck her five times with the pole and she was lying unconscious on the landing floor before he realised what he was doing. Norman threw the pole down the stairwell, picked Rita up in his arms and phoned for an ambulance.

Rita didn't die. She had a fractured skull and a broken jaw and collarbone but she would survive. When she regained consciousness and could move her jaw again she told the people at the hospital she had got up in the night and fallen over the banisters and all the way down the stairwell in the dark. The curious thing was she seemed to believe this herself.

Alone and remorseful, Norman kept thinking how odd it was there had nearly been a second murder under this roof. He went to the estate agents and told them he wanted to put the house back on the market. Hare's house, he always called it to himself these days, never 'my house' or 'ours'. They looked grave and shook their heads but brightened up when Norman named the very low figure he intended to ask.

Now he was going to be rid of the house Norman began to feel differently about Hare. He wouldn't have minded knowing what Hare had done, the details, the facts. One Saturday afternoon a prospective buyer came, was in raptures over Norman's redecorations and the tiles in the downstairs bathroom, and didn't seem to care at all about Hare. This encouraged Norman and immediately the man had gone he went down the road to the library where he got out *Murder in the Sixties*. He read the account of the case after getting back from visiting Rita in hospital.

Raymond and Diana Hare had been an apparently happy couple. One morning their cleaner arrived to find Mrs Hare beaten to death and lying in her own blood on the top landing outside the bathroom door. Hare had soon confessed. He and his wife had had a midnight dispute over a window that continually came open with a crash and in the heat of anger he had attacked her with a wooden pole. Not a very interesting or memorable murder. Robinson, in his foreword, said he had included it among his four because what linked them all was a common lack of any kind of understandable motive.

But how could I have tried to do the same thing and for the same reason? Norman asked himself. Is Hare's house haunted by an act, by a motiveless urge? Or can it be that the first time I looked into that book I saw and read more than my conscious mind took in but not more than was absorbed by my *unconscious*? A rational man must believe the latter.

He borrowed the ladder from Roy to climb up and once more wire the window catch.

'By the way,' he said. 'I've been meaning to ask you. It's not the same pole, is it?'

'Your one, you mean? The same as Hare's? Oh, no, I don't know what became of that one. In some police museum, I expect. You've got ours. When we had our window done we offered ours to Mr Hare the nephew and he was very glad to accept.'

Norman found a buyer at last. Rita was away convalescing and he was obliged to find a new home for them in her absence. Not that he had much choice, the miserable sum he got for Hare's house. He put a deposit on one of the terraced cottages in Inverness Street, hoping poor Rita wouldn't mind too much.

Alison White

School reunions have provided material for a number of success-ful crime novels and short stories; 'Secrets' ranks with the best. Alison White is a prolific writer of short stories, who served an apprenticeship in the women's magazine market before turning successfully to crime fiction. Her insight into the way people behave is matched by an ability to structure plot so that, as here, the final revelation comes as a surprise yet seems entirely cred-ible. As with Ruth Rendell, the ease with which the author tells her story conceals considerable art.

SECRETS

Alison White

Peter didn't want to go. But perhaps *not* going was worse. Because then he'd hear about it from Jenny and not know where truth ended and fantasy began. People embellished stories. Especially Jenny. So he'd agreed. Except now the time was here, he wished he hadn't.

Jenny was excited. 'I know you think it'll be boring, Peter, but it'll be fun. What I don't understand, though, is why do a reunion now? After all this time?'

He'd already had this conversation with her several times over the last few days. But he answered anyway. 'Twenty years. *That's* why. It's a kind of landmark. And I suppose by now, there'll be something to see, won't there? Most people will have made something of themselves. Those that are going to anyway.'

Jenny nodded. 'It's amazing they managed to get in touch with everyone.'

'That's if they did.' With the glare of the sunlight through the windscreen he only saw the bend at the last minute and swung round it quickly so Jenny's handbag fell off her lap, her make-up bursting out and on to the floor.

'Careful!' She reached down, gathering everything up into the bag except for her lipstick, which she reapplied. Smacking her lips together as she squinted at her reflection in the small mirror of the sun-shield.

'This heat, it's just eating my make-up. Why is it so hot?'

'It's the summer, what do you expect?' he scowled.

She ignored his testiness. 'We're the only year that hasn't had a reunion before now. There isn't the same nostalgia when a teacher's found dead on your last day,' she admitted. 'But why now?'

'I don't know. Curiosity maybe.'

And please God, only related to what became of the class of '80. Not to what had happened on their last day. Another hot July day twenty years ago. The day that changed his life.

Not much had been happening in school. Exams over, they waited for the results in a summer-hazed state of limbo. These days, kids didn't have to go into school after the exams, he'd heard. But then it was different, with talks and careers advice right up till the end of term. In theory, anyway, but mostly they just hung about, killing time and dreaming before they went out into the real world. There was a kind of reckless yet innocent freedom in the way they felt back then. Free of the constraints of school, the teachers couldn't threaten them, for they'd done the exams, yet they still had the protective mantle of the 'pupil' status. It was safe. Or at least it felt so. But exciting. They were on the edge of something new, and their teachers were in on it. Maybe they were a little envious too. Certainly some had been wistful.

'Nearly there now,' Jenny said, needlessly. Her eyes began scanning the pavements as they turned into School Lane, as though old school friends would suddenly start appearing before them. As if they'd know them after all this time.

They'd never actually left the neighbourhood. Lived within a few miles of the school. Yet Peter always took the long way round town when he was driving. He didn't like going past there. Jenny, though, had a ghoulish delight about the place – loved telling people of the tragedy that brought them together.

'We helped each other back then,' she'd say. 'Clung to one another, and when our grief was over, we realised we were in love.'

But Peter's grief had never left him.

And now, twenty years later, they were back. The scene of the crime, as it were. The school. For a reunion. Peter parked the car painstakingly between the white lines, not wanting to show to Jenny any of the tension he felt. But when he took his hands from the steering wheel it was slippery with perspiration.

'This way,' Jenny said, out of the car in seconds. Her enthusiasm was exhausting.

There were balloons pinned to the main door and a crude 'Class of 1980' banner across the archway. It looked like a bunch of teenagers had done it. The present kids, though, Peter thought, it couldn't be the banner from back then, could it? Who would have kept such a thing? He caught up with Jenny and they followed the paper signs and arrows directing to the gymnasium.

'Do you suppose there'll be *any* of the old staff here?' Inside, Jenny clacked across the polished wood floor in her high heels. Peter started in surprise to hear it from her. That's what Miss Jameson had sounded like when she walked. Clack-clack. He'd liked it. No one else had sounded like that then, the girls wore ghastly clumpy regulation things on their feet, but Miss Jameson had her heels and her wiggle as she clack-clacked around the school.

Reunions, what was the point? He closed his eyes briefly and took a deep breath as Jenny pulled open the gymnasium door. The whole place seemed barely changed. The same smell of chalk and young bodies, even the same voices carrying across the air. Or were they just in his head?

'Looks like we help ourselves.'

First things first, Jenny was focusing on the buffet table. Peter followed her. Someone had made punch in one of the big steel bowls they used to serve custard in. Twenty years on they had to dole out the contents themselves into plastic cups and look at the bits of stringy pineapple floating on top. Sophisticated it was not. It was no place for Miss Jameson. No place for him.

Jenny handed him a cup of punch and, obediently, he drank. Jenny then seized two paper plates and proceeded to work her way down the table, piling them high with food.

Last night, Peter had had a dream – a nightmare. Someone would finally confront him today. Sixty eyes would turn to look at him. Like back then. Except twenty years older and wiser. They'd see more. They'd know. He'd woken up breathless – having to reach for his inhaler. Stupid, adolescent dream. Pubescent rambling and theatrics. Twenty years. It was a long time to carry a secret.

'Not wearing your badge, then? Let me guess . . . Peter, isn't it?'

He struggled to focus his thoughts back on the present as a wheezing overweight man blustered up, peering at him. 'And you married Jenny Watts, didn't you?' He jerked his finger toward Jenny, whose tongue was poking out as she concentrated on manoeuvring vol-au-vents on to a plate. 'Lucky boy!' He gave Peter a shove, almost sending him into the punch.

'Well then, do you know who I am? Guess!' He covered his own handmade badge, with fat fingers like sausages.

'Leslie Morris.' Peter knew him straight away. He'd always been an idiot. Some things, even twenty years didn't change.

'Arrgh! Brilliant. Just the same but without hair, eh? Don't tell me, I've heard it ten times already tonight.'

Peter's eyes were scanning the crowd now. But she wouldn't be here, would she? Of course not.

Miss Jameson had been their drama teacher and he just one of her admirers. And she'd been oblivious to his feelings. At least he'd thought she had.

That last day, she gave them one of her pep talks. The last one, she said. And it was, of course. Giving them the benefit of her experience before sending them out into the wide world. It had only occurred to him much later that she couldn't have had that much experience herself, she was surely only in her twenties then. And fresh from college. But she knew how to make an impact. A good drama teacher knew how to grip an audience. He could hear her voice now if he closed his eyes. Clear and well modulated – compelling.

'Every moment is important,' she'd said. 'Each step you take leads you closer to your future and shapes it for you.'

It had been a hot day. A heavy heat you could almost taste. He'd taken off his tie and put it in his shirt pocket, as had most of the other boys. Miss Jameson wouldn't strictly enforce the dress code. Not for a bunch of school leavers in a heatwave on the last day of term.

She'd sat on her desk and crossed her bare legs. They were pale, like the rest of her. With translucent skin, mid-blonde hair and an air of fragility, she was a typical English rose. She wore fancy espadrilles with tiny little heels and ribbon straps that criss-crossed up her legs. Her floaty floral skirt had its buttons half undone. Even indoors it was hot, and she kept lifting her hair up off her neck and pulling it back, leaving just a few strands falling across her face. Outside, there had been a cricket match going on and every now and again she'd stop and stare out at the boys running down the field in their whites.

She'd turn back to the class with a well-timed sigh, and

another piece of advice. 'And it's important, you know, to go for what you want – when you can, because you might never get that moment again. If you remember anything I say to you – then remember that,' she'd said, and smiled.

And Peter had known he would. He knew he loved her. And in that moment, he knew he had to tell her. That day. She'd understand – hadn't she just told them how important it was to act when the moment was right?

He'd been carrying around with him the poem he'd written for her, trying to pluck up enough courage to show her, and when the bell finally went at the end of class, he'd taken it to her.

'Peter. For me? How lovely.' She looked at him, smiling slowly as she unfolded the page. 'A poem!' He'd felt his skin flush with colour, but she pretended not to notice.

'I'll read it over lunchtime. I'll be seeing you later, won't I? Before we finish. But don't be late for your next lesson.'

And she'd still had the poem in her hand as he backed obediently out of the classroom. He could hardly think straight for the next couple of hours. She'd made a point of saying she'd see him before they finished. Like it was important to her. Well, he could tell her then. That he loved her. And he knew she'd understand. Once she'd read his poem, then of course she would.

The day was finishing after afternoon breaktime, with a 'farewell' assembly and lecture. To be held in the drama studio, and all the teachers were going to be there. Sending them on their way. So Peter went early, towards the end of breaktime, hoping to catch her upstairs there, setting the lights. He crept in through the balcony door, not wanting to disturb her. He just wanted to see if she'd read his poem.

And she had. But her reaction wasn't what he'd expected. She'd been laughing about it when he saw her. *Laughing.*

Moments later, his classmates had found him as they walked into the studio's main entrance downstairs. He was looking down from the balcony at the twisted body below. And his classmates' thirty pairs of eyes had looked at it too. And then up at him.

There was a banging noise and Peter jumped. Back into the present. Twenty years on. He looked round wildly at faces he

213

knew from the past, but changed now. Bearded and bald, wrinkled and overpainted. And waiting.

'Oh God,' someone groaned nearby. 'Leslie's giving a speech.'

His breathing started to steady again. He shouldn't lose his nerve now. He loosened his tie. It was hot in here – all these people, that's what it was. The bodies. He was aware of the quickening pulse in his finger as he pressed down on the table for support.

'Peter.' There was a gentle brush of feminine fingers on his arm. 'I didn't think you'd come.'

He froze. Not wanting to turn around. Not for that voice. Surely not . . .?

She moved slowly in front of him, her eyes wide and unblinking. 'I'd have known you anywhere.'

There were soft, fair, waves falling around her face. Still blonde. Still lovely. With a cool elegance. She had grown up.

'Miss Jameson.'

'Most people are calling me Yvonne now. I was only a few years older than you back then.'

It was true, she blended in with the rest of them. Looked younger than several. He stared into those eyes. Those so innocent-looking blue eyes that knew his secret.

She looked over at Jenny. 'I heard that you married. I was glad.'

He swallowed, his mouth suddenly dry. 'And you?'

She closed her eyes and almost smiled. 'I never married. No.'

Peter looked away and then back at her. Forcing himself. He owed it to her, didn't he? She'd protected him all these years. He'd never known why. Finally, he found his voice. But he was an adolescent again suddenly, as it came out higher than usual and he cleared his throat self-consciously.

'I thought you'd left the area. I tried to find you but you'd gone.' Everyone knew she'd left. She never came back to the school.

'I still have some family here though. My parents. When the invitation came for tonight, they forwarded it.' She looked at him now, watchful, curious. 'Right up until I walked through the door I thought about turning away. Didn't think I could cope

214

with it. But I had to. I wondered about you, Peter. I often have. Obviously.'

'That day,' he said quickly, as though blurting it out made it easier. Not that he was trying to blame her, but . . . 'You gave us a talk.'

'I remember.'

'And said that every step you take leads to your future and shapes it. You were right. For me – in just one second, one step, everything changed for ever.'

'You pushed her, Peter.' She spoke in a whisper, then looked away into the distance as she had in class all those years ago, but there were no cricketers to focus on, then she closed her eyes.

'I did,' Peter said. 'But I didn't mean for –'

'No. I know. But it happened.' She looked back at him with a sigh, as though playing out the second act of a script. 'Cassie Moore has gone, Peter. She's dead.'

'It was . . . I wasn't thinking . . . she was laughing at me. I . . . I just wanted her to stop.'

He'd heard Miss Jameson reading out a line of his poem and had stopped, flattered, but then as he'd moved forward, he'd seen the two women together. Heads bent together and laughing.

Yvonne shook her head. 'She was laughing at the situation. Never at you, Peter, just the irony of it. Cassie was always laughing, she was such fun. You remember that. She even died laughing, didn't she? There's irony for you again.'

'Why did you protect me? Then and since . . . all these years.' He closed his eyes, remembering the studio that day. Laughter, then seeing Miss Moore, that stupid PE teacher with her tracksuit and whistle on a cord round her neck, holding his poem. Laughing at it. Making Miss Jameson laugh. And then his clumsy attempt to retrieve it in a lunge, and stop them laughing, then push her away from Miss Jameson. It was over in a split second. They hadn't heard him approach. Laughter turned to a scream when Cassie Moore fell back over the balcony . . . while Peter stood there, with his poem in his hand.

He asked her again. 'Why have you kept my secret?'

She met his eyes then, as an equal. 'Because I felt responsible, Peter. Teenage crushes were innocent – easy to deal with. But the world was not an enlightened place then. It was Cassie and

215

I who shared a terrible secret first. That's what we were laughing at – just the situation, although it wasn't funny really.'

Peter frowned. 'I don't understand.'

'No. You lost a teacher in Cassie Moore. But what you didn't know was that I lost a lover.' Her eyes misted over as she watched him take in what she had just confessed. And how she'd carried it alone for all this time.

At the time, she'd thought for both of them. Said they'd walked into the studio together, had heard Cassie Moore fall only moments before the class had walked in. That's why they'd been looking over the balcony when everyone else came in. They had heard the fall of course. He'd never forget that sound – he'd been able to describe it to the police with an accuracy that still chilled him when he thought about it. But backing each other up, there was no reason for anyone to doubt them. It was just a terrible, tragic accident.

'You still protected me,' he said.

'I protected myself,' she said softly. 'I knew how you felt about me, Peter. And I enjoyed it. I thought teenage crushes were harmless and I played up to it. What gave me the right to play with people's feelings? And it wasn't me that paid ultimately. It was Cassie. And you. So what does that make me?'

'We've carried this for twenty years,' Peter said, his eyes searching hers for something that would help. Bring solace at last. But there was nothing. Just sadness.

She spoke on a sigh again. 'We're survived, haven't we? Secrets. At least you've only got one.'

'Miss Jameson! I didn't expect to see you!' Suddenly Jenny was beside them, swaying slightly at the effects of the punch she'd been drinking. 'Peter's only got one what?'

'Wife,' said Yvonne Jameson brightly, her dramatic skills resurfacing. 'Jenny, you've hardly changed. I was just saying that some of your fellow pupils have had more wives than Henry the Eighth. I could almost die laughing.'

And with just a ghost of a smile at Peter, she clack-clacked away across the floor.

Biographical Notes of Contributors

Mat Coward was born in 1960 and became a full-time freelance writer and broadcaster in 1986. Having written all manner of material for all manner of markets, he currently specialises in book reviews, magazine humour columns and short stories – crime, SF, humour, horror and children's. His first crime story was shortlisted for a CWA Dagger and he has also published a novel. Since then his stories have appeared in numerous magazines, anthologies and e-zines in the UK, US and Europe as well as being broadcast on BBC radio. He edits the critically acclaimed crime story magazine *Crimewave*.

Carol Anne Davis has been described as 'an uncompromising new literary talent'. Four reviewers chose her mortuary-based novel *Shrouded* as their debut of the year in 1997. It was followed by *Safe as Houses*. Carol's short stories have appeared in anthologies and magazines and have been placed in national competitions. Her dark crime collection is available for publication and she says that no reasonable offer will be refused.

Eileen Dewhurst was born in Liverpool, read English at Oxford, and has earned her living in a variety of ways, including journalism. When she is not writing, she enjoys solving cryptic crossword puzzles and drawing and painting cats. Her latest novel is *Double Act*. Her other works include *A Private Prosecution*, *The House that Jack Built*, and *Death in Candie Gardens*. She wrote five novels featuring the policeman Neil Carter; currently, her principal series detectives are actress Phyllida Moon and the Guernsey policeman Tim Le Page.

Martin Edwards has written seven novels about the lawyer and amateur detective Harry Devlin; the first, *All the Lonely People*, was shortlisted for the CWA John Creasey Memorial Dagger for the best first crime novel of 1991. The series has been optioned for television. He has published over twenty short mysteries, including several with a historical setting, and is also the author of seven non-fiction books on legal topics. In 1999 he was commissioned to complete the late Bill Knox's police novel *The Lazarus Widow*. His latest Harry Devlin novel is *First Cut is the Deepest*.

Jürgen Ehlers works as a geologist at Hamburg State Geological Survey. Since his graduation from Hamburg University, he has published more than fifty articles in scientific journals as well as five books about Ice Age geology. In addition, he has contributed to a number of anthologies published in German.

Lesley Grant-Adamson was born in North London and spent much of her childhood in South Wales. She worked on provincial newspapers before joining the staff of *The Guardian* as a feature writer, then became a freelance journalist and television writer before becoming a novelist. Her first crime novel, *Patterns in the Dust*, was published in 1985 and its many successors include *Evil Acts, Lipstick and Lies* and *Undertow*.

John Hall worked as an analytical chemist and systems analyst before becoming a full-time writer. He contributes regularly to *Sherlock Holmes: The Detective Magazine* and to *The Sherlock Holmes Journal*. His books include two commentaries on the Sherlock Holmes cases, *Sidelights on Holmes* and *The Abominable Wife*. He has written several new Holmes novels, but is now concentrating on a series featuring his medieval investigator Martyn Byrd.

Edward D. Hoch has dominated the market for short crime fiction of quality for over the past forty years. Although he has written occasional novels, it is his gift for (and ability to make a living from) the short form that has earned him a unique reputation. In the course of writing many hundreds of stories, Hoch has employed a wide range of pen-names and created series characters such as Captain Leopold, Dr Sam Hawthorne, the cipher expert Rand, Ben Snow and Simon Ark, who claims to be two thousand years old. Recent collections of selected cases of Hawthorne and Snow are, respectively, *Diagnosis: Impossible* and *The Ripper of Storyville*.

Peter Lovesey received the CWA Cartier Diamond Dagger in 2000, in recognition of his outstanding career in the genre. His first book, *Wobble to Death,* was published in 1970 and introduced Sergeant Cribb, the Victorian detective who went on to feature in seven more books and two television series. His recent novels have included the much-praised series featuring policeman Peter Diamond, but his latest publication is a non-series book, *The Reaper.*

Phil Lovesey is the son of Peter Lovesey. Born in 1963, he took a degree in film and television studies and had a career as London's laziest copywriter at a succession of the capital's most desperate advertising agencies. He turned to 'proper' writing in 1994 with a series of short stories, and was runner-up in the prestigious MWA fiftieth anniversary short-story competition in 1995. His first novel, *Death Duties,* was published in 1998, to excellent reviews, and has so far had two successors.

Catherine Morrell had her first published short story in *Ellery Queen's Mystery Magazine* in April 1994. She also writes, under the name Gaynor Coules, a regular column in *Sherlock Holmes: The Detective Magazine.* Domiciled in Kent and working in London, she is only prevented from using the travelling time to best advantage by a tendency to fall asleep. That is her excuse for her failure to complete her novel. She is currently convenor for the south-eastern Chapter of CWA.

Amy Myers was born in Kent. After taking a degree in English Literature, she was a director of a London publishing house before becoming an author. She is married to an American and lives in Kent. She also writes under the name Harriet Hodson.

Ian Rankin is renowned as the creator of Inspector John Rebus who has appeared in such novels as the CWA Macallan Gold Dagger-winning *Black and Blue, The Hanging Garden* and *Set in Darkness.* He has written acclaimed short stories: *A Good Hanging* is a collection which features Rebus. His other publications include thrillers written under the name of Jack Harvey. He is a former Chairman of the CWA.

Ruth Rendell, under her own name and as Barbara Vine, has won both critical and popular acclaim for her achievement in showing the rich potential of the crime novel. Her first book about the Kingsmarkham policeman, Reg Wexford, *From Doon with Death*, appeared in 1964. Her non-series novels under her own name include *A Demon in my View* which won the CWA Gold Dagger in 1976 and *A Judgement in Stone*. *Lake of Darkness* won the Arts Council National Book Award for Genre Fiction in 1981. The much-praised Vine novels include *A Fatal Inversion* (another CWA Gold Dagger winner) and *The Brimstone Wedding*.

Alison White was born and bred in Liverpool, but returned to the North-West after some time living and working in London and is now based in Southport. She has published many stories in magazines and her work has also been broadcast on BBC Network Northwest, Radio 4 and the World Service. In recent years, she has concentrated increasingly on crime fiction, writing for magazines such as *Ellery Queen's Mystery Magazine*. She is now at work on her first mystery novel.